JOHN L. DeBOER

THE GIRL FROM BELGRADE

---

1.   http://StreetlightGraphics.com

Chapter 1

Belgrade, Serbia
April 1999

Katarina Petrovic held her hands over her ears as explosions continued to rock the neighborhood. She looked out from beneath the kitchen table at her mother's inert form.

Mira Petrovic had ushered her daughter to the fragile refuge just before the ceiling crashed down, a beam knocking Mira to the floor. She had lain there ever since, unresponsive to Katarina's shouts.

The concept of death, at least involving people, had not fully formed in Katarina's five-year-old brain. But she knew hurt, and her mother had obviously been seriously injured.

"Momma!" she kept calling out, to no avail.

The explosions finally stopped, and the apartment building ceased shaking. Katarina crawled over to her mother and brushed dust and plaster fragments from her face. Clotted blood covered a gash in her forehead. "Momma?"

Her mother's eyes opened. "Are you hurt, Kat?" she gasped.

"No, Momma. Are you?"

"I can't... breathe."

"Katarina!"

The girl turned as two men dressed in uniforms like her father wore entered the apartment. She recognized one of them. "Momma can't breathe! Help her!"

The soldiers lifted the beam off her mother's chest. Mira's eyes were still open but no longer looking at her daughter as they stared, unblinking, at the ceiling.

One of the men leaned over to put fingers on Mira's neck for a moment. "She's gone, Goran."

"Gone?" Katarina shouted. "She's right there!"

"She's dead, Kat. I'm so sorry." The man she knew as Lieutenant Stankovic pulled her into a hug as she sobbed, her eyes not leaving her mother's body.

"No!" She squirmed in his arms. "Where's Poppa?"

Stankovic held her tighter. "Kat, the bombs killed your father too."

"Oh no!" she wailed. Tears ran down her cheeks. "Where is he?"

"At the airport. He sent us here just before he died. He wanted you to be safe."

"Why... Why did they die?"

"The American planes are bombing us."

"Why?" She struggled to get out of his embrace.

"It's war. You're too young to understand."

But she did know about war and soldiers, thanks to her father. And what she understood was that war had killed her parents and that her life could never be the same. "Will I die too?"

"No, Kat. Lieutenant Kovac and I will get you to a safe place where someone will take care of you." He released her to take out a cell phone.

She went to lie between her mother's sprawled legs, her arms around her waist as she sobbed into Mira's sweater.

"The girl's fine, Major," Stankovic said into the phone, "but Mrs. Petrovic is dead." He paused, listening. "Okay."

"Kat," he said as he put the phone away, "does your mother have a suitcase?"

She looked up at her father's friend. "Yes. Poppa has one too."

He turned to the other soldier. "I'll help her pack, Darko. Look for any valuables that should go with her."

Stankovic took Katarina's hand, and the three of them stepped through the debris to the bedrooms.

The soldiers wrapped Mira's body in a bedspread and carried it out to an extended-cab pickup. They put the bundle in the bed of the truck, followed by two suitcases.

"Get in the back seat, honey," Stankovic said.

She climbed in, holding her stuffed elephant.

"Major's waiting for us at the airport," Stankovic said to Kovac, who got into the driver's seat.

"Am I going to see Poppa?"

Stankovic turned from the front passenger seat. "Uh, no. They've taken him away. They'll take your mother there, too, so they can be buried together."

She started crying again. "Like Muffin?"

"Who's Muffin?"

"Our cat. She died, and we dug a hole for her in the garden."

Stankovic nodded. "Something like that."

"Why are we going to the airport?"

"Other children who have lost their parents are there. You'll all be taken to a place where there isn't any bombing."

Her eyes got big. "In an airplane?"

"No, sweetie. It's too dangerous for that."

Kovac drove away from the damaged apartment building. They passed other bombed buildings and people searching through the rubble. The partly cloudy sky had turned a dark gray, and a slight breeze became a strong wind. Hard rain pelted the truck.

"Explains the pause in the bombing," Kovac said.

The truck went through a gate in a chain-link fence onto the tarmac of the airport. In the distance, smoke billowed from two demolished planes, the heavy rain dousing their fires. Kovac dodged craters in the pavement as he drove to an open hangar, continued inside, and stopped next to a white cargo van.

Stankovic climbed out and saluted a soldier standing next to the van. "Captain's daughter, sir." He pointed at Katarina.

"His wife?"

"Her body's in the back."

"Very well. We'll take care of it. This is a good time to move. No telling how long this weather will last."

Stankovic beckoned to Katarina. She left the truck and joined him as Kovac removed the suitcases.

Stankovic grabbed her hand and led her to the back of the van, its rear door open. Inside, two kids about her age and one a few years older sat on blankets. A woman in uniform held a baby in her lap. Bags and suitcases lined one wall.

Katarina turned to Stankovic. "Where am I going?"

"It's like your apartment building but with a school. Children without parents live there and go to school in the same place. You'll be there until a family takes you to live with them."

"But I don't know them!"

"You will, honey. You'll have a new family that loves you. Maybe you'll even have a brother or sister."

"They won't be Momma and Poppa." Tears welled up again.

"I know." He smiled kindly. "But we can't bring your parents back. You're very sad now, but that will go away with time. I lost my momma and poppa when I was a little older than you, so I know how you feel."

She wiped away tears with her hand. "Your momma and poppa died?"

"Yes. It's hard for me to remember them now. I was so young. The same thing will happen with you, Kat."

Kovac loaded the suitcases, and Stankovic lifted Katarina into the van. He wrote something on a piece of paper, folded it, and handed it to her. "Put this in your pocket. It's my phone number. When you get a chance, you can call me."

The soldier Stankovic had saluted looked into the van and said to the woman, "That's the last of the passengers."

She nodded, and the officer closed the door while Katarina stared at Stankovic, the folded paper in her hand.

Two other soldiers climbed into the front seats, and the van drove out of the hangar.

Rain continued to beat on the roof. Katarina kept to herself, trying to cope with what had happened. The other children were quiet as well.

After a trip that seemed to take forever, the van slowed then stopped. When the back door opened, the van was in front of a large square brick building with lots of windows. Katarina realized her new life was about to begin.

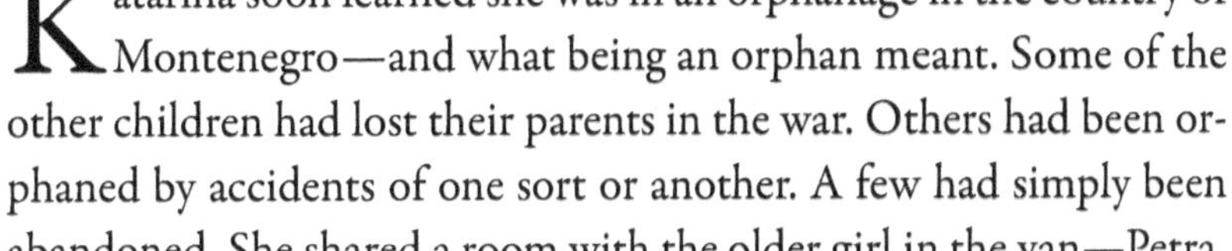

Katarina soon learned she was in an orphanage in the country of Montenegro—and what being an orphan meant. Some of the other children had lost their parents in the war. Others had been orphaned by accidents of one sort or another. A few had simply been abandoned. She shared a room with the older girl in the van—Petra, who was eight. Petra's mother had died of cancer, and her father, like Katarina's, had been killed by the enemy.

The orphanage did contain a school, so she began her formal education there. Much to her surprise, that included learning English. She wondered why she was being taught the language of the terrible Americans.

The Kosovo War, as it was called, ended two months after it had killed her parents. The Americans had gone home. So had the Albanians, who were fighting against soldiers like her father. The Russians, who had been on Serbia's side in the conflict, also left her country.

Why? she often asked herself. *Why did Momma and Poppa have to die?* She didn't understand what had started the war, only that different groups of people wanted the same land for themselves. And the Americans had decided what group should win and butted into something that didn't involve them. She found a similar hatred of the United States as well as an affinity for Russia among her teachers.

So why aren't they teaching us Russian? Later, they did.

The years went by, and no families arrived at the orphanage to take her under their wing, as had happened with several of the other students. Petra had left two years earlier but not because she'd been adopted. The headmaster had recommended her for a higher-level school in Moscow. Katarina had been granted permission to call the number she had saved, but the number didn't work. Her last connection to the world she had known as a small child was gone. Lieutenant Stankovic had been right—the memories of her parents were fading.

One day, the headmaster summoned fifteen-year-old Katarina to his office, where two other men waited. Mr. Milosevic directed her to a chair in front of his desk. The two strangers stood next to it.

"Katarina, you've reached the age when you need more education than we offer here at the school. And you've done very well with your studies. As a result, you've been selected for special training."

"Like Petra?"

"Yes." Milosevic smiled. "These men will take you to the new school."

She looked at the strangers. "Are you Russians?"

One of the men said, "We are."

Good! She turned to Milosevic. "Thank you, Headmaster. I am honored to be selected, and I will do my best to justify your faith in me."

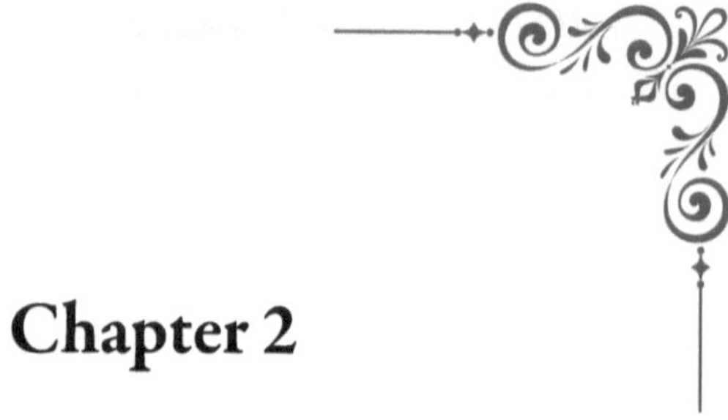

Chapter 2

San Francisco
Present day
September 29, 8:00 p.m.

The panoramic view from the Top of the Mark was spectacular. That was why I'd wanted to make the Intercontinental Mark Hopkins Hotel on Nob Hill part of my San Francisco tour. I'd closed the deal with management, and I was celebrating with a martini as I looked out at the night cityscape from the lounge on the nineteenth floor.

I checked my watch, though I knew it was too late to call my father in Virginia. Dad had a big day scheduled for the next day, including a celebration of his own. I would call him in the morning to congratulate him, hoping he wouldn't bring up that issue between us again.

I had one more day to wrap up other details of the latest itinerary in the Baker Tours portfolio. Trish, my assistant in New York, would still be up and anxious to get an update. I pulled out my cell phone. She answered after two rings.

"Did you get it?" Trish asked without preamble.

I chuckled, visualizing her excited face. She was my age, thirty-eight, and presented an attractive and outgoing client contact for our growing company. If she weren't already happily married to a good man, I might have considered taking our business relationship in a romantic direction.

"I'm celebrating, Trish."

"Great news! Clients will love it. When will you be back?"

"I'm taking the red-eye tomorrow. How's the Chicago tour go-ing?"

"Greg called me an hour ago. No problems."

"We should start looking for someone to run San Francisco."

"I'll get on it tomorrow. Alex?"

"Yeah?"

"We have Boston and New England, Chicago, Charleston, New York, of course, and now San Francisco. Maybe..."

"Maybe what?"

"We should think about Europe."

Europe. During my optimistic what-if moments, expanding overseas had occurred to me, but that would be a huge step. "And compete with the likes of Perillo?"

"Why not?"

I chuckled again. "Let's get Frisco up and running first."

"You'll think about it?"

"Promise. Now get a good night's sleep."

"See you day after tomorrow, boss."

I rose early the next morning and called my father.

"Congratulations, Dad. I wish I could be there, but I'm tied up in San Francisco on business. Did you get my card?"

"Yes. Thank you. You know, Alex, in three years, you would've been eligible to retire. And you'd still be a young man."

There it was again, as I'd feared. But maybe with my father finally taking off the uniform, I could put the issue to rest at long last.

"Dad, we've been over this many times. The only reason I went into the Air Force originally was because I didn't know what I want-ed to do in life, and I thought it would please you."

"It did. I was disappointed you chose a different career path in the service, but I got over that, and I was proud of you. If only you hadn't resigned your commission."

"Can we finally let this go? I've got a good business, and I'm happy. I was hoping you and Mom would be happy for me too."

He was silent for a moment. "I'm sorry, son. It's just that what will happen today brought it all back. Your mother and I *are* happy for you and wish you every success."

"Thanks. I wish you the best as well. Any idea what you'll be doing in Denver?"

"Trying to get used to civilian life. After that, who knows?"

"Maybe you and Mom can go on one of my tours."

"Would we get a family discount?"

I laughed. "Of course!"

"We might take you up on that."

"Have a great send-off, Dad."

"Stay in touch, okay?"

"Count on it. Bye."

I stared out the window of the hotel room. The fog hadn't yet started creeping in on "little cat's feet," as Carl Sandburg had famously penned. Below, a cable car was clanging its way up the hill.

My morning and early afternoon called for a visit to Fisherman's Wharf for photos and meetings with restaurant managers. Later, I would get details on what plugging into an Alcatraz tour would entail. Other attractions we would offer in various packages included the Lombard Street experience, a visit to Chinatown, Golden Gate Park, North Beach, Telegraph Hill and Coit Tower, a trip through the wine country north of the city across the Golden Gate Bridge, and tours of various San Francisco museums. All packages would, of course, include that Nob Hill cable car ride.

My plan to make San Francisco a jewel in the Baker Tours portfolio was taking shape. But the phone call had dampened my mood by dredging up an incident that, despite putting it behind me, still rankled.

Four years ago, I'd been an Air Force major in command of an Office of Special Investigations unit. Our mission was to investigate crimes committed against or by Air Force personnel and counterintelligence threats against the Air Force, the Department of Defense, and the US government. I had not followed in my father's footsteps to become a flier, and that disappointed him. I wasn't sure why I'd chosen that different path. An obvious explanation was that I wanted to get out of Dad's shadow, to avoid always being compared to him. Deep down, I knew that could have been the reason.

Lieutenant Melissa—"Call me Mel"—Willoughby was a member of my team. She was intelligent and eager. She had the kind of intelligence that made its owner believe they were always the smartest person in the room and an eagerness that compelled them to let everyone in the room know it.

I appreciated robust enthusiasm, as long as it made for a good team player. But that didn't apply to her. She considered her hunches to be insight and acted on them outside the framework of a diligent by-the-book investigation. And it could put the prosecution of miscreants in jeopardy.

I'd counseled her about it on several occasions, as was my duty, and stressed that insubordinate behavior had consequences. I couldn't fire her, but as I was her commanding officer, it was my responsibility to fill out the Officer Performance Report form for the officers under me. Promotion in the Air Force depended on a good OPR.

When my assessment of her concluded with "Does not meet standards," she went to the Inspector General, claiming I'd demanded sexual favors in return for a positive OPR. The IG, per regulations, called for a written response from me as the first step.

The military was hardly an activist in the Me Too movement, but complaints of sexual harassment in the service were on the rise then, and the powers that be started to take them more seriously.

The charge was baseless—there had never been even a hint of flirtation between us—and I, of course, denied the charge. But I knew two things would follow. She couldn't prove what she claimed, and the likelihood of formal charges being brought against me was minimal. But the allegation alone would mar my record, making subsequent unsatisfactory OPRs for female officers under my command automatically suspect.

Adding to that, a recent investigation by my unit had been close to nailing the airman in question when it was torpedoed by Willoughby's impetuousness. It made me, as her commander, look foolish if not downright incompetent. That had been the final straw that led to her negative OPR.

My unit came under scrutiny, its integrity in question. One of my best officers requested a transfer, and I couldn't blame him.

I saw no positive way forward in an Air Force career. I'd been tarnished irrevocably. So I resigned my commission on my terms rather than being forced out later.

When I told Dad my decision, he argued that I was being too hasty. That I was taking the easy—the coward's—way out.

It became a constant source of friction between us. He told me sometime later that Willoughby had also left the service. Not surprising. Her career had been on the line too. That was why she'd filed the complaint in the first place.

So I was suddenly without a job in my midthirties. I had training and experience as a cop, essentially. And I had administrative skills. Well, I used to, anyway. I could have found a police department to hire me. But law enforcement bureaucracy had already done me in, and I didn't want to take that on again. A lot of ex-cops took the private investigator path, and I briefly toyed with the idea. The sleaze involved in what would be the bulk of my contracts, though, turned me off. But I had to make a living somehow, so I landed a decent-paying job in a Las Vegas security firm.

Boring.

Then my sister called me. Connie, four years my senior, owned a travel agency in Manhattan, just south of the Columbia University campus. She had done well for years, but then the internet entered the travel scene in a big way. Folks started planning their own vacations online, and her business suffered. So she'd started organizing tours of New York and New England, and this stemmed the tide of red ink.

"How are you doing in Sin City, Alex?"

"I'm doing. What's up?" She never called me just to chat.

"I'm pregnant!"

"Pregnant? How did that happen?"

She laughed. "Really?"

"I mean, well, you know."

"Yeah. Stupid me, I thought I was beyond that age. Megan'll be a senior in college next year." She laughed again. "I'm closer to being a grandmother than my days as a mom!"

"Congratulations. I think."

"Thanks, but there's a problem besides being too old for this. My OB says I've got hypertension, which could be an issue as the pregnancy advances. I have to take it easy. And that means I can't have the stress of my business."

"What're you going to do? You considering abortion?"

"Heavens no! I'm having this baby, come hell or high water. So I need your help. Would you consider coming back to New York to run my agency for me during my forced vacation? I'll make you a partner. No buy-in necessary. Your contribution will be sweat equity.

You'll be doing all the work while I'm on the couch at home, watching Turner Classic Movies."

"What does Frank say?"

"He's in favor of it. He's always wanted a son, bless his heart, and the ultrasound says he'll get one—if I follow doctor's orders. C'mon, wouldn't you like to be back in the Big Apple?"

I'd spent four years there while attending Hunter College, and I had enjoyed living in the vibrant city.

"Well..." I started, thinking about it.

"What are they paying you there?"

"Seventy-five."

"I'll make it a hundred to start. The business is on an uptick that I see continuing. I can send you the figures for the last six months."

"Tell you what, Connie. I'll put in for a leave of absence—family emergency. My boss is a good guy. I'll give it a month. If it doesn't work out, I'll help you find someone else. Fair?"

"Yes! Thank you, Alex! You can stay with us while you decide. When can I expect you?"

I laughed. "Give me a couple of days to settle things here."

"You're a lifesaver. Thank you so much."

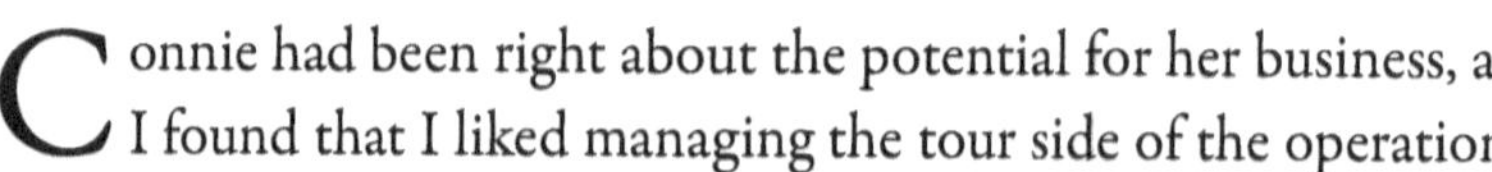

Connie had been right about the potential for her business, and I found that I liked managing the tour side of the operation. I cut my ties to Vegas and became a businessman for the first time in my life.

Connie had to have a C-section, but mother and baby did well. Despite her concerns about taking care of an infant after so many years, old memories came through, and she managed just fine. In fact, she loved being a mother again so much she didn't want to resume her other job. We worked out a deal for me to buy her out in payments spread over two years, and I became the owner.

I continued the regional tours Connie had started but looked to branch out to include America's popular tourist cities. Chicago followed Charleston, and I'd just added San Francisco.

As I flew back to New York, I thought about Trish's idea for an expansion to Europe. Competition would be tough, especially regarding Italy, where Perillo Tours had established a strong foothold. Other countries in Europe were already well-represented tour-wise as well. We would be starting from scratch, creating tours much more complicated for us than those we managed within the US. And we would have to offer something unique to stand out. But what?

Visions of the Scottish Highlands and the French wine country were my last thoughts before I drifted off to sleep.

She'd flown from Heathrow Airport in London to Washington Dulles International on an American passport.

The safe house in McLean, Virginia, stood about a mile from CIA headquarters, and the irony was not lost on her. An agent of the Russian Foreign Intelligence Service—the SVR—met her there with what she would need for her mission.

She'd requested the particular assignment—for personal reasons, she'd said. Her controllers, who had supplied her with the information, knew what those reasons were. And they were fine with it, as long as it didn't impede their more important plans. Like James Bond, she'd become a semi-independent operative, and they let her have her way for the most part. She was that good.

She drove the rental car south on I-95 to Richmond then southeast on I-64 toward the coast. A few miles west of Joint Base Langley-Eustis, she checked into a Holiday Inn Express, where another car waited for her in the parking lot.

In her room, she set the alarm for a three-hour nap. She had a long night ahead of her.

Chapter 3

Air Force Brigadier General Patterson Baker said goodbye to the last of the well-wishers at his retirement party. In a ceremony earlier that day, he'd passed the command of the base to Colonel Brett Perry. The next day—in just two hours, actually—he'd be a civilian for the first time in almost forty years.

He turned to his wife. "What time will the movers be coming, honey?"

"They said around eight." She took his hand. "Are you ready for the change, Pat?"

He gave her hand a squeeze and leaned over for a kiss. "Are *you*, Janice?"

"I'll miss the social life. It'll be pretty quiet in comparison. But having a home of our own will be nice."

"For you to decorate and me to maintain." He chuckled. "I'll have to buy tools and a lawn mower!"

Her face took on a wistful expression. "We've made some good friends over the years."

"And we'll see them again. We have the time for travel now, Jan."

She laughed. "Without orders, for a change."

He looked at the club staff cleaning up. "Time to go, love."

They headed to their Lexus in the dimly lit, nearly empty parking lot. He hit the key fob button, and the car's lights came on.

As he opened the passenger door for his wife, a figure exited a car nearby and approached—a young woman in an Air Force uniform. Captain's bars adorned the epaulettes of her tunic.

She saluted. "General Baker?"

He returned the salute. "Yes?"

"I'm sorry I missed the party. It's been an honor serving under you."

"Thank you, Captain"—he read the name tag—"Wilson."

"Could you..." She shook her head. "No, I shouldn't ask."

"What?"

"I was wondering if I could take a selfie with you. I doubt I'll ever see you again, and I'd cherish the memory."

"Sure. I'd be happy to."

She stepped closer, invading his space, as she reached into her tunic. Before he could react, she pressed the barrel of a snub-nosed revolver against his sternum and pulled the trigger. Eyes wide in shock, he fell to the pavement without making a sound, and the woman trained her weapon on Mrs. Baker before she had a chance to scream.

"That was for Belgrade." The woman lowered the revolver and hurried to her car.

Manhattan
The next day, 9:00 a.m.

I was heading toward the door of my condo when my cell phone rang.

Patience, Trish. I'm on my way. But I didn't recognize the number. The area code, though, was quite familiar.

"Hello?"

"Alexander Baker?"

"Yes."

"This is Colonel James Truax of the AFOSI."

I didn't know him, but I recognized the name. He'd been a lieutenant colonel in the OSI when I left the Air Force. *Why is he calling me?*

"Has anyone contacted you about your father?"

I squeezed the phone, suddenly worried. *Heart attack?* "What happened?" I went back into the living room.

"I'm sorry to break this to you so abruptly, but General Baker was shot to death last night."

No! I stopped my aimless pacing. "Oh my god! Is Mom—Mrs. Baker—all right?"

"She was with him at the time, just after the retirement party in the parking lot of the Langley Club, but she wasn't injured."

Thoughts swirled madly in my head, trying to find purchase. "Was it a robbery?"

"No. It appears to be an assassination."

"I don't understand."

"Neither do we, but we have a lead we're investigating. That's all I can tell you over the phone."

"I'll fly down later today."

"Out of courtesy for your former position and your relationship to the general, we'll share with you what we know."

"I appreciate that, Colonel. Do you know where my mother is?"

"She's staying in the BOQ. I'm sorry for your loss."

"Thank you. I'll call you when I arrive. Bye." I sank into an armchair and called my mother.

"Oh, Alex!" She started to cry. "It's been a horrible, horrible night. You know about Dad?"

"Yes, Mom. I just got off the phone with OSI. I don't know how or why it could have happened. You must be going through hell."

"I can't believe he's dead. Dead! Shot by some crazy woman. Why? It doesn't make sense!" She was sobbing now.

"I'm flying down today to get a briefing. After that, I'll tell you what I've learned."

"They put me in the BOQ."

"I know."

"Connie! She doesn't know about Dad. I can't think straight, Alex." She moaned. "I should have called you two, but it's like I'm paralyzed. My mind's a mess. I don't know what I should be doing."

"Don't worry about that. The Air Force will take care of your needs for now. I'll call Connie, and I'll see you in a few hours."

"Thank you, Alex."

"Bye, Mom."

I called Connie. After the initial shock waned a bit, she got practical. "Mom's all alone. Where is she staying? She and Dad were supposed to be moving to Denver today."

"They put her up in the Bachelor Officers' Quarters for now."

"I'll fly down. Probably not till tomorrow, though. Frank'll have to make arrangements at work so he can take care of Frank Junior."

"I'm going there today, Connie."

"Good. I'll call Mom now."

I caught the shuttle to DC and drove a rental to the base. The sentry at the gate had me on his list. I'd been stationed at Langley early in my career, so I knew my way around. The Security Forces building hadn't changed in the interim.

We met in a conference room. Seated at the table were Truax, who'd come down from DC; Lieutenant Colonel Michael Cassini, the officer in charge of Langley's OSI unit; and two airmen of the Security Forces, formerly known as the Air Police. They had been the first to respond to my father's murder. Each of them had the up-all-night look I remembered so well.

After the airmen gave their report, Truax excused them and handed the ball to Cassini, who looked down at his notes.

"Mrs. Baker described the assassin as a woman, late twenties, early thirties, medium height, with blond hair. She wore an Air Force uniform with captain insignia. Using the subterfuge of taking a selfie with General Baker, she was able to get close to him and fired what Mrs. Baker thought was a .38 Special in direct contact with the general's body in the area of his breastbone." Cassini looked up. "The autopsy is pending, but all indications are of a direct wound to the heart, resulting in almost instantaneous death." He read from his notes again. "After shooting the general, the woman said, quote, 'That's for Belgrade,' then got into her car and left."

"Any idea what that means?" I asked.

"Your father took part in the 1999 NATO bombing of Belgrade during the Kosovo War. He led a squadron of B-2 bombers," Truax explained. "That could be the reason for her statement."

"So it was a revenge murder?"

"The woman had to be a young child at the time," Cassini said. "We're working on the assumption that she or someone she knew was a victim of the bombing."

"She's Serbian?"

"Possibly. She had no accent, according to your mother. She could be an American who had a relative in Belgrade. She had 'Wilson' on her name tag, and we're looking for all female Captain Wilsons in the Air Force, to be thorough, but the name was likely bogus. This assassination was well-planned and had considerable support. For one thing, she had to have military ID to get onto the base. And a uniform, of course. By themselves, not that difficult. But consider this. Somehow, she had to know General Baker's role in the Belgrade operation."

"*I* didn't even know," I said. "If he didn't tell war stories to his own son, I can't believe he'd share that with other civilians."

"I agree," Truax said. "Which leaves her having his personnel record." He pointed at a thick folder in front of him. "Your father's record was paper-based because he was still on active duty, and it's intact."

Paper-based. A thought occurred to me. "But she'd have to know which record to look for in the first place. Have any members of his squadron or superiors in that NATO mission retired?"

Truax gave me a tight smile. "You've put your finger on it. The answer is yes. And those records would be archived—and computerized—at the National Personnel Records Center. We know the NPRC has been hacked on at least one occasion since 1999. The techies are looking into whether there's been a more recent one, but it's irrelevant. Once is enough."

I shook my head. "Sifting through thousands of personnel records would require massive detective work. They'd have to look for all officers who flew planes, who were in an appropriate age range in 1999, their duty assignments, chains of command, then correlate the data to narrow it down to those involved with Belgrade."

"That's what Colonel Cassini meant by 'considerable support.' I'm thinking the Russians. They were on Serbia's side during the Kosovo War, and they certainly have that kind of computer expertise."

As I pondered that, a ringing cell phone broke the silence. Cassini picked up his from the table and answered.

"What's up, Bill?" He listened for a few moments. "It might tie in to something we're working on here" He paused to listen. "Yeah. Ours looks like an assassination, so I think yours might be, too, but better treat it publicly as a robbery gone bad for now. If you come up with any leads, let me know. I'll reciprocate if I can. Thanks, Bill."

Cassini put the phone on the table. "That was Bill Talmadge, the sheriff of York County. We've worked together before. A Bethel Manor citizen was shot to death in his home last night. The victim was retired Air Force Colonel Lloyd Hogan." He looked at me. "Is the name familiar?"

"No."

"Colonel Hogan was your father's second-in-command in the NATO mission."

"So that makes our theory more tenable," Truax said. "Why Russia—or whoever—would be involved in payback so many years later is puzzling. But we'll have to alert all surviving officers involved in that mission." He eyed Cassini. "Anything else?"

"I think that's it for now."

Truax looked at me next. "Thanks for coming in, Mr. Baker. I'll keep you informed on any progress we make in the case."

The landline phone rang, and Cassini picked up the handset.

"Yes, Marcia." He paused to listen. "Okay. Bring them back after Mr. Baker leaves." He ended the call and addressed me. "We'll keep in touch."

"I appreciate that." I nodded to them and left. Passing through the reception area, I noticed two men in suits sitting in visitors' chairs. They kind of looked like cops but not quite. *Why would they be waiting to see Cassini at this particular time? An unrelated matter?* But my still-intact investigator's mindset didn't believe in coincidences.

As I headed to my car, an old memory surfaced of an involvement I'd once had with a certain government organization when I was in the OSI. And Russia possibly being behind my father's assassination bolstered my assessment.

They're CIA.

C onnie arrived the next day. We moved Mom to a hotel off-base. The funeral, an Air Force affair, was held a week later—after the forensic pathologists finally released Dad's body. Since it would be transported to Denver for burial in the family plot, the honor guard ceremony was held on the side lawn of the base chapel. It was an impressive affair, including an eleven-gun salute, the presentation of the flag draping the coffin to the widow, and a bugler playing "Taps."

Connie accompanied Mom to the Denver house and helped her move in when the household goods held in storage were delivered.

I wondered how Mom would cope on her own in an empty house in a city where she'd never lived. A bungalow in a retirement community closer to her family would probably be more suitable, and Connie and I would have to look into that. Connie, of course, knew about financial matters, so she could help Mom with settling those things.

I'd been so preoccupied with learning why my father had been murdered then worrying about how my mother would manage now that he was gone that it suddenly hit me—I would never see him again. I wouldn't ever have the opportunity to bond with him, to assure myself of his acceptance—and approval—of the life decisions I'd made. I would never know the civilian Patterson Baker who was no longer burdened with the Air Force risks and responsibilities he'd had for my entire life.

As I flew back to New York, a profound sadness gripped me along with anger at the cause of it. But when the pilot announced we were starting our descent, I had to put thoughts of Dad into the back of my mind. With the OSI and likely the CIA involved in the case, I would have to depend on their sharing the investigation progress with me. Truax had said he would do that, and I was going to hold him to it. Meanwhile, I had a business to run.

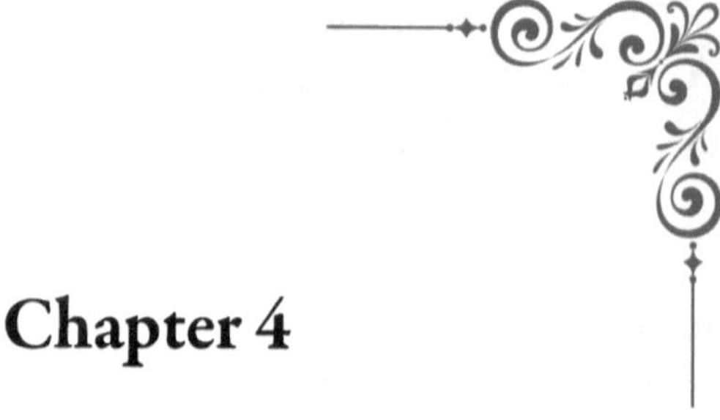

Chapter 4

Manhattan
Two weeks later

Trish and I had our hands full getting the San Francisco tour off the ground. She had the task of lining up candidates for the two positions we would need—the tour director and the driver of the shuttle bus that would ferry our clients around to the various venues. My job was to create the tour packages.

To flatten the learning curve and avoid problematic relocations, we wanted residents of the area for the positions. We brought the top contenders for director to New York for interviews and agreed on our final choice: Ann Renfro, age forty-five, had managed tours for a Sonoma Valley winery, so by necessity, she knew what the other wineries north of the city had to offer. After losing her job due to the COVID-19 pandemic three years earlier, she now worked in sales for a car dealership in Oakland, where she'd grown up. And she had an Uber-driver friend who was happy to take our offer of a better salary and benefits. Two birds with one stone.

I had to come up with attractive tour packages, assign prices, and sign up clients. We would send emails to our previous customers and advertise to find new ones.

Except for New England, where we had Vermont ski packages, our tour business was essentially limited to the summer. Not too many people would want to visit San Francisco during the cool, rainy season. *And Chicago in the winter? Forget it.* Charleston was popular from March through December, but it still left off months for our boots-on-the-ground employees. So they would need other jobs during the downtime, and they knew that going in.

Trish wanted to expand to Europe, but I thought we should consider year-round destinations in the good old USA first, like San Diego and Key West. Maybe even Hawaii.

I had just pulled up "Things to Do in San Diego" on my laptop when my cell phone rang. It was Rick Buie, our man in Charleston.

"What's up, Rick?" I answered as I scrolled down the website.

"Hey, Alex. This is probably nothing, but with what happened to your father, I thought you should know."

That got my attention. "Go ahead."

"I was at a bar last night when this woman sat down next to me. Good-looking, nice figure. She gave me the eye, and I thought, 'Okay, I'm game.' But I soon found out it wasn't me she was interested in. She introduced herself as Angela, and when I gave her my name, she said she knew I ran our Charleston tours. And then it got strange."

I waited. His pause was typical of the way he baited our clients during the tours to pique their interest and get them involved. "In what way?"

"She said she went to high school with an Alexander Baker and wanted to know if it was you."

High school? "So she'd seen our website."

"Either that, or she talked with one of our tourists. But accidentally finding you when looking into a tour doesn't compute. I mean, she's already in Charleston, right? She could do her own itinerary. And she had to have followed me to the bar, which isn't in the hotel we use."

"You're right. Seems fishy."

"Well, she was fishing, all right. She said she wanted to get ahold of you for old times' sake and asked me for your phone number. I gave her the website number, but she already had that. I said, 'Sorry, that's all I have.' So if an Angela—she didn't give me a last name—calls your office and asks for you, you should have your guard up."

"Thanks, Rick."

"Did you happen to know an Angela in high school?"

"That was in Ohio, and no. Not that I recall."

"You think she could be... you know... the one who shot your dad?"

Is she? "Probably not. But I appreciate the heads-up. How's the weather down there?"

"Still pretty warm. I see we have one more group after this one. Then a break before the Christmas season."

"That's right. What was the color of Angela's hair?"

"Dark brown, medium-length."

"Okay. Thanks, man. Talk to you later."

I hung up. The woman in Charleston had brown hair, not blond, but a wig would be an easy disguise. And maybe Dad's killer had worn a blond wig.

Am I being paranoid for no reason? I hadn't thought of being a target of the assassin until now. I'd assumed Dad's history had fueled the revenge—if that was what it was. But maybe this woman, who'd perhaps experienced the bombing as a young child, had lost not only a parent, but also a sibling. Closure for her might mean killing the bombers' children as well.

Jesus.

I got my secretary on the intercom. "Lisa, if an Angela—I don't have a last name—calls and asks for me, get her number and let me know."

"Sure, Alex."

I checked my phone contacts and called Truax. I passed on what Rick had told me.

"You sure you didn't know any Angelas in high school? It's been—what? Twenty years?"

"Right, a long time. A good-looking girl who remembers me after all those years, and I can't remember her? My high school wasn't that big, Colonel. I knew all the pretty girls and dated a few of them. Yeah, I'm positive."

"I'm not sure what to do with this, Mr. Baker. Tell all those NA-TO pilots to warn their kids about attractive women showing an interest in them? Huh. I don't see that working."

"Speaking of that, have there been any other deaths in that group?"

He paused. "One. Active-duty colonel stationed at Scott AFB in Illinois. Similar to the Virginia case. Shot when he answered his doorbell. He either ignored our warning or forgot about it. A neighbor heard the shot and saw a woman leaving the premises."

"Colonel, I'm trying to get my head around this, but I can't."

"How so?"

"Okay, we have a woman getting revenge for something that happened as a result of the Belgrade bombing. A lone wolf isn't logical. It would require a ton of legwork, high-level computer savvy, and preparation—as you pointed out. You were thinking the Russians were behind it, right?"

"That was my guess."

"And you met with the CIA about it."

After another pause, he asked, "What makes you say that?"

I chuckled. "That was *my* guess. Those two men waiting to see you when I left the debriefing."

"I see."

"My point is, why would Russia be behind it? Unless the assassin is Putin's daughter, it doesn't seem credible they would use their resources to help her. Does the CIA have any answers?"

"Mr. Baker—"

"Call me Alex."

"Alex, I can't continue this conversation over the phone."

"How about in person? If I'm a target, I deserve to know what you know."

Truax sighed. "Okay. If you fly down to DC, I'll meet you at the airport, and we'll talk."

"Thank you. I'll call you with my flight info."

I took the shuttle again to Reagan National the next day. Truax met me at the Arrivals exit and led me to his Suburban outside at the curb.

After we'd climbed in, I asked, "So, the CIA?"

He started the engine and headed toward the airport exit. "There was an orphanage..." He paused to turn onto the terminal access road again. Apparently, we would be making a circuit as we talked. "An orphanage in Montenegro active in 1999. Children orphaned by the bombing were taken there. The rumor was that some of them were selected for training in Moscow."

"Spy training?"

"Yes. Those kids would have a natural hatred of Americans."

"One of them is our assassin?"

"Possibly. There've been reports of political figures in Belarus, Ukraine, and other former Soviet republics being killed by a woman."

We passed my terminal. "A female Russian operative doing political assassinations. If she's *our* killer, then she must have two agendas—one for Putin and one for herself."

He nodded. "That's the current theory. She'd have to be one of their primo agents for them to help her with a personal vendetta that they logically shouldn't give a damn about. Of course, these assassins could be two different women."

"You think?"

"No. I'm a believer in Occam's razor—the simplest solution to a problem is usually the right one."

I smiled. "Like what I used to tell my OSI team—when you hear hoofbeats behind you, don't think of zebras."

"Your Angela thing might be completely innocent. Or at least not involved in the assassinations. Doesn't seem like what a skilled agent would do. Too revealing. Your man smelled a rat right away. And it was unnecessary. She had your business number. That would be enough for her to get at you with some concocted story without giving you a tip-off ahead of time."

"Yeah, I have to agree with you." I laughed. "But being paranoid doesn't rule out that someone's really out to get you."

"I hear that." He cracked a smile. "Seems we've reached our daily quota of useful axioms." He stopped in front of the Departures entrance of my terminal. "Take precautions with Angela, whoever she is. Let me know if it amounts to anything."

"I will." I grabbed the door handle. "Thanks, Colonel."

"It's Jim."

I nodded and got out of the car. He drove off, and I went inside the terminal for my flight back to Newark.

Isle of Palms, South Carolina
Same day, 2:00 p.m.

She was running out of time to check off the targets on her list. Soon, Moscow would insist she address theirs.

He had a house on the waterfront, not too far from the gated community of Wild Dunes. The old two-story home was in good condition, with well-kept landscaping. Moscow had found him for her, but she'd done the additional research on her own. He was a widower with adult children living elsewhere. The newer houses on either side were second homes, currently unoccupied.

She parked in the driveway, behind a late-model pickup, and adjusted her wig in the rearview. After grabbing her handbag containing the .38, she headed to the front door, pressed the strange-looking doorbell button, and waited.

A few moments later, the owner suddenly appeared from around the corner of the house. Tall and lean, with thinning gray hair, the sixty-nine-year-old reminded her of Clint Eastwood in his later years. He wore jeans and a T-shirt. But what captured her attention most was the pump-action shotgun in his hands.

"You looking for me?" he asked, the shotgun pointed to the side.

She stepped back on the small porch, hands raised. "Sorry to disturb you, Mister..."

He didn't respond.

She lowered her hands. "I'm Sally Richards of Low Country Realty. I've been checking out homes on the island and wondered if you'd be interested in selling your house."

"You have a card?"

"Certainly." As she made a show of rummaging in her handbag, she noted the barrel of his weapon was now pointing her way. "I'm sorry. Looks like I'm out."

"Uh-huh. Anyway, this house isn't for sale."

"I see. I'm sorry to have bothered you." She stepped off the porch and returned to her car.

She backed out of the driveway, and the man moved in closer. As she drove off, she saw him in the rearview staring at her car.

— ⚬ —

The next day, 11:00 a.m.

Truax called me as I was going through our Manhattan brochure, looking for ways to update it.

"I wanted to give you a heads-up, Alex."

"Shoot." I immediately regretted saying that.

"A woman claiming to be a real estate agent showed up at the house of retired Air Force General Blake Sizemore, the commanding officer of our Belgrade bombing mission. He had one of those security cameras and took precautions because of our warning. He ran her off with a shotgun."

"Maybe she *was* a real estate agent?"

"He got the license number of her car. We traced it to a rental agency at Dulles. Obtained using a bogus credit card with a stolen number. Two weeks ago."

"Okay. She's still at it but was foiled this time. Good news, Jim. But why is it a heads-up for me?"

"The intended victim lives on the Isle of Palms—just across a bridge from Charleston. Your Angela has now taken on new importance."

For sure. "What was her hair color?"

"Brown."

"Did the camera record her?"

"Unfortunately, his unit didn't have that capability. Live-viewing only."

"Close but no cigar."

"If she contacts your office, call me immediately. If she wants to meet, put her off. We can have people there in a matter of hours. And stay away from the office if you can. She doesn't know where you live."

"Jim, if the Russians can hack into the NPRC, how hard could it be to hack into the DMV? She might even be able to do that on her own, for all we know."

"Good point. Okay, just be careful. You've had the training and know the tricks. And, Alex?"

"Yeah?"

"Angela notwithstanding, you are not to get involved with this case. I know you have a personal stake in it, and for that very reason, I'm sure your superiors would have kept you out of it if you were still in the OSI. You're a civilian now, and I can't order you to stand down, but any action on your own initiative could be considered interfering with a government investigation. Do I make myself clear?"

Yeah, right. "Yes, sir. I'll keep you informed of any developments on this end."

"Thank you. Stay safe."

I hung up, already thinking about what I would do if and when Angela made an appearance. I'd expected to get blown off by Truax, but I was still gratified he'd confided in me. Must have been the cop brotherhood at play.

I would take his proscription under advisement, but there was no way I would sit idly by while my father's killer remained at large and there was something I could do about it.

Chapter 5

Manhattan

The call came the next day. An Angela wanted to talk to me. Lisa told her I was unavailable, got her call-back number, and gave it to me. I immediately called Truax.

"Charleston area code. Good. We'll get on it."

"If she's the assassin, Jim, I doubt it'll help. What spy would let her phone number get out?"

"I agree. But we have to check it. A negative search will still mean something. I'll let you know what we find."

"Okay, thanks."

I hung up. Part of me hoped this was a breakthrough, but the realist in me held sway. I couldn't dismiss my concern about being a target. But I had to try putting thoughts of Angela aside.

I leaned back in my chair, thinking of what I'd planned before the call from Angela had me on edge: a Circle Line cruise around Manhattan to update photos for our brochure. The forecast called for sunny skies, though a little on the chilly side with a temperature in the low sixties, but it was mid-October, after all.

I wasn't about to just sit around, waiting for an assassin to come gunning for me. I donned my black leather jacket, grabbed my sunglasses and camera, and was out the door.

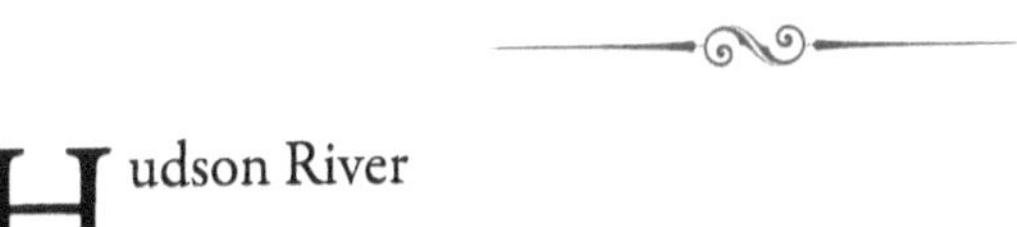

Hudson River

I stood at the railing near the bow on the port side of the cruise ship, idly watching the waves caused by the ship's passage roll toward Manhattan Island. I'd just taken photos of the World Trade Center. That group of buildings, dominated by what had been known as the Freedom Tower, had not been updated for our brochure since 2019.

With nothing new to document regarding the Statue of Liberty and Ellis Island, I had some time to kill before we rounded the southern tip of the island and approached the Brooklyn Bridge. The Brooklyn waterfront had developed several attractions in recent years, and I wanted some shots of that.

A crisp breeze from the west engulfed the ship, but I expected the wind to die down once we entered the East River. I was about to go inside for a cup of coffee when a woman stepped up to the railing next to me. She gave me a smile before directing her gaze at the passing downtown skyline. A nice, inviting smile. The kind a man wouldn't get from a woman who didn't have the slightest interest in him.

But in light of recent events, I was suddenly on guard. She could be interested in me, all right, and her friendly smile might mask a sinister intent. I was glad to see both her hands on the railing.

She wore jeans and a quilted jacket with a Chicago Bears logo on the front. Her auburn hair was pulled into a short ponytail through the gap at the back of a Chicago Cubs cap. Auburn, not blond or dark brown. I relaxed a little.

Not the smartest thing to do, I thought at the same time I reasoned that being suspicious of every friendly woman I met would be not only ridiculous but also counterproductive. So I shoved aside my paranoia in favor of a more primitive reaction. Her attractive face and figure undoubtedly had something to do with that.

"Are you visiting New York?" I asked. A lame approach on a level with, "Do you come here often?" *I'm not exactly Mr. Suave.*

She turned to face me and gave me that smile again. "How did you know?"

So far, so good.

I pointed at her cap and jacket. "A Chicago sports fan on a Manhattan sightseeing boat? Not the wildest of guesses." I held out my hand. "Alex Baker."

She shook it. "Nice to meet you, Alex. I'm Dee Norton, and I *am* from Chicago. Where are *you* from?"

The investigator in me saw an opportunity. "All over. My father was in the Air Force, so I was a military brat growing up." I looked for a tell but didn't see one. "I live in Manhattan now."

She wrinkled her brow. "So why are *you* being a tourist?"

I chuckled. "Actually, I'm here *for* tourists. I run a travel agency that organizes tours in various cities—including New York." I held up the Nikon strapped around my neck. "I'm taking pictures for our advertising. What's your line of work?"

"Fashion design. At least, that's what I want to do. That's why I'm here—to learn. Chicago is great, but New York is where it's at. I thought taking this cruise would be a good way to get the feel of the city. I've never been here before."

"So you've never seen the Statue of Liberty up close and in real life." I pointed to the starboard side of the ship. "There she is. Got a camera?"

She took a cell phone from her jacket, and we walked to the opposite railing. She snapped a picture. "Impressive."

We chatted for a while, and I learned she had grown up in a Chicago suburb. I told her I'd followed in my father's footsteps and joined the Air Force before going into my current business. Again, I caught no sense of recognition from her.

I added details to the information coming from the loudspeakers concerning landmarks we encountered. She showed no signs of wanting to be left alone and appeared to enjoy my company. If so, the feeling was certainly mutual.

I took my pictures of the Brooklyn waterfront, and after we passed under the Brooklyn Bridge, I got wine for us from the bar. I started to entertain the possibility of a date with her that evening.

It had been a while since my last romantic relationship. When I was a lowly lieutenant stationed at Joint Base Lewis-McChord near Tacoma, Washington, I thought I'd found a life partner. But she'd also been an Air Force officer with ambition, and after a promotion she transferred overseas. We exchanged letters for a few months, but they grew farther apart until she stopped writing. I never saw her again. A marriage of two officers would likely mean many long-term separations, so I rationalized it was for the best.

Thereafter, I confined my flings to civilian women. Pleasant and satisfying for what they were, those relationships never led to anything serious.

Then *I* was a civilian, in the category of eligible bachelor, but my business took up most of my time. But now, opportunity was standing next to me.

"Where are you staying?" I asked.

"At the Hobart Hotel—until I can find an apartment. Any suggestions?"

The Hobart wasn't a dive, but it was cheap by Manhattan standards. I wondered about her financial situation. "I can look into that for you."

"That would be great. Thanks. Something reasonable." She smiled. "Money's a little tight. I have a salesclerk job at Macy's here. I want to enroll next semester at the Fashion Institute of Technology, and I need to have the tuition ready by the deadline."

We exchanged phone numbers—hers wasn't the one Angela had given my secretary—as the United Nations Headquarters building came into view.

"Where do all the foreign diplomats stay when the UN is in session?" she asked.

"Huh. I don't know. Embassies, maybe. Hotels." *But not the Hobart.* "Why?"

"Just curious."

The ship continued north past Gracie Mansion, the mayor's residence, and entered the Harlem River flowing between Manhattan and the Bronx. We were on our second glasses of wine, the day had warmed up, and I felt pretty good about my chances with Dee. Most of the major landmarks were behind us, and my photography duty was over. I pointed to the east. "See that big round building?"

She followed my gaze. "The Mets stadium?"

I laughed. "I forgot you were a National League fan. No, Citi Field's in Queens. You're looking at the home of the New York Yankees—in the Bronx."

She gave me a mock pout. "You're a Yankees fan, I suppose."

"Yup."

"Uh, Alex, how have your Yankees done lately, hmm? My Cubs have won the World Series more recently than your team. When was their last title, by the way?" Even her challenging smirk was attractive.

"Ouch! Thanks for reminding me." I thought it was time to make my move. "Do you have plans for the evening?"

"Are you making an offer?" Her grin encouraged me.

"Would you like to have dinner with me?"

She looked away, apparently thinking it over—or just being coy. When she turned back to me, she was grinning again. "I would!"

"Great! What kind of food do you like? Italian, French, Indian... Russian?" I couldn't help it. Despite pushing thoughts of the assassin to the back of my mind, my training kicked in uninvited.

She looked at me funny. "Russian?"

I scrambled for a smooth answer now that she'd called me on my impetuous suggestion. "Uh, sure. Caviar from the Black Sea, chicken Kiev, beef stroganoff." I spread my hands. "New York has any kind of restaurant you want." I chuckled. "Even those serving British cuisine."

She rolled her eyes. "I like any kind of food that tastes good. You choose the place."

"I'll pick you up at the hotel. About six?"

"No need for that, Alex. I'll meet you there. Just call me with the name of the restaurant and its address when you've decided."

She was likely hedging her bets, and I couldn't blame her. I could be a charming serial killer, after all. "Will do."

We headed around Manhattan's northern tip then passed under the George Washington Bridge. I had a slight buzz going from the wine, and that enhanced my anticipation of an enjoyable evening. By the time we docked at Pier 83, I'd decided that meeting Dee was pure serendipity, a chance encounter out of the blue. Still, I couldn't escape the thought that those metaphorical hoofbeats in my mind were probably not coming from zebras.

Chapter 6

She didn't have a plan yet. Worse, she had no idea how much time remained to come up with one.

Baker's office was out. The travel agency, located on a busy street, had people coming and going all the time. His condo had an enclosed garage, and if he was already on alert, as she assumed, she couldn't surprise him at the front door, like the other two targets she'd eliminated.

So it would have to be done when he was on the move, alone, on business or personal errands. That meant surveillance. And that's why she'd ended up buying a Circle Line Cruise ticket.

As she made contact with Baker then engaged him in conversation, she wondered how a hit on a ship teeming with tourists could be possible and still allow for a getaway. After concluding such an assassination had a dangerously low chance of success, she relaxed, the intensity of the hunt winding down. And that was when she noticed a woman on the opposite side of the ship staring at them: late twenties or early thirties, with blond hair, she was wearing a calf-length coat.

Maybe the woman had been attracted by Baker. Though not movie-star handsome, he *was* good-looking. Or maybe the female tourist was actually checking *her* out. In either case, the woman wasn't a threat. But she couldn't afford to assume such an innocent motive in a woman who happened to be there just for the enjoyment of a scenic boat ride.

Her hand found the comforting presence of the Beretta 92 Compact in her jacket pocket as Baker asked her for the date. When she turned away as if considering the question, the woman was now holding up a cell phone to take a picture of them.

Damn! She turned her eyes back to the clueless Baker, his eyebrows raised in anticipation of her answer. She forced a smile. "I would!"

I'd chosen a cozy Italian restaurant near my condo for our date. Having eaten there a few times, I thought it had just the right ambiance for seeing if meeting Dee on the ship could lead to something more.

I'd decided it *had* been a chance meeting. If Dee were a skilled assassin, surely she could have dispatched me, ditched the weapon overboard, and become lost amid scores of tourists as I fell to the deck, mortally wounded.

My death wouldn't have had to come from a bullet. I was aware of claims that Putin's enemies had been attacked with poisons in public places. A covert stab with a needle, a powder surreptitiously poured into my wineglass, a toxic aerosol suddenly sprayed in my face—any of these techniques could have done me in with little risk to the killer.

But I was thinking of these scenarios after the fact in my condo while preparing for our date, and hindsight was always twenty-twenty. I could have stayed in the office and not taken the photo tour. But having decided to do what was needed for the business, I could have kept to myself and not struck up a conversation—with a woman, no less. But even without that social contact, I would have to be watching all the women all the time if I were to be completely careful. And I *had* semi-interrogated Dee so I could semi-eliminate her as a suspect. Bottom line: nothing bad had happened.

I was rationalizing my decisions, for sure. But there was no way I would be a recluse because a woman *might* be out to kill me. In fact, being out in public, presenting myself as a target, could give me an active role in catching the woman who'd killed my father. I mulled that over as I got dressed in business casual—white button-down shirt, navy blazer, gray slacks, and loafers.

Having planned for a possible next-level step after dinner, I had wine and liquor available. I'd also cleared the condo of clutter, turned down the bed, and set the bedroom lighting on dim. Satisfied with my preparations, I headed for Palumbo's on foot.

When he emerged from the building and walked north briskly, she followed. Noting the abundant foot traffic in both directions, she looked for the blond woman. After he entered the restaurant, she slowed her pace.

Theresa Palumbo, the owner's wife, smiled at me from the hostess lectern. "Mr. Baker. So nice to have you with us again. Your table is ready."

"Thank you." I scanned the bar but didn't see Dee. "I'm expecting a lady to join me."

She looked over my shoulder. "Is that her?"

I turned. "Right on time, Dee."

"I'm never late for a first date." She gave me a wink and grinned.

Dee wore a dark-green jacket over a white blouse. Her matching green knee-length skirt let me confirm my guess as to the shape of her jeans-clad legs on the ship. Hoop earrings and a red-pink lipstick completed the picture. She looked great.

She took an exaggerated sniff of the air. "Smells heavenly in here. I like it already."

Theresa grabbed menus and led us to the corner table I'd request-ed. After we sat, Theresa said, "Your server will be right with you. *Buon appetito!*"

She left, and I smiled at Dee across the white-linen-covered table. A candle flickered in a glass bowl against the wall next to a collection of condiments. "I hope you like Italian food."

"Oh, I do. The aromas are making me ravenous."

That was encouraging.

The thirty-something son of Salvatore Palumbo appeared at our table. "Good evening. I'm Chris and will be taking care of you. Wel-come back, Mr. Baker."

"Thanks, Chris."

"May I start you off with wine or a cocktail?"

I looked at Dee.

"Go ahead, Alex. I haven't decided yet."

She wants to see what I order. "I'll have a Bombay Sapphire marti-ni. Straight up, icy cold."

Chris looked at Dee. "And the lady?"

She looked at me as she said, "The same."

"Very good. I'll be right back with your drinks."

Chris left, and I picked up my menu.

"You've obviously been here before, Mr. Baker."

"A few times."

She perused her menu. "What do you recommend?"

"Anything with their marinara sauce. It's the best I've ever had. And their meatballs are excellent. But the prosciutto-and-spinach pasta is very good, as is the fettuccini and mushrooms."

Chris returned with our martinis and a basket of garlic bread. "Are you ready to order?"

"Give us a minute, Chris," I said.

"Certainly." He went to a table of two young couples, notepad in hand.

We took sips, and she looked over the menu. I had already decided. After a few minutes, Chris returned, and we gave him our selections, including my request of a bottle of Chianti Classico with our meal.

Dee gazed around the room and was frowning when she turned back to me.

"Something wrong?" I asked.

"That woman at the bar. Don't be obvious when you look."

I tried to make it casual. "The middle-aged one talking with the bald guy?"

"No. Wearing a blue dress." Dee looked straight ahead at me.

I snuck another peek. "I don't see her."

Dee looked at the bar then scanned the room. "She's gone."

"What about her?"

"I saw her on the boat today. She seemed interested in us. And I caught her looking our way from the bar."

"Young, old?"

"Early thirties, maybe. Blond hair, attractive."

Angela? My good mood dissipated. "Do you know her?"

"No."

I pretended to be unconcerned and changed the subject to Chicago, a city I'd visited several times and gotten to know and like. As we drank our martinis, we talked about the Magnificent Mile, the Field Museum, Adler Planetarium, and Navy Pier. Then I brought up the subject of pizza.

"Have you tried New York pizza yet?"

"No. Is it special?"

I chuckled. "Well, New York pizzeria owners claim that Chicago pizza isn't authentic. That it's not even pizza, in fact."

"Really? Why's that?" She seemed confused.

"The deep-dish part. Personally, I like Chicago-style pizza. To each his own, right?"

"Absolutely. Who cares about the shape?"

Shape? I thought that was a strange comment, but then Chris arrived with our meals. As he uncorked the Chianti, I said, "Chris, there was a woman sitting at the bar a little while ago, wearing a blue dress. Did you notice her?"

He evinced a slight smirk as he poured a sample into my glass. "I did."

"Have you seen her before?"

"I don't think so. Not here, anyway."

"Okay, thanks." I tried the wine and nodded my approval.

Chris filled our glasses. "Enjoy."

As I watched him go to the bar, I wondered about Miss Blue Dress. Her presence on the ship then here with us at one of the thousands of Manhattan restaurants on the same day couldn't be a coincidence. Yet she'd let herself be seen both times. That could mean it didn't matter—she was planning to eliminate me tonight. *She could be waiting outside to ambush me.*

She must have followed me earlier from the office and tonight from my condo. That conclusion made me think of my conversation with Truax. It did not look good.

I went through the motions of starting on my meal, thinking of my next move. I didn't want to endanger Dee. As I twirled angel-hair pasta on my fork, I decided what I had to do. But it would entail telling a story that would ring true without scaring a woman I hardly knew.

"You have any idea who she is, Alex?" Dee asked as if reading my thoughts.

"I didn't see her, so I can't be sure. But from your description, I have a guess. An old girlfriend. When I broke it off with her, mainly because she was a control freak, she went ballistic. Actually threatened me."

As I spun the tale, Lieutenant Melissa Willoughby popped into my head. She could possibly hold a grudge against me, though she had only herself to blame. But I hadn't seen or heard from her for several years. Still, having that real history to draw on helped me fabricate my story.

"Threatened you how?" Dee looked concerned.

"That she would bad-mouth my business, tell potential clients I was dishonest, spread lies about me on Yelp and Facebook."

"Did she?"

"Not as far as I know—yet." I took a sip of wine. "But she could be waiting outside now, ready to create an ugly scene for your benefit. I want to avoid that."

"You think she could be violent?"

If you only knew! I shrugged. "I didn't think so, but if she's that unhinged to stalk me like she did today, who knows what she might try." I needed a reasonable enough excuse to do what I'd been considering, and Dee had just given it to me.

"Maybe you should call the police."

And look like a wimp afraid of a hysterical woman? I immediately thought, then realized I was reacting to my own concocted tale. Angela was no jilted girlfriend, but someone who could kill us both. I had to walk a line of logic consistent with the imaginary threat while defending against one that could be quite real.

"I'd rather not go down that road, Dee. It'd be messy for all of us. But I have an idea. Did you come here by taxi?"

"Yes."

I caught Chris's eye, and he came over to us.

"Chris, that woman I asked you about is an old girlfriend of mine. When we split up, she didn't take it well. I'm afraid she might be waiting for us outside to do something drastic. Her meathead of a brother could be with her."

"Uh, we don't have any security people, Mr. Baker." Worry lines on his forehead deepened.

"I understand. But you must have a back entrance, right?"

"Yeah, off the kitchen. It's on the alley that runs behind the restaurant."

"Would it be okay if Dee and I went out that way when we leave?"

"Sure, no problem."

"Thanks, man."

Chris crossed the room and went through the swinging door to the kitchen, presumably to tell his father, the head chef, of our predicament.

"So here's what we'll do, Dee. I'll call Uber and have the driver pick us up in the alley. You can be dropped off at your hotel."

She picked up her wineglass and peered at me over its rim. "Did you have another plan for us before your girlfriend showed up?"

I gave her a sheepish look. "Actually, I did. I thought we'd take an after-dinner stroll to my condo. It's only a couple of blocks from here."

Her eyebrows went up a tad. "I see. Do you have etchings to show me?"

I like this woman! Despite the potential danger, I chuckled. "No, but I can order tiramisu to go, and we could have dessert at my place. It'll be the shortest Uber ride in history, and Cheryl"—I made up the name—"can have a conniption all to herself when we don't show up."

"I love tiramisu."

She ran her tongue over her upper lip, and I felt a stirring in my groin. I looked down at my plate. "Maybe we should go before Cheryl gets impatient and storms into the restaurant."

"Good idea."

I poured the last of the wine into our glasses and signaled Chris, who hurried over.

"We're going to leave before something happens," I said. "Can we have doggie bags and two orders of tiramisu to take with us?"

"You bet. I'll get right on it."

Maybe Baker believed his scorned-girlfriend explanation, but she couldn't afford to.

His condo could be staked out, and she'd been seen twice in his company. She would have to continue playing the role Baker had apparently already accepted. She was reasonably sure her cover hadn't been blown, but she had to be careful.

But she had an advantage the woman had stupidly given her. Finally, there was a face to put with the heretofore anonymous threat, while her Dee character ostensibly remained an innocent bystander. For the time being.

Chapter 7

The Uber driver, a pretty young woman working her way through City College, dropped us off in front of my building. I had her drive by slowly first, so I could scope out the area. The streetlights had come on, but shadows remained where an assassin could lie in wait.

My escape plan from Palumbo's had been prudent, but Angela could have anticipated our ultimate destination and beat us there. And for all I knew, she had a confederate providing surveillance backup.

I realized I should've called Truax with this latest development. But even if I had, no way could he have managed to get the cavalry here in time.

I had a Beretta M9—the sidearm I was familiar with from my Air Force days—but it was sitting in my nightstand. Although the Supreme Court had mandated New York loosen its concealed carry law, I hadn't seen a reason to apply for a permit. Until then.

"I don't see her," I said to Dee and led her quickly to the front door. I tapped the code into the security pad, and we went into the foyer, which was empty of residents or would-be assassins at that moment.

We took the elevator to the fourth floor and came out into an empty hallway. My condo was about halfway down. I was about to turn the key in the lock when the door at the far end of the hall opened. I tensed before seeing Tim Harris and his wife, Barbara, emerge and head toward the elevator.

"Hey, Alex," Tim said.

"What're you guys up to?" I asked, trying to be sociable.

"Going to the movies."

"Have a good evening."

"Thanks."

I opened the door. When it closed behind us, I relaxed.

"Let me get this stuff squared away." I took the bag of goodies from the restaurant to the kitchen. I set the bag on the island and was removing the cartons when I felt something small and hard poke into my back.

I raised my hands, instantly knowing I'd made a stupid—and fatal—mistake. Hoping for a romantic interlude, I'd invited the killer into my home. "Angela?"

"Turn around."

I did. Dee had a big grin on her face—not surprising, since she had successfully conned me big time. Then I looked down, expecting to see a pistol. But her right hand was formed into the classic pretend-gun shape, the index finger pointed at me.

"Bang," she said and laughed.

"What the hell?"

"You can put your hands down, Alex." She shook her head. "Really? You thought I was going to rob you—or worse?"

I forced a chuckle. "Of course not. I was just playing along."

"Well, you're a good actor. You looked pretty scared to me." Her grin disappeared. "Who's Angela?"

"Angela?"

"The name you shouted out. Is there a woman here I don't know about? I thought we were alone."

Great. How do I explain that? I temporized by deflecting. "Why did you pretend to put a gun in my back?"

"It was a finger, Alex. C'mon. I wasn't pretending anything until I saw your reaction. I wanted you to stop with the food and pay attention to *me.*"

"Mission accomplished, for sure."

"So, who's Angela?"

"That was part of my act. I thought you were making a joke about my paranoia regarding my old girlfriend, and I played along."

"But you said her name was Cheryl."

Oops! She had me. "It's a long story."

"There is no Cheryl, is there?"

"No."

"I thought so. But you *did* think that woman in the bar was a threat. That was Angela?"

"Maybe. I really don't know." I stepped closer to her, put my hands on her hips, and drew her to me. She lifted her face, the invitation there. We kissed. "Is that the kind of attention you wanted?"

"Bingo."

"Do you want the tiramisu now—or later?"

She grabbed my buttocks. "Later would be good."

D ee was an enthusiastic, uninhibited lover, as I'd anticipated. After a second round of pleasure, we lay side by side, temporarily sated.

"Would you like something to drink?" I asked.

"Do you have chardonnay?"

"I do. Be right back."

I went to the kitchen, poured a glass of wine for Dee and uncapped a Molson Golden for myself. When I returned, she was sitting up against the headboard with the sheet gathered at her waist, her generous breasts exposed to my admiring gaze. I handed her the glass and crawled in next to her.

I took a swig of beer and reached beneath the sheet to stroke her thigh. "I have an extra toothbrush if you can stay the night."

"I have to be at Macy's by nine." She looked at me questioningly.

I leaned over to nuzzle her neck. "We'll have an early breakfast, and I'll drive you to your hotel in time to get ready for work."

"Well, that'll give us plenty of time for you to tell me your long story."

I took another pull from the bottle and grinned. "I'll tell you mine if you tell me yours. I'm the home team, so you bat first."

She frowned as she sipped her wine. "I already did—on the boat."

"I think you left out a few things. You have secrets too."

She looked away. "Don't we all?"

"Yes, but if you want to hear mine, you'll have to share yours. Like where you're really from, for instance."

She tried to hide her surprise by taking a drink from her glass. "What do you mean by that?"

I smiled to put her at ease. It wasn't a cross-examination. *Well, maybe a little.* "You made a slip when we were talking about pizza. You didn't seem to know what a Chicago-style pizza is. Which made me think you really weren't all that familiar with the Windy City."

She stared at me. "But we talked about those city landmarks."

"Easy to look up, and I did most of the talking, as I recall."

She looked annoyed. "Here I am, lying naked in your bed, and you're giving me the third degree. What are you? A detective?"

"I used to be, and that'll be part of *my* story. But it's still your turn. I just want to get to know the real you, Dee."

She sighed. "Okay, you got me. I fudged my resume. I thought Chicago was a more exciting origin than the small town in Iowa where I really grew up. I've never even been to Chicago."

"Those team logos you wore were part of the charade, then."

"Kind of, but I am familiar with the Bears and the Cubs. Dad was a fan, and we watched them play on TV a lot."

"Are you actually here to pursue a fashion design career?"

"Yes!" She rolled her eyes. "That part is true. And now I think it's your turn, Detective."

She already knew part of his backstory, but she wanted to know how much more he would reveal.

That damned pizza thing! She should have done more Chicago research. She'd almost got away with it. Only her quick thinking had kept her looking innocent. But all she knew about Iowa was that it was rural and had a lot of farmers, hogs, and corn. *Please don't quiz me on Iowa!*

She liked him, though, and that wasn't a good thing for what she had to do.

"How about hearing my secrets over tiramisu?" I asked. "I'll make some coffee."

"Won't that keep us awake?"

I gave her a lascivious grin. "I hope so."

She borrowed my robe, and I slipped on my boxers and a T-shirt. I didn't own pajamas.

We sat at the island, finally having our dessert.

"So are you going to tell me who Angela really is?" Dee asked.

"I'll get to that, I promise. But there's some background needed first."

Without being specific, I told her about my father's murder. That the killer was a young woman who appeared to want revenge for something he did during an Air Force mission more than twenty years in the past. Her reaction seemed appropriately shocked.

"Wow. That's terrible! And after all those years. But revenge can be a powerful motivator."

Then I told her about the inquiry in Charleston and the phone call to my office—both made by the mysterious Angela.

"No chance she remembered you from high school?"

"Extremely unlikely."

"But the killer coming after you seems a stretch. If she wanted revenge, she already had it. This woman didn't kill your mother, after all. Why do you think she'd focus on the son next?"

I went to the counter for the coffee decanter and refilled our mugs as I thought about how much more I should reveal.

"You made a comment about me being a detective earlier. When I was in the Air Force, that was my job, essentially. I was in charge of a criminal investigation unit. Because of that, and my being the general's son, I was made privy to other murders connected to my father—men who also had been involved in that same mission. I can't divulge any details of those incidents. But an unsuccessful attempt was made by a woman on the life of an officer in Dad's unit. That happened in Charleston, just before Angela started asking about me. Her description matched what we knew of the assassin—around thirty, attractive."

"It could be a coincidence. Lots of women meet those criteria."

I ate the last of my tiramisu and followed it with a swig of coffee. "I hope you're right. But that woman in the blue dress also matched the killer's description. So I'm going to keep my threat radar turned on."

"Like you did with me on the boat?" She gave me a smirk. "I could have been Angela, for all you knew. The right age. Do you think I'm reasonably attractive?"

"Of course."

"In fact, you thought I *was* Angela and got the drop on you earlier tonight. Your radar alert malfunctioned."

I spread my hands and gave her my sheepish look. "What can I say? I screwed up because you dazzled the radar out of me. That's why the gun in my back caught me by surprise. It shouldn't have. Even letting you get behind me was a mistake I shouldn't have made. In fact, I should've checked you out before setting myself up to be alone with you."

She squinted at me. "Aren't you a little concerned that I could still be Angela and looking for the right opportunity?"

"What a way to go!"

"Seriously."

"Yeah, I suppose you could kill me in my sleep and slip away unseen. But you *were* seen—by my neighbors. And you were undoubtedly caught by the security cameras, which a trained assassin would have noticed. One outside the entrance, one in the vestibule, and there are two on each floor."

Her eyes got big. "Oh my god! Thanks for telling me. I didn't notice them." She grinned. "Because I was dazzled by *you*. I'll have to think of another plan now."

I stared into her eyes for a moment then leaned over for a kiss. But she cut it short.

"There's a flaw in your reasoning," she said. "Okay, I'd be caught on tape and by witnesses. But what about the woman at the bar? Lots of people saw her there. Hard to miss, apparently. Chris certainly noticed her. Your agent in Charleston got a close-up look. As did your mother. Not to mention having to show a passport in order to enter the country and a driver's license to rent a car, stuff like that. Doesn't seem to have mattered much. She's still on the loose."

"Now who's being a detective?"

"Just thinking out loud."

"And you're right. Merely being seen at the potential crime scene wouldn't have to stop you. You'd have to be captured to make a definitive identification." I shook my head in mock dismay. "And here I thought I was safe."

"You think the woman I saw today could be her, don't you?"

"Actually, I think that was Cheryl." I laughed, and she punched me in the shoulder. "Yes, I have to assume she's the one we're looking for."

"We?"

"The Air Force, probably the FBI, and the CIA. And me."

"She must have followed you to be in both places today."

I nodded. "That's what I figured."

"She knows where you live."

"Stands to reason."

"Doesn't that scare you?"

"Sure." I smiled. "Like your finger scared me." I put up a hand to stop her protest. "But I'll bring in reinforcements through my connection in the Air Force. Meanwhile, assuming you're not a killer, I'm safe here, my car is secure in the garage, and I'll take precautions at the office."

"Sounds reasonable."

I undid the belt of the robe, causing it to gape open. "This talk about being hunted by an assassin is a downer. I need a distraction. Can you help me with that?"

"Absolutely."

After another lovemaking session, Dee got up to use the bathroom, and I slipped the Beretta under my pillow. Just in case.

Dee was certainly smart. Her analysis of my situation had been spot-on. Not the kind of sharp deductive thinking I'd expect from an untrained small-town girl from Iowa. And that bothered me just a tad. I would have to ask her more about her years as an adult. All

I had at that point was that she'd watched TV with her father while growing up.

But as I drifted off to sleep with her lying next to me, I felt reasonably content. I'd made my bed and was literally lying in it. I wasn't sure who Dee really was, but if she was the assassin, she was the most cold-blooded killer I'd ever come across. She'd had ample opportunities to off me, cameras and witnesses notwithstanding. Instead, we'd made love. Still, I had to wonder if meeting Dee and the other woman showing up were coincidences or dots that could be connected in some way. But Morpheus claimed me before I could analyze it further.

I woke five hours later, according to the nightstand clock, with the same contentment. Her scent still lingered in the bedclothes. Dawn light seeped through the drawn curtains. I looked over to find the other side of the bed empty.

I listened for sounds coming through the open bathroom door, but the condo was quiet. The 9mm remained under my pillow. I grabbed it and got out of bed. My discarded boxers from the night before lay on the floor, and I slipped them on. I didn't see her clothes. She wasn't in the kitchen or the living room.

She was gone.

Chapter 8

After spending the morning scouting the area, she'd found a suitable location. The old hotel stood less than a block from the flashier Westin New York Grand Central across the street. She guessed it had been built in the fifties, probably in response to the establishment of the UN Headquarters a mere half-mile away at the end of East Forty-Second Street. She didn't know if the room windows opened, but she was prepared if they didn't. All she needed was an unobstructed sightline.

A middle-aged doorman tipped his hat as she entered. The lobby's tiled floor supported several tasteful seating areas with furniture that had likely been replaced within the last few years. There was no concierge desk, lobby bar, or a restaurant entrance. The Pillsbury was a no-frills, budget-friendly hotel.

She approached a young man wearing a burgundy blazer with the logo of the hotel featured on the breast pocket.

"May I help you?"

"Do you have any vacancies? I don't have a reservation."

"How many nights?"

"Well, that depends on how well my business meetings go, but at least two, I think."

As he tapped on a computer keyboard, she added, "I'd like a room facing the street if possible. High enough to dampen traffic noise but not too high." She smiled again when he looked up. "I have a slight fear of heights."

The clerk nodded and went back to the computer. After a moment, he said, "I have a queen-bed room on the sixth floor, on the Forty-Second Street side. One forty-nine a night." He looked at her expectantly.

"That will do nicely." She reached into her handbag for a credit card she hadn't used yet.

He slid a registration form in front of her on the counter and took the card. After processing it, he handed it back to her, glanced at the registration, and eyed her wheeled suitcase. "Do you need help with your luggage, Ms. Oliver?"

"No thank you. This is all I have."

He gave her a paper folder. "Room 611. You're entitled to a discount at the restaurant next door, Café Armand. Your key card serves as the coupon. It opens for breakfast at six a.m. and provides lunch and dinner as well."

"Thank you."

"Enjoy your stay."

She wheeled her case to the elevator.

Why did she leave without even saying goodbye? As I took a shower, the mystery surrounding Dee dominated my thoughts. I replayed the previous day and night in my mind, searching for explanations.

I couldn't ignore the most obvious one—that I had been completely wrong about her and Dee was, indeed, Angela. *If so, did she change her mind about killing me? Because I'd won her over with my sex appeal?*

More likely, she'd concluded it was too risky to exact her revenge last night and decided to get at me in another, safer way. But it would be more logical if she kept up the pretense of a burgeoning romance to provide a better opportunity to complete her mission later.

And who was the woman in the blue dress? Was she the real threat? Both? Neither?

I dressed for work as those questions swirled in my head. The belt holster for the Beretta was buried in my sock drawer, and I strapped the weapon on. I would be armed from then on, New York's gun laws be damned.

I slipped on a sport coat, grabbed my cell phone, which I'd turned off the night before, and went through the kitchen to the door that led to the garage elevator. I would get coffee at the office.

Maybe she'll call me with a reasonable explanation, I thought as I drove the SUV toward my place of business. Checking the rearview for a tail was a habit, but it was even more pertinent now. No one had followed me into the parking garage.

I grabbed the camera from the passenger seat and walked the two blocks to the office, on the alert for any young woman giving me more than a passing glance.

There were no customers in the reception area when I entered. "Morning, Lisa," I greeted our secretary.

"Good morning, Alex. Looks like we'll have another nice day."

"Anything going on?"

"Not much. But she called again."

"Who?" I asked but already knew.

"Angela. She wants you to call her."

"Same number?"

"Yeah."

"Okay, thanks." I went past her desk to Trish's office. She was on the phone, so I placed the camera on her desk and helped myself to a cup of coffee from the pot on her credenza.

She ended the call. "Those the Circle Line shots?"

"Yup."

"I'll set up a meeting with the graphics guy to plan a new brochure."

"Okay." I plopped into a visitor's chair and sipped my coffee.

"What's wrong?" She knew me too well.

"I have a stalker."

Her eyes got big. "Really?"

"I think so." Trish knew about my father. I filled her in about the other assassinations and the calls from Angela.

"You think she's coming after you?"

I sighed. "I don't have proof, but the coincidences bother me." I told her about Dee and Miss Blue Dress.

"Could be this Dee person is the stalker, and she's working with the other woman to distract you."

I hadn't considered that. *Good thinking, Trish.* "And the calls from Angela? Another distraction?"

"Maybe. Three different women with a sudden interest in you and acting independently seems a stretch. They must be related in some way."

But how? I forced a grin. "Didn't know you had a CIA background."

"Just trying to be logical. So what're you going to do about it?"

I got up from the chair. "I'll call Colonel Truax. He's in charge of my father's murder investigation. He's aware of Angela but doesn't know about the other two women."

"You think we should hire a security company?"

I frowned. "To watch over me?"

"And the office. Something I just thought of scares me. Have you seen the movie *Three Days of the Condor*?"

"Yeah." Confused at first, I realized where she was going.

"The bad guys were after Robert Redford, but he wasn't there when they got into the building and killed everyone he worked with."

She had a point. I thought such an assault was unlikely, but I didn't really know much about anything in this case.

"Let me talk to Truax. Redford and his people were clueless, but the FBI and CIA are already alerted to the assassin." I smiled. "They might provide protection for the office at no cost to us. And they're pretty good at it. Meanwhile, though, you can look into getting a security camera installed. And a doorbell with an intercom. We should keep the door locked. There's not much foot traffic."

"There is some, not counting the mailman."

We both had the same thought and stared at each other. In the Redford movie, there was a security camera and a locked door, but the killer got buzzed in by posing as a mailman.

"We'll get a mail slot for the door," I said lamely, knowing we had a problem should an office invasion be planned. *How would we know if the customer at the door was really a killer? Damn it!*

"Maybe we should close the office, Alex."

"I'll call Truax, see what he can do. Let's not get carried away because of some movie. The people in Redford's building were all CIA, and the bad guys didn't know who they had to kill, so they didn't take any chances. I'm the target, not you or Lisa. Shooting up a travel agency to get at me is not how this assassin works."

As I gave this reassurance, I didn't know if I believed it. *So why take the risk?* "But to be on the safe side, we'll close the office temporarily. Put a sign on the door saying we're closed for renovations and include a contact number. You and Lisa can work from home and vet potential clients."

She sighed, looking relieved. "Thank you. I feel a lot better."

I gave her a thumbs-up and went to my office next door to call Truax.

"Hey, Alex. Anything new about Angela?"

"That was going to be *my* question."

"Verizon had her number. Only two calls—both to you. She called again?"

"This morning. So who is she?"

"Unknown. It's a prepaid phone, purchased with cash."

"She's using it just to call me?"

"So far. But if she's our assassin, she must have other phones. Whatever, this moves her way up on our suspect list."

For sure. "There've been developments at this end." I told him about Dee and the other woman.

"The plot thickens." He chuckled. "You're a popular guy with the ladies."

"Tell me about it."

"Be careful with Dee. I don't believe in love at first sight. Call it a corollary to my anticoincidence doctrine."

"Well, that's moot now, with her leaving me last night. I called her, and she didn't answer."

"She still might call you. If so, set up a meeting we can cover. Did she tell you where she was staying? Or where she works?"

"The Hobart Hotel, and she's a clerk at Macy's."

"We'll check those out. You already caught her in one lie. If no Dee Norton was registered at the Hobart and nobody at Macy's has heard of her, there's two more. Not a great way to start a relationship."

"You think?" I ran fingers through my hair. "Look, I'm concerned about my office people if she comes looking for me. I don't want a *Three Days of the Condor* thing happening."

"What's that?"

"It's a movie that... Never mind. The point is, we're a business open to the public. No way can we prevent an invasion. We're going to close the office for a while."

After a moment of silence, he said, "Don't do that. We have agents watching it."

Huh? "I didn't notice."

"Well, that's the whole idea, right? You should know that. Your condo building is covered too."

When did that start? "Including last night?"

"Yes. They saw Dee go in with you. Got some good shots of her, and we have the security camera footage."

Ah, so I wasn't the only one who took a chance. "Let me get this straight. You let me be alone with a possible killer?"

"There was a discussion about that. They decided not to spook her and that you could take care of yourself if necessary."

"How thoughtful of them." They were more interested in catching the assassin than in protecting me, obviously.

"Anyway, when she came out around three, they called you."

"To see if I was still alive, I suppose. And when I didn't answer, they rushed to my condo and broke in, right?"

He stayed silent for a moment. "Alex, if you were dead, they couldn't help you. Besides, they didn't know the access code. She called a cab, and the agents followed her to Grand Central, where they lost her."

"Great."

"Getting back to the travel agency, we want you to continue business as usual. We know what Dee looks like. She or any other young woman goes in, an agent will go in after her. Tell your secretary to pretend Mr. Brown is a customer."

"Brown rather than Bond?"

"Funny."

"You think so? I meant it to be sarcastic."

"Another thing," he went on, ignoring the comment. "With the different hair descriptions we have for the assassin, we haven't ruled out a hit team, rather than just one woman. Wigs are an easy enough disguise, but still. One could have been in Charleston while another was in New York scouting you out."

"Blue dress and Angela?"

"Throw Dee into the mix, and we have more possible combinations. Maybe all three are involved." He chuckled again. "Like *Charlie's Angels*, huh?"

Maybe he was trying to put me at ease with his attempt at humor, but I wasn't in the mood. "Want me to call Angela?"

"Absolutely. We need to eliminate somebody. Oops, no pun intended. You know Dee's voice. If Angela sounds different, we've ruled out they're the same person. Find out what she wants. Again, try to arrange a meeting in a public place."

"Okay."

"The good news is that all these possible bad guys are out in the open, and we have a heads-up. Better than flying blind."

"I guess. Okay, I'll get back to you after I call Angela."

"Take care, Alex."

I hung up and took a sip of my now-cold coffee. I had no idea what to expect, and that gave me pause. But then the old excitement I used to have when pursuing leads in the OSI kicked in, invigorating me.

I tapped out Angela's phone number on the desk phone.

Upon entering the hotel room, she set her suitcase on the bed and stepped to the window. Looking down the street, she was pleased with the view of the Westin's entrance. And the window opened. *Perfect.*

She unzipped her bag and withdrew an aluminum case. Five minutes later, she had assembled the Dragunov SVDS rifle, loaded it with 7.62x54mmR rounds, and brought an armchair to the open window. Using the chair's back as a fulcrum for the weapon's barrel, she looked through the scope and adjusted the focus.

Satisfied, she checked her watch. She had a little more than two hours to wait if he kept to his schedule. After setting her alarm for ninety minutes, she stretched out on the bed for a nap.

Chapter 9

Angela answered after the second ring. "About time you called, Alex."

"Angela?"

"That's me. As far as you know."

Dee had a sultry voice, and Angela's was throaty too, but more like a smoker. She wasn't Dee. *Cross that one off.*

"Who are you?"

"I'm Angela."

So that was how it was going to be. "What do you want with me?"

"Not with. *From* you."

"I don't understand."

"And here I thought you were a smart man. Money, Alex. That's what I want from you."

Money? What the hell? "Why should I give you any money?"

"Because you owe me. And it's time to collect."

"I don't know what your game is, but this conversation is over. Goodbye."

"Not so fast, buddy. Don't you want to know what I'll do if you ignore me?"

Too late, I wished I had set up a recorder or even prepared to trace the call. But Truax had never brought it up. And the stakeout agents, whoever they were, didn't think of getting the condo building's passcode? I was beginning to lose faith in the competence of my so-called protectors.

"Still there, Alex?"

I sighed. Might as well see what the crazy woman wanted—and why. "Why did you choose me to extort? And what makes you think you'll succeed?"

"Because of what you did. That's answer number one. Number two is because of the grief I can cause if you refuse to cooperate."

"What did I ever do to you?"

She laughed. "Nice try. That's the beauty of it. So many possibilities. I'll give you a hint. I know about your years in the Air Force. Remember all those people you went after? No, you probably don't. But you think one or more of them might want some payback?"

"You're not going to tell me."

"And let you figure out who I am? I'm no fool."

"So this has nothing to do with my father."

She didn't respond for a few moments. "He already paid his price."

I'd eliminated her as the assassin as soon as money entered the picture, but now the suspicion returned. Our theory of the killer's motivation could be all wet. She might be driven by not just what had happened in Belgrade, but a hatred for the Air Force in general.

"My father was a pilot. He had nothing to do with my job in the Air Force."

"The sins of the father..."

Well, that was vague. Implying a connection between my father's missions and my putting away bad guys didn't work. But Dad's murder was widely publicized. *She's blowing smoke, trying to act the badass.*

I chuckled. "So if I don't pay up for this harm I did you or someone you know, you'll kill me?"

"Oh dear, Alex. I don't want to do that. Really, I don't. But I will if you give me no choice. First, though, will be that girlfriend of yours to show I mean business."

Now I knew I was talking to Miss Blue Dress. "You were on the boat and later in the restaurant."

"She gave me away, huh? Yup. That was me."

Angela had just ruled herself out as a skilled assassin. "Not too smart, showing yourself like that."

"But *you* didn't notice me, did you, love? This isn't my first rodeo. I know how to get what I want."

"You've killed before?"

"Nice girls don't kiss and tell."

It was going along too easy for her. I had to shake her tree, get her mad. "You've got nothing to tell, *love*. I'm not buying this bull-shit you're peddling."

"No?" Heat edged her voice now. "Well, you're gonna find out I'm not a rookie."

"You killed men because they didn't pay up. Do I have that right?"

"Now you get the picture."

"Too bad about your mark in South Carolina."

After another pause, she asked, "What about him?"

"You see, I heard about that. My manager in Charleston—the one you talked to in the bar—told me. It was on the local news. Had to have been a real bummer for you to be defeated by such an old fart."

"I'm not done with him yet."

She doesn't know what I'm talking about. I had to hand it to her, though. She was quick on her feet. I laughed. "Good luck with that."

"Focus on *your* debt, okay?"

"What is that, exactly?"

"Two hundred fifty thousand."

"Well, golly. That seems to be a downright reasonable amount, considering all the bad shit I've done. Let me think it over and get back to you."

"Don't call me. I'll call you. In twenty-four hours. That's the deadline to make up your mind." She disconnected.

Angela represented a whole different ball game. She hadn't killed Dad and the other Air Force guys, and I thought her threats were bluster. A crazed woman with blood in her eye could still be dangerous, though. I wasn't worried about Dee; if I didn't know where she was, Angela wouldn't either. As if the assassin conundrum weren't confusing enough, we now had a wild card in the mix. I wished I'd spotted her when Dee did.

I sat back, musing about this latest wrinkle and how Truax would react to it. Then I had a thought that concerned—no, irritated—me. The feds were using me as bait—on their terms, not mine. The matter of Angela couldn't have played into their hands any better if they needed a patsy. An old saying came to mind: *If you look around the poker table and can't tell who the sucker is, you're it.*

Dee could have been playing me too, but what she said made sense. Dad's killer targeting me wasn't logical. Truax, though, had enthusiastically gone along with my idea, something I wouldn't have thought of if not for Angela. In fact, I seemed to be the one producing suspects for the investigation. I wondered what the OSI, FBI, and the CIA discovered that I knew nothing about.

I called Truax.

"How did it go?" he asked.

"We need to talk. In person. And I want the watchers at the meeting. When can you get here?"

"I'm already in New York. Have been since yesterday."

That took me by surprise. "Good. Where are you staying?"

"The Westin Grand Central, on East Forty-Second Street."

"Set up the meeting there, and call me when it's arranged." I hung up before he could protest. I was pissed. Truax had some explaining to do.

T ruax called me back thirty minutes later.

"The Chrysler Boardroom, four p.m." Terse, no friendly greeting. He was pissed too because I was telling him what to do for a change.

"Full transparency, right?"

"See you at four."

He hung up.

S ince the stakeout agents would be at the meeting, I had Trish close the office early, and I headed to the Westin.

When I entered the conference room, four men and a woman were seated at the table. Truax was the only one I recognized. He introduced the others, who were all FBI agents—three white guys and an African American woman. One of the men was older than the three other thirty-something agents.

Truax waved me to a chair near him at the head of the table. "Let's get started. Alex, you called for this meeting. Tell us your concerns."

The faces around the table stared back at me without expression, except for the woman—Michelle Simpson—who wore a Mona Lisa smile.

"I learned this morning that some of you were watching my condo last night and saw me go in with a woman who fit the general description of the assassin you want to capture. I assume you weren't staking out my place to keep tabs on *my* activities, but to catch the killer if she came after me. But apparently, you had no plan to intervene if that event ensued."

Their deadpan expressions didn't change, and Simpson's wistful smile disappeared.

"Had you clued me in to your presence beforehand, we could have worked out a more secure surveillance."

"Like what, Mr. Baker?" Sid Morganthau, the older agent, asked, looking annoyed. I had just questioned his competence, and he didn't like it. *Too bad.*

"Communications capability, for one thing. I could have been rigged with a way to signal you if there was a problem. You do know how to do that, right?"

"Alex," Truax began, but I held up my hand.

"If I'm going to be bait, I need to be an active participant, not like some goat tied to a tree while you wait for the tiger to come."

"I agree," Truax said, looking at Morganthau, who was obviously the other agents' superior. "Alex is an experienced investigator in his own right. He should be part of the team."

Thanks for that, Jim.

"We were going to set him up with communications equipment," Morganthau said.

"How long had you been on station?" I asked him.

"Two days."

I spread my hands. "Better late than never, I suppose."

Truax clasped his hands together and thumped them down on the table. "Okay, Sid will take care of that issue. And, Alex, you'll furnish him with the security code for your building and a key to your condo."

I nodded.

"Now tell us about Angela."

I reiterated the phone conversation, gave my interpretation of it, and looked at Truax. "Did you really think Angela might have been the assassin?"

He rubbed his face with his hands. "Frankly, the CIA doubted it. Angela wasn't acting like a professional spy would. But Angela coming into the picture when she did made us think the theory of your being a target could have merit. So the surveillance was there for a reason. And when you told me about Dee, it gave credence to what I considered to be a weak theory, and she became the prime suspect. You know I hate to accept coincidences, but in this case, the coincidence of Angela put us on what looks to be the right track."

That cleared up a lot, but something still wasn't quite right. "You thought the assassin coming after me was unlikely, right?"

"We all did, actually. Unlikely but still possible."

"Enough of a possibility for the FBI to tie up four agents in the surveillance and for you to put your boots on the ground in New York?"

"Good point. But it happens that I had another reason to be here that didn't involve you. At least I didn't think it did until you told me about Dee."

With the window open, she watched through the scope as the limousine stopped at the Westin entrance. It was not accompanied by the two plain-marked sedans and the police cruiser this time.

The bodyguard climbed out from the passenger compartment, looked around, then beckoned to the passenger still inside. Bohdan Tereschenko emerged from the car and headed to the entrance, the bodyguard following.

She squeezed the trigger, sending a supersonic round toward her target's head. The bullet would reach Tereschenko before the sound of the shot did, giving him no time to even flinch. His head exploded in a red mist, and he fell to the pavement. The bodyguard, gun in hand, crouched as he put his head on a swivel, looking for the shooter.

She backed away from the window and dismantled the rifle. After storing the parts in their designated cutouts, she returned the aluminum case to her luggage bag and made her way to the lobby.

The young reservation clerk was still on duty. "Wish me luck," she said as she headed to the front door, and he gave her a thumbs-up.

"Need a taxi, ma'am?" the doorman asked, though his eyes were on the chaos up the street.

"No thank you. It's not far." She wheeled the suitcase in the opposite direction from the Westin and soon disappeared around the corner.

Truax started to tell me the real reason he had come to New York, but at that moment, sounds of shouts and screams and the pounding of running feet penetrated the closed door.

"Don't tell me!" Truax went to the door and opened it, the rest of us following.

People were running down the hall in both directions, but mainly away from the lobby. Truax, dressed in civilian clothes, held up his Air Force credentials and stopped a wild-eyed desk clerk. "What's going on?"

"A man got shot," the clerk blurted.

"Where?"

"In front of the hotel. I think he was some kind of diplomat staying here."

Sirens blared on Forty-Second Street, getting nearer.

Truax let the man go as security personnel rushed past. He turned to Morganthau. "Find out if that's our guy."

"Gotta be." Morganthau left with his people in tow, and Truax and I walked slowly after them.

An ambulance had arrived, and two EMTs huddled over a man lying on the concrete outside the glass door. Flashing lights from numerous official vehicles created psychedelic strobes of color on lobby surfaces and gawking onlookers.

Morganthau went to two patrolmen who were talking to a burly bald man. After showing his badge, he joined the conversation. His colleagues, looking down at the pavement beyond the victim, stepped to a large potted plant on the far side of the hotel entrance.

Two plainclothes cops replaced the patrolmen, who went to stand guard at the door. The burly man, as he'd done with the patrolmen, pointed down the street. The detectives looked in that direction.

The EMTs had draped a sheet over the victim and stood idly next to the body—waiting for the medical examiner to arrive, I assumed.

Morganthau's agents said something to him, then they all returned to the lobby a few moments later, Morganthau holding a phone to his ear.

When he got within earshot, I heard him say, "Right. The Westin Grand Central on East Forty-Second Street... Okay." He hung up. "It was Tereschenko, all right. Looks like a sniper. The bodyguard thinks the shot came from a height down the street. Blood splatter and a bullet hole in a planter confirm that. The field office is sending people. It's their screwup. Let them fight it out with the NYPD."

Truax nodded. "Our part of the mission hasn't changed, though."

"It hasn't?" Special Agent Reinhardt asked.

"Let's go back to the conference room, and I'll explain."

After we retook our seats, Truax eyed me. "As I was going to say before we were interrupted, the CIA got word that Ukraine's Minister of Defense, Bohdan Tereschenko, had been targeted for assassination by Putin. Naturally, we figured the woman we were after would be tasked with the job. Tereschenko was scheduled to give a speech at the UN, so that is what brought me to New York."

"And since you were here because the assassin would likely be here, you borrowed some agents to cover me as well." That resolved my last loose end.

"Yes. We thought the hit would come before he had a chance to give the speech because he was going to denounce Putin in the most scathing way. When nothing happened, somebody obviously let down their guard. But that's irrelevant at this point. She's still out there, and it's possible she has more business in New York, so we don't stand down yet."

"If she's working for Putin again," I said, "maybe I've been put on hold."

"Maybe. She had her chance with you, but I think she decided against it because Tereschenko was more important, and she didn't want to raise alarms. That's why she left you last night. Had to prepare. But she could still take care of personal business before she leaves town."

"So Dee is the primary suspect now, and we've eliminated Angela?" I asked.

"Yes, in my view. Including her being part of a hit team. Dee wouldn't have mentioned seeing her, otherwise. Angela was stalking you when she came upon Dee." He smiled. "Coincidences do occasionally happen. We're back to a one-woman-assassin theory again."

"Agreed," Morganthau said. "Which means this Angela, whoever she is, is a matter for local law enforcement."

"But we still have to find Dee Norton if she's hanging around," Truax said. "So we'll check out her cover story and continue the stakeouts."

"Not to be a downer here," Special Agent Townsend spoke up for the first time, "but I don't think we can discount Angela yet."

"Because?" Morganthau asked.

"What if she uses extortion in her personal hits? Like an old-school protection racket. She demands money in return for not destroying them. Then she kills them anyway—revenge with a profit."

I shook my head. "Interesting theory, but Dad would've told my mother about such an attempt."

"Ditto with the families of the other Air Force victims," Truax agreed. "No reports of extortion."

Townsend shrugged. "Just trying to cover all the bases."

Truax stood. "Thanks, everyone. We all have our jobs to do. I'll have to fill the CIA in about Dee. Sid, your team will check out the Hobart Hotel and Macy's. And make sure Alex gets his communications equipment. Alex, give Sid the security code for your building and a key to your condo. Questions?"

No one answered, and we started filing out of the room. Truax held me back. "Feel better now?" he asked.

"I guess. But now I have *two* women after me."

"At least you're no longer tied to that tree, Billy."

He chuckled as he stepped out of the room.

Chapter 10

I drove to my condo after the meeting. After making myself a martini, I sat at the kitchen island with a writing pad and pen.

The reason for Angela's extortion, if her story was to be believed, involved a target of OSI when I commanded the team. Logically, the years I spent as a junior officer in the investigation unit wouldn't apply. So I had about an eighteen-month window—almost four years ago—to consider.

It had to be someone who'd ended up with more than a slap on the wrist, probably significant prison time. That made me think Angela was the wife or girlfriend of the perp in question, because her man would still be locked up, most likely, and unable to come after me himself. And it would have to be a man; I'd prosecuted no major crimes perpetrated by women during that time. Angela was a go-between.

I sipped the drink as I started creating a list of names I could think of. Getting the records for those eighteen months would be the best way to go about it, but Angela's deadline didn't allow enough time for Truax to get them for me.

By the time I'd finished the martini, I had ten names: two Michaels and two Jacks. The other six first names were different. That gave me a chance to narrow the list to two, depending on Angela's reaction to my planned bluff. That was a long shot, but it was all I had.

Satisfied I'd done all I could to pin down the threat, I peered into the fridge, looking for something to eat, and spotted the forgotten containers from Palumbo's. My cell phone rang, but I didn't recognize the number.

"Hello?"

"Mr. Baker, this is Special Agent Reinhardt."

"Peter, right?"

"Pete's fine."

"And I'm Alex. What's up?"

"I have that equipment for you."

"Oh, good. But I haven't had the chance to get a key made yet."

"That's okay. You can have the communicators regardless."

"Where should I meet you?"

"Uh, I'm actually parked down the street from your condo. It's my shift."

"Great. Come on up." I gave him the security code.

Reinhardt fixed me up with a wireless receiver that tucked behind the ear and a voice-activated transmitter disguised as a pen.

I offered him a drink, but of course, he refused.

"I'll get that key made first thing tomorrow, Pete."

"You can give it to Nicole. She'll be on duty then."

"Okay, man. Thanks."

Reinhardt left, and I went back to the fridge.

Completing her handler's most recent mission earned her a brief "vacation" to devote to personal business. Conveniently, she wouldn't have to travel far.

I had a tape recorder ready to go when Angela called me at the office the next day—right on time. I put the desk phone on speaker.

"Time's up, Alex. You going to pay up?"

"Nah. I've decided not to."

"Big mistake!"

Here goes. "You weren't going to give Mike the money anyway, right?"

"Who's Mike?" No hesitation.

"The man you're fronting for."

"I don't know what the hell you're talking about."

I believed her. With a twenty percent chance, I'd guessed wrong.

"Well, it doesn't matter, because you're not getting the money. I'm calling your bluff. I suggest you get a real job, because this extortion thing is not working out for you."

"Is that so?"

"Your threat makes no sense. Kill me if I don't pay you? Where's the profit in that? And you wouldn't even get the credit for it to use to scare your next target, because nobody knows who you are!" I chuckled. "Now, the Mafia, they do it right. Break a leg, cut off a finger first, show the victim they mean business. They only kill when the sap still doesn't pay. But then they get the rep for violence to send a message to other folks. You're an amateur with no idea how the game is played."

"I told you I've done this before." She was backtracking and sounding defensive.

"With no names that could be checked out for proof."

"Your father."

"C'mon, give me a break. I would have known if you tried to extort him, and his murder was in the papers. But not all the details, which I know. You can't give me any of those, can you?"

She was silent for a moment.

"Okay, you got me there," she said. "Worth a try. But I don't have to break your leg to send a message."

"My so-called girlfriend again?"

"You got it."

I laughed. "I met her the day you saw her. We had a dinner date. That's it. Haven't seen her since. I don't know where she is, and neither do you. Try this game with somebody else. I'm not buying."

"I know where you work. You have employees. It would be a shame if something happened to them because of you." She was getting desperate.

"Look, why don't you forget all this foolishness and come to the office. My employees can show you our upcoming vacation packages. I'll leave word to give you a discount. Do you ski?"

"And I know where you live."

"Excuse me if I don't invite you for a visit."

"You'll regret this."

"Angela, the only thing I regret is humoring you this long."

I hung up and turned off the recorder. I hadn't come closer to learning Angela's identity, but she had revealed some tells suggesting she wasn't much of a threat. I had sarcastically dismissed her, though, and it was possible that could push her into an aggressive move. Hell hath no fury, et cetera. But Angela didn't know about the protection from the FBI, so if she tried anything stupid, she would be in for a big surprise.

He owned a hardware store in Brooklyn that his grandfather had started in 1947 when he mustered out of the Army after WWII. It was a good business with local customers and had so far survived the competition from the big chains. She admired that, but it was irrelevant. He had to pay for what he'd done as Captain Aaron Feldman in 1999.

He was always the last to leave the store after it closed at six. Then he would ride his hybrid bicycle to his home, a mile away. He had a daughter in college, and his wife worked the middle shift as an RN at Kings County Hospital. No one would be home.

Feldman came out the front door, secured it with a key, then unlocked the Schwinn chained to a tree at the curb. He wore a helmet, making the hit a bit trickier.

Her driver, a big man known to her only as Boris, started the sedan's engine and took off after the cyclist. After a quarter of a mile, Feldman looked behind him before signaling for a right turn, then left the busy thoroughfare for his much quieter street. He would slow as he neared his driveway and use a remote to open the garage door. That was when she would do it.

She lowered the rear passenger window and took the silenced pistol from her handbag. As expected, Feldman looked behind him again, signaled for another right turn into his driveway, and reached into his windbreaker for the remote. Boris pulled the car abreast of him.

As she took aim, Feldman stopped the bike and turned to face her. The surprise of seeing a pistol in his hand pointed at her caused her to hesitate for a fraction of a second—enough time for her target to shoot.

The bullet banged into her below the clavicle, and her gun dropped to the pavement. Boris accelerated and turned right at the next corner, where a van waited, its rear door open.

While she gasped for breath, Boris helped her into the van then closed the door after her. The van took off, and Boris followed. She unzipped her jacket, ripped open her blouse, and looked down at the wound. Not too big, and not bleeding much. But it was frothy.

"Blyad'!" She reached behind her back with her left hand, making her groan in pain. The hand came back clean. The bullet had not passed through.

She knew what she had to do and took a lipstick from her handbag. She took off the cap and, gritting her teeth, plunged the waxy cylinder into the sucking chest wound.

"Klinik!" she shouted at the driver.

———— ❧ ————

The next day
Trish and I sat down in the afternoon with Ole Nilsen, our printer, to plan the new brochure with the photos I'd taken. It took about an hour, after which Trish returned to the office, now knowing the surveillance setup.

Trish was tough. Although not happy about it, she'd accepted the risk of keeping our business open to the public because she wanted the manhunt to be over—for both our sakes. But our secretary, Lisa, was an innocent bystander, so she worked from home. As I'd discovered, Truax found it easy to use people as bait. I wondered how blithe he would be if he were the one with a target on his back.

I'd forgotten to get the key made, so I did that at the Lowe's on Second Avenue then went home. Reinhardt was on duty again, and I gave him the key.

I had just fixed myself a drink when the bait master called.

"Alex, your girl's still in the city. At least she was as of last night."

"You saw her?"

"No. But she tried to take down another of our Belgrade pilots in Brooklyn. A drive-by as he was coming home from work. But he was armed and got off a shot. Thinks he might have hit her. She was in the rear passenger seat."

"So she had help this time."

"Yup."

"License plate?"

"Stolen. We've got the local hospitals covered, but I doubt she'll show up at one of them if she's wounded. There's a strong Russian community in Brighton Beach. We're working on that."

"She could be dead or wounded or..."

"Alive and not injured at all. We have to assume she's still active."

Naturally. "Angela called again. But that was yesterday. My deadline had expired."

"Great! What's the deal on getting her the money?"

"There isn't one, Jim. I told her I wasn't paying."

"Not good. We want to grab her, and that would be the perfect opportunity."

There it was again—the unknown. *Were Angela and the assassin the same person?* "You haven't given up on Angela as the shooter?"

"I've been thinking about that. Could be the money thing's a dodge—a way to get you out in the open. Anyway, it'd be nice to be sure. Call her back, say you changed your mind. If she doesn't answer or call *you* back, that tells us something."

"That she can't."

"Exactly. But if she gives you instructions for the drop, tell her it'll take at least a day to get the cash together. That'll give us time to set things up."

With me as bait, of course. "Okay, I'll call her now and get back to you."

I hung up my cell and used the landline. After five rings, I didn't expect her to pick up. And no way would there be voicemail. But she came on the line.

"Change your mind, Alex?"

"Not that I believed you, but why take a chance a crazy woman would do something... well, crazy?"

"A wise decision."

"Once you get paid, that's it, right? No coming back for a second helping?"

"That's the deal."

"And I'm supposed to trust you on that?"

"You have no choice." She was back being the badass again.

"There won't be a second round. I can afford this one—barely. But that's it. I'll be tapped out. The Air Force didn't pay that great, you know?"

"But your travel agency is doing well. I calculated a figure you could live with."

"Very generous of you. Okay, where do we meet?"

"Meet? I may not be smart like the Mafia goons you seem impressed with, but I'm not stupid. There won't be a meeting. And there won't be a drop that can be watched. I've seen the movies, okay?"

That threw me a little. "How do I get the money to you then?" A disturbing thought suddenly popped into my head. *Could she have?*

"You're going to wire the funds to my bank in the Caymans."

Oh boy! "The Caymans?" I asked lamely, no longer cocky. She was a step ahead of me. I'd lost the advantage.

"Yes. You have something to write with?" She gave me the account information.

"It's gonna take a day or two to get the money together. I have to call Merrill Lynch, get some stocks sold."

"You do that. I want to see the funds in my account by thirty-six hours from now. And don't call me with any excuses. This number won't work anymore." She disconnected.

Back to square one. Of course I wasn't going to wire the money. Let her come after me if she dared. That was the original plan anyway. I called Truax.

"Christ, a Caymans bank," he said when I told him the good news.

"Jim, isn't it about time we think of Angela as a competent criminal after all?"

He sighed. "And our international woman of mystery?"

Is she? "At this point, I have no idea. But we're back to being on the lookout again, whether it's for Dee, Angela, or both, right?"

"Afraid so."

"Are you still in New York, Jim?"

"Yeah. I was going to fly to DC today, but then last night's hit attempt happened."

"What about the Ukrainian killing? Did you learn anything about the sniper?"

"They found the room she used, got a description of her we already had—blond hair this time—and that was it. God, I hate this case."

"You and me both."

I hung up, dismayed at the lack of progress. Despite the considerable resources of the OSI, the FBI, and the CIA, we still had two women with murder on their minds and no idea who or where they were.

They took her to a doctor's office in Brighton Beach. The chain-smoking, middle-aged fat man with red curly hair knew enough about surgery to treat her.

He'd stuck a tube into her chest through the bullet hole and jerry-rigged an underwater trap to collect the air that was compressing her lung.

She breathed much easier immediately, despite the damned tube coming out of her chest. By the second day of lying on a cot in the back room, the water in the jar had stopped bubbling.

Dr. Nikita, as he called himself, removed the tube the next morning and slapped a bandage on the wound. He took another X-ray.

"The pneumothorax is resolved," he announced to her in Russian after lighting up a Marlboro. He put the film on a view box mounted on the wall. "See, the lung is fully expanded, like on the other side. Fortunately, you only had air causing the problem, from both outside and the damaged air sacs inside. Not much bleeding."

She pointed. "What about the bullet?"

He smiled and blew a cloud of smoke toward the ceiling. "Permanent souvenir. Should cause no trouble. Scar tissue will wall it off. These kids in gangs today—many are walking around with bullets in them." He chuckled. "I, too, have some steel fragments in my back, but that's a long story."

"Thank you, Doctor."

"It will be painful still for a few days when you breathe deeply. The muscle has to heal. I've given you an antibiotic, but if you get a fever, you might have to go to hospital."

"I can leave now?"

"Your people are coming to pick you up."

And then what? She started to think about where she would like to go to finish her recovery.

Chapter 11

My snarky remark to Angela the day before reminded me of the coming ski season. The leaf-peeping tours had ended in northern New England as we headed into November.

I called our Vermont tours manager in Burlington. A lifelong resident of the Green Mountain State, Blake Allen claimed Ethan and Ira Allen in his ancestry. When not working for us, he sold insurance.

"Any snow up there yet?" I asked. We had an app that reported snow conditions on the slopes, but only when the season had begun.

"Stowe got a dusting over the weekend. Killington's still dry. Temp's still too high for snowmaking, but a cold front is due in the next couple of days. Barring a crazy warm spell, we should be okay for Thanksgiving."

"Good to hear. I'll mention that to inquirers." I appreciated his optimism, but late November was always iffy, and in the last couple of years, even December ski conditions were problematic.

"You have anybody lined up yet?" he asked.

"Negative."

"Just so you know, the renovations on the Inn at Bolton Valley aren't done. They say they'll be ready by Thanksgiving, but I'll keep you updated."

"Okay, thanks, Blake."

Vermont was still pending, Ann Renfro was getting San Francisco organized for next year, and Rick Buie had Charleston covered.

Nothing major was left for me to do. It would be a good time to look into the Florida Keys, primarily Key West.

Keys. That triggered a vaguely uneasy thought in my mind I couldn't quite grasp. Something I'd forgotten to do, perhaps. The extra key to the condo had been taken care of. That wasn't it. The condo. Something about that. Then I had it.

I called Truax.

"What's happening?" he answered.

"No news to report. The reason I called is you never told me what you learned about Dee."

"I didn't?"

"Not that I recall."

"Sorry about that. Okay, there was no Dee Norton working at Macy's, and no Dee Norton registered at the Hobart Hotel. So she *was* lying and figured you wouldn't be able to verify those things."

My heart sank. I had so hoped Dee was legit. But she'd become a major suspect again... unless she didn't want me to find her for another reason. Maybe she was afraid I might stalk her. Or wanted to avoid getting serious this soon in our relationship. My hope increased a tad.

"Did you check the other hotels?"

"Which ones out of the thousands do you suggest? Not to mention rooms for rent, boarding houses, and the same for New Jersey."

He was right. *Stupid thought.*

"But we did contact the DMV in Iowa. No Dee Norton registered. Ditto Illinois, though there was an old lady registered there as Deidre Norton. But if Dee is just an initial, then the database is huge. And if she kept the last name but changed her given name, it's even larger."

"But you're looking into it?"

He sighed. "Alex, what's the point? We already know she's not who she claims to be. Say we get lucky and find a Dolores Norton whose license photo kinda looks like our girl, and she used to live in Des Moines but doesn't anymore. How does that help us?"

"You could talk to the family, her friends, acquaintances, get clues to who she is, where she might be. That's standard missing-person investigation."

He sighed again. "If that fortunate scenario happens, we'll look into it. But as far as we know, there is no Dee Norton. We've checked with the IRS and credit card companies. Nothing that fit our suspect."

I was about to end the disappointing call when the mention of DMV photos came back to make a new synaptic connection in my brain. "Those photos of Dee at my condo. Did you share them with the CIA?"

"Of course."

"And?"

"Didn't match anyone in their files."

I couldn't think of anything else. "Sorry to bother you."

"Hey, no bother. Brainstorming can be fruitful. By the way, we've got the NSA involved."

NSA? "What do you mean? How?"

"The assassin is a terrorist, right? And a foreign one operating in the US, to boot. That gives the authority to monitor her, including calls from her phone. Angela's phone too."

"Angela said she wasn't going to use that phone again."

"Okay."

"Are you still in charge of the investigation?"

Truax chuckled. "The NSA thing, huh? Yeah, I'm still the lead, but I've got people literally above my pay grade with a big interest in this. Helps get stuff approved, though. And the powers that be have egg on their faces because of Tereschenko, so what we need, we get. That, for your information, is why you still have FBI stakeouts."

"Which'll end if there're no further developments in New York."

"Right now, however, we're still in full-court-press mode. So keep me informed of anything suspicious."

"I will. Thanks, Jim."

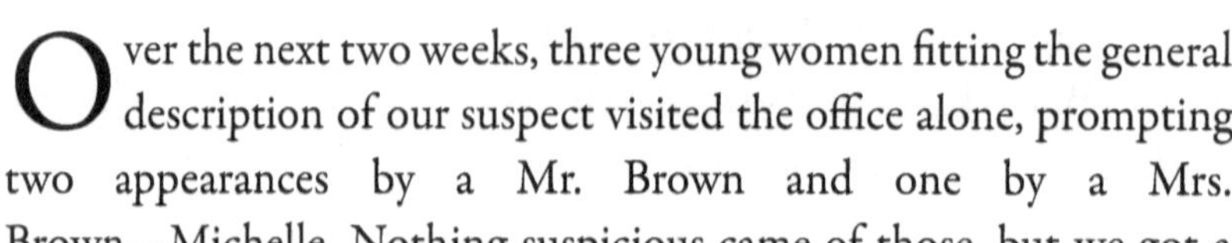

Over the next two weeks, three young women fitting the general description of our suspect visited the office alone, prompting two appearances by a Mr. Brown and one by a Mrs. Brown—Michelle. Nothing suspicious came of those, but we got a contract for a Charleston tour out of it.

The ski areas in Vermont were making snow, we had significant interest in our San Francisco packages, and I was researching Key West in earnest in preparation for a visit. My business hummed along as if everything were normal. Locked-and-loaded normal. Somebody with clout had expedited concealed carry permits for me and Trish. I didn't know she already had a pistol at home.

Angela had not been heard from since our last phone conversation. No news was good news, and my threat level naturally waned as the days went by without incident.

The woman Alex knew as Dee Norton flew into BWI Marshall Airport from Owens International on Grand Cayman Island. Her handler, a medium-height man in his forties sporting a light-brown crew cut, picked her up. They drove to a high-rise apartment building in downtown Baltimore and parked in its underground garage.

Two men in suits were in the tenth-floor apartment when they entered—one, tall and trim with silver hair; the other, equally tall but thinner and about twenty years younger.

"Refreshments are in the kitchen," the older man said and sat on a couch in front of a coffee table. His colleague sat next to him.

The handler, known to the woman as "Norman," poured himself a cup of coffee, and she grabbed a bottle of water. They returned to the living room and took armchairs facing the couch.

"So," the silver-haired man began, "what do you think of this Angela person?"

The woman took a sip from her bottle before answering, "She's not an amateur, exactly, but if she's in the business, she's not very good at it. I think we can forget about her."

"But she's apparently focused on the general's son. Do we forget about him too?"

"He's irrelevant, sir."

"You're no longer interested in him then?"

Am I? "No."

"The FBI and the OSI continue to believe he's a target." He smiled. "We might have had something to do with that."

The younger man next to him spoke up. "We shouldn't disabuse them of that. Despite what Petra says"—he glanced at the woman—"we can't afford to dismiss Angela as a threat. In my opinion."

Norman agreed. "We figured she'd show up at the bank, but she didn't."

"Because she suspected a trap." Silver Hair smiled at Petra. "And she was right."

"Sir," the younger colleague said, "if she suspected a trap, doesn't that tell us something?"

"That's my point," Norman said.

Silver Hair sipped from his coffee cup. "Gentlemen, Angela discovers that her account has been cleaned out. Would she think it's a bank error? Or a hack that coincidentally singled her out? I think not. She tried to extort money from Baker without thinking it through. Too late, she's realized he had access to considerable resources capable of launching a counteroffensive. That's why Petra did not see her at the bank."

"But she couldn't know about the FBI," the leader's young colleague insisted.

"Probably not for certain. But she does know Baker's Air Force history and likely presumes now that his position then had provided him with a number of contacts he could call on to fight back. I agree with Petra. Angela is an unintentional distraction—a criminal, yes, but not an espionage agent."

"Do you have anything else for me, sir?" Petra asked.

"Not at the present time. Norman will contact you with your next assignment." Silver Hair put his coffee cup on the table and stood, signifying the end of the meeting, and his underling followed suit. "Thank you for your report."

I was packing for my trip to Key West when Truax called.

"I take it everything's still quiet on the Angela front?" he asked.

He was just checking in. I relaxed. "Not a peep."

"That might change. I think she'll be hopping mad now."

That got my attention. "You found her?"

"No, but that Cayman bank account of hers went from a hundred thou and change to zero."

I threw the pair of shorts I was holding at the open suitcase but missed. "You bastard!"

"What?"

"She'd backed off, didn't call our bluff, and now you could've pushed her into doing something rash. I thought I was supposed to be a member of the team."

"Now hold—"

"You didn't ask for my opinion. I'm staked to that tree again with no clue what you and the feds are doing."

"Look, it wasn't my idea, Alex. The CIA thought it would be a way to flush her out. Like I said—above my pay grade. They didn't want you to know. I'm telling you now so you'll have a heads-up. And you've still got the FBI watching out for you."

"Thank you very little." I sighed and tried to calm down. "All right, what's done is done, and I appreciate the warning. I'm about to leave town and plan to be away for a few days, so she won't find me here anyway."

"Where're you going?"

"Why? So you can tell the spooks where I am?"

"So *I'll* know. The CIA will find out, believe me. Morganthau and the other shadows don't just report to me. Their main loyalty is to the FBI, man. And the New York SAIC has a direct line to Langley. You flying?"

"Yeah."

"Under your real name, I assume."

I sighed again. "Okay, I get it. I'm going to Key West to check it out for a possible addition to our tour business."

"I don't expect them to lure Angela there, but they'll likely have someone keeping an eye on you."

"Why doesn't that comfort me?"

"I like that you're getting out of town. Have a pleasant trip."

"Maybe I won't come back."

"I'll burn his office to the ground!" she had said after the deadline passed with no funds wired to her bank account. "He's not going to fuck with me and get away with it. For the second time!"

She'd paced around the living room of the rental house in Pennsylvania's Pocono Mountains, seething. But after gulping down two glasses of wine, her temper cooled enough for her to think more rationally.

Baker had gambled she wouldn't back up her threat—because he didn't know who she was. He didn't know about the years she'd spent hating him, until that day in the Charleston hotel when she came upon a travel brochure a tourist had left in the lounge. There he was, smiling at her from the glossy page. And that was when she'd begun her plan of revenge.

Vinnie came into the house while her anger still smoldered. "What's the matter, babe?" He took the two grocery bags he was carrying to the kitchen. Vinnie Carozzo, like her, worked in the casino at the Oakmont Stream Resort.

She followed him into the kitchen and watched him unload the bags: a six-pack of Rolling Rock, a bag of Doritos, two steaks, two russet potatoes, and a bagged salad.

"Baker didn't pay," she announced.

"The Air Force guy?" He turned to look at her.

She rolled her eyes. "Yes, Vinnie, the Air Force guy. Who else was I hitting up for money?"

He popped a beer and took a sip. "Don't take it out on me, Mel. I don't need that shit, okay? It was your thing, not mine."

She reached for the can, and he gave it to her for a swig.

"I'm sorry, Vinnie. I'm upset, is all. I thought he'd cave."

"I wouldn't have." He went out the back door to turn on the grill. He came back in. "You had nothing to back it up, and he figured that."

He grinned at her in that cocky Italian way of his that had won her heart three years earlier, when she was a detective for the Chicago PD. She and her partner had busted Vinnie for running a sports book. Ironically, it was what he was doing on the side now at the resort with her help luring the gamblers to him. She'd been taken with his confident charm and his gangster moxie.

The case against him had been dismissed—she'd never understood why—and a month later, they were living together. His brother in Philadelphia had told him about gambling opportunities opening up in the Poconos, and off they'd gone for new starts.

They were supplying high rollers from New York and Philly what they couldn't get from the resorts in the Poconos: a chance for higher returns than the maximum payouts allowed by the casinos. *Hey, we can take care of that. Why go down to seedy Atlantic City or fly all the way to Vegas when we can handle your action here in the beautiful, peaceful Poconos?*

Vinnie had interrupted her reverie as he washed the potatoes in the sink. "My people can take care of him if you want." He stabbed the spuds several times with a steak knife and wrapped them in foil. "It'll come out of your end, though."

At first, she hadn't really wanted to kill Baker or hurt him physically. Just bring the smug bastard down by hurting him in his wallet and put a speed bump in his current career. That would have been enough to satisfy her. But his condescending intransigence changed that.

"You know, he brought up the Mafia when he was dissing me. Said they'd break a leg or something to show they meant business."

Vinnie laughed and took the potatoes to the grill. He was still chuckling when he returned. "Yeah, my guys can do that. Philly guys. Not known in New York."

"Like Paulie?" She'd met that thug once and now shivered at the memory.

"Yeah."

"I'll have to think about it. What kind of steaks you get?"

"New York strip." He laughed again. "Appropriate, huh?"

Over the next two days, as she mulled over using Vinnie's people, she kept checking her account, hoping Baker had come through after all.

Then came the awful discovery. Her money was gone. All of it.

How could that be? The bank computer must have screwed up. She would have to go to the Caymans to straighten it out. *Damn it!*

But then another possibility broke into her distress—and made it worse. *Not only was Baker not going to pay, but he had fought back!* But that kind of hack involved a skill way beyond what she knew about him.

In her years as a cop, she'd been aware of the feds' tech people doing such things. A chill went through her. Baker must have gone to the FBI. To set a trap. To catch her when she showed up to ream out the bank.

Using somebody like Paulie to punish Baker appealed to her now. She had no assets to pay for it, though. She would have to owe Vinnie.

Chapter 12

I ended my trip to the Florida Keys undecided. The island chain—islets for the most part—stretched from the southern tip of Florida to the western terminus of US Route 1 at Key West, a distance of some one hundred eighty miles.

Key West was the most happening place among the chain, having the most bars, restaurants, and entertainment. But all the islands were known for their excellent fishing and coral reefs that were inviting to snorkelers. There were few specific attractions beyond the Hemingway House and Museum on Key West, where one could see six-toed cats, the descendants, as legend would have it, of a ship captain's gift to Papa Hemingway.

The Dry Tortugas National Park, featuring the nineteenth-century Fort Jefferson, lay seventy miles farther west, two hours away by boat. A cocktail cruise could be arranged for that trip, I supposed. There were already several sunset dinner cruises around Key West. We could possibly grab a piece of that action.

The climate made the Keys a good candidate to fill our winter gap in the business with nonskiers wanting to escape the frigid months of the Midwest and Northeast. The ocean temperature made swimming and snorkeling possible even in January, according to my Google search. I discovered the water to be quite comfortable in November. Basically, the Keys presented a place to relax in shorts and flip-flops and enjoy laid-back island life—a respite from a harsh winter elsewhere in the country.

I would run it by Trish before making a decision. I trusted her judgment, and if she wasn't keen on the idea, I wouldn't be either.

After three days of recon, I drove back to Miami. If a CIA agent had been shadowing me, I hadn't been aware of it. But as Truax had pointed out to me before, that was the whole idea.

I wondered if Angela would be waiting for me in New York. I would welcome it. I wanted it to be over.

Paulie had a friend. Well, she didn't know if Tony was a friend, exactly, but they usually worked as a team for such jobs. And their method of choice was kneecapping. Simple, nonlethal, and effective. The victim would have a good chance at a permanent reminder of his intransigence in the form of a painful limp, though surgical remedies were sometimes successful. Mel was fine with that, though she would give Baker one more chance to make good before giving the goons from Philly the go-ahead.

Using another prepaid phone, she called Baker's office.

I was in Trish's office, filling her in on my trip, when her desk phone rang. She ignored it at first because Lisa, still working from home, had office calls routed to her cell phone. But when the ringing continued, Trish answered before the call went to voicemail.

"Baker Tours. How may I help you?... One moment." She put the line on hold and looked at me. "It's that crazy Angela woman. Wants to talk to you. Are you in?"

Great. "I'll take it in my office."

I went to my adjoining office, closed the door behind me, and sat at my desk. Lifting the handset, I pressed the lit button.

"What do you want?" I asked, but of course, I knew.

"My money, Alex. What you stole from me and what you already owed me."

"Stole from you? What the hell are you talking about?" Rule number one—deny.

"Don't give me that innocence shit. You hacked into my account and cleaned it out."

"Huh. I wish I'd thought of that. But even if I had, I don't have the faintest idea how to do such a thing."

"You probably don't, but you know people who do. I want it back. And for pissing me off, you now owe me an additional hundred K. Three hundred fifty thou, total."

"Hey, you could make it a zillion, for all I care. I'm not paying you anything. Zip. Nada."

"I hoped you wouldn't take that attitude, because now I'm forced to hurt you. Like what those gangsters you mentioned are good at. If I can't get my money, at least I'll have the satisfaction of knowing you suffered for it."

Her newfound confidence, unlike her previous bluster, chilled me. *She must have help now.*

"Last chance, Alex. I'll give you until this time tomorrow to have your computer geeks return my money and do whatever it takes to get my fee plus the surcharge together and wire it to the bank. There will be no more calls, no more warnings. Twenty-four hours."

She hung up before I could respond. If only the damned CIA hadn't hacked her account, she might have left me alone. But it didn't look like that would be happening, unless the spooks saw things my way and returned the stolen funds. No harm, no foul, maybe.

Regardless, there was no way I would submit to her extortion. If she had muscle willing to do her bidding, I would just have to be ready for them. And that could be the breakthrough I needed.

Mel thought she'd handled the call well. Strong, determined. Vinnie was right. She should've been prepared to back up her original threat. But now she could.

And there was still a chance to get what she wanted when push came to shove. A gun in his face would focus his mind. He would come around. She would finally get retribution for Baker ending her Air Force career. Without that, of course, she wouldn't have met Vinnie. But still, Baker had to atone for what he'd done—and especially for what he was doing to her now.

Vinnie had volunteered the cash for Paulie and Tony when she told him her account had been wiped out. She and Vinnie sat on the couch in the living room, going over the plan.

"It'll go down like this, Mel," he said. "My guys'll force him into their car. You know where he works, right?"

"Yeah."

"He's gotta park his car somewhere."

"A garage down the street."

"Perfect. So he walks there from his office. That's when they grab him. Paulie has a cousin with a chop shop in the Bronx. They take Baker there and do their thing."

"But I want to persuade him to cough up the money. If he's disabled, how do we get him to go to the bank?"

Vinnie frowned. "I thought you'd given up on that? This was just supposed to be punishment."

"Well, I was thinking he'd cave if we gave him some incentive, you know? Pay up or I shoot you right here. We hurt him *after* he gives us the cash."

"Shit, that complicates things. You're right—if we mess him up, he can't traipse into his bank. Let me think about it."

He rubbed his chin for a few moments. "Okay, how's this? They grab his secretary. She's the hostage. Gets him to cooperate. She goes with them to the bank, stays in the car with Tony while Paulie and

Baker go into the bank. After, they take him to the Bronx for his punishment."

Mel shook her head. "What about the hostage? We're not killing her. If we let her go, she's a witness, gets the license plate or something."

"They blindfold her."

She thought about that for a couple of minutes, looking for another hole in the plan. Vinnie was street-smart, but not the sharpest knife in the drawer.

"He said he'd have to sell some stocks to come up with the money."

"Takes too long, Mel. We can't be waiting around for that. It's already gonna take a while for the bank people to collect the cash and count it. And they'll probably have to get a vice president or somebody to approve it. Those guys love raking it in but hate giving it out. Anyway, you'll have to settle for what he's got in the bank. But he's the owner of the company, so he can get his hands on the business account too. Could add up. Maybe not what you were hoping for, but still a good piece of change."

That made her think of another flaw. "Paulie and Tony will have the cash. How can we trust them not to skim?"

Vinnie smiled. "Good thinking. We can't. So that's why I'm going with them."

"I like it!" She leaned over for a kiss as she put her hand on his groin. "This is making me horny. Let's go to bed."

I informed Truax of Angela's call, and he passed it along to the FBI. We all agreed the threat appeared actionable, and the number of stakeout agents was doubled.

At my request, he asked the CIA to return her funds, but they balked. They wanted her to stay mad. If she were back to financial

normality, she might decide to avoid any risk and forget about getting even—and thus end any chance of capturing her. I didn't quite
get the CIA's motivation for this, why they would care about arrest-
ing an extortionist whom they must have determined by now was
not the assassin.

But the FBI had skin in that game. Extortion was a crime, after
all. Maybe Truax hadn't been completely honest with me when he
put all the blame of the account hacking on the CIA. *Oh, what a tan-
gled web we weave...*

Regardless, I was still in Angela's crosshairs, and I didn't care
much which federal agency would come to my aid when needed.

When I went to bed that night, I thought of when I should start
the clock on my code red alert. In twelve hours, the deadline would
be up. It could happen any time after that, depending on the logistics
of Angela's plan.

Maybe she would make me sweat for a day or two, but I doubted
it. She would make her move as soon as she could.

"Where to?" Norman asked Petra Nikolic as they drove away
from the meeting.

"The airport, please."

He nodded. "What're your plans?"

"I'm going to hang out in New York."

He glanced at her. "Baker?"

She didn't respond.

"You said he was irrelevant."

She stared straight ahead. "He is, and he isn't. Thanks to our boss,
Angela remains a threat to him. We know nothing about her, what
resources she could call on. Why would they push her like that? She's
not AOD. So what's the point?"

He shrugged. "Being thorough, I suppose. Ours is not to reason why. The FBI is still looking for you, and they have Baker covered, so be careful. And the satellite is looking for your phone calls."

"I've got another phone. I'll give you the number at the airport."

He took the exit to BWI.

"What will *you* be doing?" she asked.

"You're my only agent, love, so I'll be hanging out too. But at Langley. Something will break soon, and we'll be active again."

"The key is AOD's vendetta. We can't possibly anticipate all of Putin's potential enemies. But those involved in the Belgrade bombing constitute a finite, manageable list."

"As far as I know, they've all been warned and told to report any suspicious activity to the FBI. I agree that's how we're likely to get her."

Petra reasoned that the best base from which to keep tabs on Alex was the hotel the FBI had already checked. Though there was a small chance someone there would remember her photo, a simple disguise would take care of that. And it did.

Norman hadn't asked about her interest in Alex because he'd probably guessed. And as long as she was on her own time now, it was none of his business. Everyone knew about that night in his condo.

She couldn't help it. Besides the sex, there had been a connection between them, she was sure of it. *But which came first? The sex? Or the affection, if not love?* It was a classic chicken-or-egg conundrum.

She surmised that was how most relationships began. The initial attraction involved a sexual desire, albeit perhaps on an unconscious level, and consummating it cemented the connection. Sometimes it fell flat, but that certainly didn't apply in her case. She'd hated having to leave him in the middle of the night, but she'd needed to prepare.

It made her look suspicious, but there'd been no other choice. Alas, it had not been enough to save the Ukrainian official.

The Angela thing had been a red herring from the get-go. She'd told them that in the beginning. Still, they wanted to be sure, but now must know she was right. They were keeping the FBI in the dark about not only Angela, but Petra's identity as well. There could be only one reason for that. Her superiors were using the FBI's manpower because they still thought it possible that Alex was a target of the Angel of Death,—or AOD, their colorful nickname for the unknown assassin. And the night she'd spent with Alex had fortified that view for their federal colleagues. Without her as a suspect, the FBI might lose interest in him.

Angela, whoever she was, had unwittingly sidetracked the intelligence community and led them down a path that ultimately led nowhere. But it had been responsible for setting up her supposedly accidental contact with Alex on the boat. And that, she didn't regret.

They knew the killer was a woman. Reliable sources said she had attended the same "finishing school" as Petra and likely even came from the same orphanage. Her age, based on eyewitness reports, could mean she and Petra were in that orphanage at the same time and had known each other.

Young girls orphaned because of the war. Living together, learning together, developing hatred for Americans, especially for those who could have made them orphans. One of them had become an assassin carrying out Putin's political needs when not seeking personal revenge. That was the current CIA theory.

What wasn't hypothetical was that another of those girls had become a Russian covert operative as well. But then she'd been turned into a double agent—first by the lure of American dollars, then by conviction after seeing the true nature of Putin's regime and learning the facts that had led to the Kosovo War.

Those days were behind her, and Petra Nikolic was now the CIA's chief hunter, an assassin in her own right, seeking out Russian killers and removing them from the game. Despite the plausible theory that she and AOD had once known each other, it had been too long ago to help Petra identify her. But that worked both ways.

Chapter 13

The deadline passed with no change in her account, as Mel had known it would. But because she had a plan to focus on, some of the sting went out of her anger. She had nixed the kneecapping part that could get her charged with assault with intent to inflict serious injury. But Alex would pay for ruining her Air Force career, then for adding insult to injury by stealing from her. She would have to be satisfied with that.

She'd never figured out what he had against her when she worked for him. His accusations of insubordination and not being a team player were clearly bogus. She'd been the best officer in the unit. Maybe he was pissed she'd shown no romantic interest in him. But he'd never come on to her. Whatever the reason, the inexplicable bad OPR had stopped her career in its tracks. And she had no recourse in going against a superior officer's prejudice except for the tried-and-true sexual blackmail charge. It was all she'd had, and it'd backfired. Baker had resigned over it, but she'd become a pariah as well.

They would still need the Philly muscle to overpower Baker and his secretary. But since they couldn't blindfold *him*, obviously, blindfolding the secretary made no sense. The team would wear simple disguises instead. Ball caps and sunglasses would do the trick without raising any premature alarms.

And Mel decided she would be part of the team. She wanted to be there to savor the look on Baker's face. In addition, although she loved Vinnie and owed him for his help, she wanted to ensure he didn't take more than his cut from the proceeds. He was a gangster, after all.

They'd also decided that abducting the two targets would be less complicated if they took them when both were inside their workplace, out of public view. The staff would be held hostage while Baker was taken to the bank to get the money.

Paulie and Tony arrived to pick them up in a big Lincoln with stolen plates. They wore sport coats to conceal their guns and brought their "disguises" with them.

On the I-80 drive to New York, they went over the details of the plan. By the time they reached the George Washington Bridge, they were all set.

I'd gotten in the habit of checking in with my FBI watchers every morning after I arrived at the parking garage, partly to stimulate them into alertness from what had to be a brutally boring duty, but mostly for me to know they were still on station. I couldn't count on Truax to notify me in a timely fashion if the surveillance had been lifted.

This morning, I had Michelle Simpson and Pete Reinhardt on the stakeout.

"Angela's deadline passed yesterday, guys," I said into the transmitter as I walked toward my office.

"We know," Michelle responded. "We're ready. Look across the street. Black SUV in front of Starbucks."

I spotted the car as Michelle lowered the driver's-side window. She gave me a wave. I nodded and continued to the office.

The front door was unlocked. Trish usually arrived before me. When I went to her office to say hi, she had a cup of coffee ready for me.

"Thanks." I smiled as I took the mug. "I guess I can't catch you unawares anymore."

"Ha! You never could."

We'd had buzzers installed in our offices to signal us when the front door opened and camera feeds to show us who had opened it. "This could be the day, if Angela was serious about the deadline threat."

She patted the middle drawer of her desk, where she kept her 9mm. "She'll be sorry if she tries anything with me."

I forced a chuckle. "Yeah. She doesn't know Annie Oakley is waiting for her. Anything scheduled today?"

"Lisa has referred two prospects. One couple interested in Chicago and a woman wanting info on San Francisco. Both have done business with us before. Sometime today. Couldn't pin down times."

"Well, they must be legit. Angela wouldn't give us a heads-up. Anyway, the FBI is standing guard outside per usual."

"Mr. or Mrs. Bond today?"

"Both, actually. They've doubled up the stakeout." I turned to go to my office.

"I like the Key West idea, Alex. I think we should do it."

"Okay. I'll work on an outline. We can go over it later today." I paused. "Barring any distractions."

An hour later, I was making out itineraries for Key West tours when Michelle's voice came through my earpiece.

"Alex, we have activity. White Town Car parked down the block. Two men in ball caps and sunglasses exited and are coming your way. We saw the same Lincoln cruise slowly by five minutes ago. Pete's calling for backup."

"Thanks." With adrenaline coursing through my body, I called Trish on the intercom. "Lock your door. We're going to have visitors, and I don't think they're customers."

I locked my door, drew my pistol, and watched the camera feed from my desk.

Two large men who met Michelle's description came through the front door. One stayed by the door; the other took a semiautomatic from inside his coat and approached the vacant reception desk. He looked around then headed for the hallway to the right of the desk that led to our offices.

A camera in the ceiling of the hallway captured him nearing my office door. On the other screen, I saw Michelle and Pete through the glass front door.

As the two men entered the travel agency, Michelle looked back at the Lincoln. She had seen two passengers in the back seat when the car passed earlier. She couldn't make them out now at that distance. A dark-blue sedan pulled to the curb about twenty yards behind the Lincoln.

"They're here, Pete. Let's go!"

She and her partner climbed out of the SUV and quickly crossed the street as two men emerged from the sedan, guns held at their sides, and slowly approached the rear of the Lincoln. Pete kept behind Michelle while she opened the front door and was immediately confronted by one of the intruders.

"I'm sorry, we're closed," the man said.

Michelle pushed her way in. "But I made an appointment. My husband and I—"

"Listen, lady, I told you—"

"Hands up!" Pete shouted, coming around Michelle, his gun pointed at the man's chest. "FBI!"

"Paulie!" the man called out as he backed up and Michelle drew her weapon.

"What's going on, Vinnie?" Mel asked, wide-eyed, as she watched the man and woman race across the street.

"Looks like an ambush. Shit! We have to get out of here!"

"You in the car!" shouted a voice behind them. "FBI! Get out with your hands up!"

They turned to see a man on each side of the Town Car's trunk, guns pointed at them through the rear window.

"Vinnie!"

"Fuck! They knew!" He reached for his gun. "I'll take the one on my side. You—" He looked at her empty hands. "Get your gun out, Mel!"

"No, Vinnie! They got us. We'll get a lawyer. We haven't done anything serious yet."

"Now!" one of the men behind them yelled.

As Vinnie hesitated, shots rang out from the area of the travel agency.

I saw the confrontation at the front door, and the hall camera showed the gunman suddenly turn to look back. He hesitated then stepped slowly toward the lobby.

I unlocked my door and opened it quietly. The gunman made his way past the conference room to where the hall opened into the lobby. I heard voices, one of which belonged to Michelle, but I couldn't distinguish the words.

The gunman peeked around the corner then backed up. He turned to retreat and found me blocking his path, my Beretta held in a two-hand grip.

"Drop the gun!" I shouted.

He brought his pistol up to shoot, and I sent two quick rounds into his chest. The man fell to the floor, and Pete appeared from around the corner, pistol in hand. He looked at me then at the still form lying on the floor, and back at me. "You okay?"

"Yeah." I stepped on the man's wrist and reached down to retrieve the weapon still in his hand. I held it up to Pete, who took it by the barrel and put it in his coat pocket. The man had a glassy-eyed stare, but I put a finger on his carotid to confirm. "He's dead. What about the other one?"

"Under control."

Trish came out of her office, holding her Glock. She stared at the dead man then moved next to me.

Pete put a hand to his ear. "We have one perp dead, the other restrained... Roger that."

He looked at me. "Two more perps in the Lincoln. Man and a woman."

Angela? "I want to see them. Maybe I know who they are."

"Sure. But I'll need your weapon."

"Oh. Yeah, of course."

Pete took out a plastic bag from his coat and held it open. I dropped the Beretta into it.

Pete addressed Trish. "You'll have to come outside too, ma'am. Without your weapon."

I told her, "Lock it in your desk."

"Sure." When she returned a moment later, Pete had recovered the man's wallet.

We stepped into the lobby as the sounds of approaching sirens came through the front of the building. The other man, handcuffed, sat on the floor. A presumed FBI agent—one I hadn't met—stood next to Michelle, speaking into a cell phone.

An ambulance came to a stop outside, followed by two patrol cars. Lightbars flashing, they blocked the street in both directions. Two EMTs carrying equipment rushed in, and Pete directed them to the hallway.

Michelle eyed me. "That was you who got him?"

"Afraid so."

"Righteous, Alex. Not to worry."

I forced a smile. "From your lips to the DA's ears."

Before Pete could lead Trish and me outside, Special Agent Morganthau came in and began to confer with the other agents.

The crowd in the lobby became even larger when two men in suits entered.

"NYPD," one of them said. "Who's in charge here?"

"That would be me." Morganthau stepped over to them, and the three cops flashed their credentials.

Pete, Trish, and I made it outside while the turf battle raged between Morganthau and the detectives. I heard Morganthau say something about "national security" before the door closed.

We followed Pete down the street to a white Lincoln. Behind it, a man with dark curly hair and a blond woman sat on the curb next to each other, their hands behind their backs. Agent Townsend, whom I recognized from the meeting that seemed so long ago, stood guard, most likely waiting for the disposition resolution being debated half a block away.

As I got closer, it suddenly became clear why Angela was after me. I knew the woman was Angela, and I knew her real name.

She watched me approach, hatred in her eyes.

"Hello, Mel," I said. "Or should I say Angela?"

"You know them?" Pete asked.

"Him, no. Her, yes. Melissa Willoughby."

"Matches her ID," Townsend said. "The man is Vincent Carozzo. Both have the same East Stroudsburg, PA address."

I turned to Pete. "Go tell Morganthau that NYPD can have them. They aren't involved with the one he's after."

He raised his eyebrows. "You sure?"

"Positive."

He shrugged and left.

I shook my head at my former colleague. "What was your plan, Mel?"

"I don't have to tell you squat, Baker."

I nodded. "True. But a man is dead, thanks to your attempted crime, whatever that was. You know the law. Doesn't matter if you didn't pull the trigger. Felony murder applies. So sad. You threw away a promising career. And now you've sacrificed years of the life you have left."

If looks could kill... "Because you—"

Carozzo rammed his shoulder into hers. "Shut up, Mel," he said. "The only one we talk to is our lawyer."

I turned away to look toward my building. A man and a woman wearing blue windbreakers were going into the office. CSI, I figured. Morganthau passed them as he came out. He saw me and approached at a brisk pace.

He gestured at Mel. "You know her?"

"Somebody from my past. Nothing to do with national security."

"So all this..." He shook his head in disgust, took out his cell phone, and stepped away. He was calling his boss, no doubt.

Petra had followed Alex as he walked to his office from the parking garage. She went to a Starbucks across the street and took her coffee to a booth by the window facing the travel agency.

When two large men wearing sunglasses—on a cloudy day!—went into Alex's building, she got up, ready to intervene. But then a man and a woman rushed across the street to the agency, and she relaxed somewhat. The FBI was on it.

The agents went in, then two gunshots erupted from within the building.

Alex!

Starbucks patrons drew close to the window where she sat, murmuring with excitement. They were soon rewarded with the arrival of an ambulance and police cruisers. They went outside to get a better look, leaving Petra alone with her anxiety as she kept watching the front door, hoping to see Alex emerge uninjured.

After what seemed like forever, during which more law-enforcement types poured into the agency, Alex came out with a woman and one of the FBI agents. *He looks okay.*

The trio headed toward a large white sedan parked halfway down the street. She took out a compact telescope from her handbag and looked at the scene around the white car. Alex was talking to a woman sitting on the curb, her hands behind her back.

The woman on the boat. It's her!

I stepped away from Mel, relieved that part of the mystery had been solved, but also dismayed how a less-than-satisfactory Air Force OPR could have set the events of the last month in motion.

I wondered what Mel's intent had been. To get back at me, for sure. *But in what way? Rob my agency?* We only kept petty cash in the office. A travel agency was not commonly an attractive target for thieves. And it wouldn't take two gunmen to accomplish that. Killing me wouldn't get her the money she wanted either.

Then a scenario that made some kind of sense occurred to me. She'd planned to kidnap me and hold me for ransom. *But from whom?* My mother didn't have that kind of money. Trish could write checks on the company account for routine expenses. But only I had access to our profit accounts in the bank and with Merrill Lynch.

Trish interrupted my musings. "What do we do now, Alex?"

Yes. What? "Either the FBI or NYPD or both will want my statement. We'll be temporarily denied access to the office until the crime scene procedures are over—probably not more than a day or two."

"That woman—Angela—you know her."

"I'll tell you the whole story later."

Morganthau had finished his call a few minutes earlier but had stayed nearby. The reason soon became clear.

A large SUV pulled next to the Lincoln, and the passenger, a man in his fifties wearing a suit, got out. Morganthau hurried over to him. His boss, I assumed: the Special Agent in Charge of the FBI's New York City field office. I didn't know him and didn't want to.

Petra saw SAIC O'Connor arrive. Still wondering who the blond woman was and how Alex knew her, she decided she'd better leave before the cops started canvassing the area looking for witnesses. She left Starbucks and walked past the onlookers on the way to the parking garage.

Chapter 14

SAIC O'Connor was not about to let the NYPD have the Pennsylvania criminals until he had more info on them and had checked with his CIA colleagues. I was not surprised when that process started with my interrogation at 26 Federal Plaza.

All the agents who had participated in the takedown were present at the meeting chaired by O'Connor. One of the men I'd seen waiting for Truax after the debriefing at Joint Base Langley-Eustis sat at the conference table—the CIA had representation. The tapes recorded by my cameras were available for everyone to see.

After I related the whole story, O'Connor said, "So this woman—Willoughby—came after you for revenge. And it had nothing to do with your father or the Belgrade bombing."

"That's right."

"You knew this all along?"

"At first, no. The Charleston coincidence had me going. But then after talking to her on the phone, I decided she wasn't a foreign agent. That it was just an extortion attempt." I leveled my gaze at him. "And I didn't think she presented a real threat to me until you feds decided to push her with the hacking stunt. Pissed her off enough to get aggressive, and I had to kill a man as a result. Thank you for giving me that pleasant experience."

O'Connor stared at me for a moment, glanced at the CIA guy, then looked down at his notes.

I had just shifted the responsibility for Paulie Aschettino's death away from me, and O'Connor knew it. The feds could cover up their involvement in the hacking under the claim of classified information, but having me on the witness stand would not be good. I had played my get-out-of-jail-free card.

O'Connor looked up at me and changed direction. "Do you have any idea where Dee Norton is?"

"No. I haven't seen or heard from her since that night in my condo."

He smirked slightly when he asked, "You don't consider her a threat, I take it."

"To me?"

"Yes."

"No. If she wanted to kill me, she had several opportunities. Now that we know she's not Angela or working with her, what would be the motivation? Even if she's the assassin?"

Ask *him* a question for a change. Put him in the hot seat to either acknowledge a now-untenable theory that had sent Willoughby on a rampage, mobilized his field office, risked multiple lives, and, yes, resulted in a death—or blame the CIA, who had run with it without thinking of the consequences, even though he'd been fully complicit.

But he ignored my question and looked around the table. "Anything else for Mr. Baker?" He was wisely wrapping it up.

"When can we get our equipment back?" Morganthau asked.

"Right now." I removed the earpiece and pen and placed them on the table. "When can I have my office back?"

"I'll take care of it," O'Connor said. "You can open your business tomorrow morning."

"And my Beretta?"

Morganthau looked at Reinhardt. "Pete?"

"I'll check on it." Pete then addressed me. "Ballistics and fingerprints should be done by tomorrow morning. I'll drop it off to you."

"Thank you." I eyed O'Connor. "May I go now?"

"Yes." He gave me a half smile. "Thank you for your cooperation, Mr. Baker. Special Agent Reinhardt will take you to your car."

I rose from the table and left the conference room, with Pete following. On the way to the parking garage, neither of us spoke for a few minutes. Then Pete chuckled.

"That was a good move you made, Alex."

"With O'Connor?"

"Yeah. He'll make sure no prosecutors have you in their sights."

"That's my hope. Anyway, you and your buds can forget about me now. Once the FBI traces Willoughby's history, you'll know she's not the assassin."

"You think Dee Norton is?"

"All I know is she's not who she claims to be. Maybe she's a fugitive for another reason entirely. Or she's escaping an abusive husband or a stalker. But she doesn't strike me as a trained killer."

Pete dropped me off at the garage entrance, and I walked up the ramp to my Escalade on the second level. I pressed the key fob button to unlock it and was about to open the driver's door when a female voice behind me called out my name.

I turned to find Dee Norton standing ten feet away. I yelled, "Pete!" before realizing I no longer had the comm gear. Dee's hands were empty, thank goodness.

"Dee?"

She smiled. Another good sign, I hoped. "Who's Pete?"

"Uh, the FBI agent who dropped me off."

"It's about time. I've been waiting hours for you to show up."

"To get me alone without being spotted?"

"Yes. It hasn't been easy with all the people watching you."

But they're not watching me now. Though I'd been hoping to see her again, a current of unease ran through my body. "They were FBI agents."

"I know."

"And they're looking for you."

"I know that too. So who's that blonde they arrested?"

"You were there?"

She nodded. "I followed you today because I had something to tell you."

I forced a smile. "Will I like to hear it?"

She smiled in return. "I hope so."

That relaxed me a little. But the clickety-clack of heels on concrete caused me to turn. A young woman had emerged from the elevator and was headed toward us. I watched, holding my breath, as she went to a sedan four slots away and climbed in. A moment later, the car backed out and drove to the exit ramp. I noticed that Dee had been watching too.

"I guess she wasn't after me," I said. "Or you."

"She wasn't the assassin, Alex."

Her smile was gone, chilling me. "Because you are?"

She chuckled. "You still have doubts about me?"

Before I could answer, a man, woman, and two middle-school-aged kids came up the ramp and headed to a minivan.

"Why don't we have this conversation in my car?" she asked. "For privacy." She gave me a smirk. "Unless you don't feel safe doing that."

Do I? "How about *my* car?" I said before I realized how stupid that was. If I died in the familiar surroundings of my Cadillac, I would still be dead. And if she were going to shoot me, she wouldn't want to mess up her car.

"I'd prefer mine, Alex. Yours might be bugged."

I hadn't considered that, but it made sense. She had me, anyway. Nothing I could do. I just hoped my good vibes about her could be trusted. "Okay."

She led me to an Audi, and we climbed in. I had to remove her handbag from the passenger seat and put it on the center console. It felt heavy.

"The blonde?" she asked again. "She's the one I saw on the boat and later in the restaurant. Who is she?"

"Someone I used to work with in the Air Force. It's a long story."

"I remember you using that line before. Are you in a hurry to get somewhere?"

"I was looking forward to an icy-cold martini at my condo, but I guess it can wait."

I told her about Mel.

"So that's why she was stalking you."

"Yes. Why are *you* stalking me?"

"That's a long story too."

I grinned. "You have some other place to be now?"

She laughed. "Touché. I can tell you some of it, but not all. It's classified."

Classified? Who is this woman? "Let's start with your real name."

"That's one of the classified parts. Sorry. You know, I could use a martini too." She smiled. "Maybe if you ply me with alcohol, I might let some secrets slip."

I liked that idea. "I'm not sure the surveillance has been lifted yet. We'll have to go in my car."

"I'll duck down and won't say anything during the drive."

I pointed at the handbag. "Is there a gun in there?"

"Yes."

At least she was open about it. *Who is she?*

"It was also there during our date, Alex." She looked at me with eyebrows raised.

"Oh, hell, why not?"

I climbed out, and she followed me to the Escalade.

The garage elevator to my condo opened to a hallway outside the door to my kitchen. After letting us in, I headed to the fridge for the martini makings. Something small and hard pressed into my back.

Not again!

When I turned, hands in the air like before, Dee wrapped her arms around my waist and drew me to her.

"My, my. You just don't learn," she said and parted her lips invitingly. We kissed, softly at first, then with ardor, and a part of my anatomy rising, the kiss intensified, our tongues touching, my hands massaging her lovely backside.

I finally broke away from her lips, but not her pelvis, which was grinding against my erection. "The martinis?" I asked.

"Later."

It was like the first time. No, this was better, with the cloud of possible danger no longer hanging over me.

We lay side by side, musing at the wonderment of it happening again. At least that was *my* reverie. I couldn't guess Dee's thoughts—until she shared them.

"I didn't think I would ever see you again."

"Ditto. You were like a ghost suddenly entering my life, then just as suddenly disappearing. It didn't seem real. Except..." I turned onto my side to look at her. "There was a reason to explain that, but I hoped it wasn't true."

She gazed at the ceiling. "That I was the assassin who killed your father and now wanted you dead."

"Yeah, that definitely occurred to me, thanks to Angela coming into the picture at the same time. And meeting you on the boat—especially when I caught you in a lie—seemed contrived."

She grinned at me. "Yet you ignored that, brought me here that night, and made love to me."

I leaned down to kiss her breast. "Your charm overcame my caution."

"But you were right to be suspicious of me. That boat meeting *was* contrived. We thought you might be targeted by the assassin and wanted to be there if she did."

"We?"

"What?"

"You said, 'We thought you might be targeted.'"

"The CIA, Alex. I work for them."

Oh. I stared at her as pieces of the puzzle were trying to come together.

"Is it starting to make sense to you now?"

It was, if I believed her. And I did. Those vibes I had from our first meeting were fully formed, no longer nebulous. If I was wrong, it would be the biggest misjudgment of my life. "I think it's martini time."

We dressed like we had the first time, as if we were recreating the memory. Perhaps, subconsciously, we were. She used my robe to cover her nakedness, and I slipped on a pair of shorts and a T-shirt.

I found a can of Blue Diamond almonds in the pantry and poured some into a dish.

She sat at the island and watched as I made the martinis. I stirred them with ice in a glass pitcher while I thought about how I had become a blip on the CIA's radar screen and how that had led to one of their operatives keeping tabs on me—very close tabs, it had turned out. The CIA was keeping Dee's identity a secret from the FBI. *Why would they do that?*

"Olive or onion?" I asked. "I don't have a lemon."

"Onion, please."

Ah, a Gibson girl. I liked that. I took two martini glasses from the freezer, plopped toothpick-impaled cocktail onions into them, and poured the drinks.

I sat next to her, and we clinked glasses.

"Cheers," I said, and we took sips.

I asked her about the identity thing.

"I can guess, but I really don't know for sure." She took another sip. "This is really good."

"Thanks. Okay, guess."

"The obvious reason is that the Agency likes to keep secrets. It's what we do. Need to know always applies."

"But the FBI *did* need to know. They were supposedly working with the CIA to find you."

"Maybe, maybe not. The FBI can be crafty too. Could be they knew I was CIA, so finding me could get them closer to finding the real assassin."

I shook my head. "Is the relationship between them really that convoluted?"

"It can be. And I can see some logic in what they did in my case. The Agency didn't know who Angela was, how she fit in the picture, and that bothered them. But the FBI knew about me. If the Agency revealed that the suspicious Dee Norton was actually one of them, would the FBI have been as active in protecting you? I was in New York, had been seen with you. Eliminating me as the assassin would then leave Angela, who was just a voice over the phone, after all."

"And not a very convincing one."

"Exactly. But the Agency had to make sure. The FBI has many more agents than we do. The CIA needed the FBI's manpower to find out who Angela was."

"By luring her into a trap."

"I was against the hacking. I told them my opinion that Angela was not the assassin." She sighed. "A lot of good that did. The feebs were already watching over you, so they forced the issue."

"Wow" was all I could think of to say. The FBI and the CIA weren't sharing information. I guessed my brief experience with the CIA back in the day had not been as representative as it could have been. And there were a slew of other government intelligence agencies. *Did they work at odds with each other too?* No wonder 9/11 could have happened as it did. Interagency cooperation had supposedly been beefed up as a result of that disaster, but sitting next to me was proof more needed to be done.

"So your job in the CIA is finding the assassin?"

"That's my current assignment. Now that we know it's not Angela, we can direct our focus away from you."

"Do you know who she could be?"

"Possibly someone I knew as a young girl."

"In the orphanage?"

She looked surprised. "You know about that?"

"Truax told me. Your CIA did share that with him at least."

"That must have been before I got involved. Anyway, we think her name is Katarina Petrovic. Her parents were killed in the Kosovo War. I had already lost my mother to cancer when my father died in the fighting. I was bitter and enthusiastically began training as a Russian spy—a few years before Petrovic entered the same program."

"But you left the Dark Side."

"Huh. I wish it were a fictional story like *Star Wars*, but yes. I saw the light"—she smiled at me—"and was recruited by the CIA. And that's all I can tell you." She drank the last of her Gibson and laughed. "And it's more than I should have said."

"Candy is dandy, but liquor is quicker."

"What?"

"It's a line from Ogden Nash, an American poet and humorist. Something about breaking the ice." I smiled. "You were right about the alcohol."

She looked me in the eye. "Or maybe it's just that I feel I can confide in you." She laughed again. "But the martini helped. And I trust you will not repeat anything I've said. Right?"

I leaned over for a kiss. "Of course. You'll be leaving New York soon?"

"I don't have orders yet."

"I want to make the most of the time we have left before you run off to Bulgaria or someplace."

"You've read my mind, Alex."

She took my hand and led me back to the bedroom.

Chapter 15

Caracas, Venezuela
5:00 p.m.

Michael Sosa entered the apartment on Avenida los Totumos and was surprised to find his roommate, Carlos Hernandez, already there.

"Happy last day, Mike!"

Sosa smiled. "Thanks. I thought you went to Valencia today to follow that tip."

"I did, but I wasn't there long. I trailed Perez to the airport, where he met someone who flew in on a private jet. He looked Eastern European. I got a good frontal and sent it to Langley. Perez drove him right back here to the Miraflores Palace."

"To see the president."

"He must be important. I'm betting he's Russian. But it's not a problem for you anymore, amigo. Let's have a drink to celebrate you leaving this shithole. I made us some mojitos. And I got reservations at Casa Pakea."

"Sounds great, man."

Hernandez held up a hand and grinned. "Wait here a sec." He left Sosa in the living room and went to the kitchen. After a few moments, he called out, "Okay, Mike, come on in."

A small cake adorned with a single lit candle sat on the dinette, flanked by two glasses filled with a clear liquid over ice and a lime wedge and garnished with a mint leaf.

"Make a wish and blow it out. Then we'll have our drinks."

Sosa paused for a second then blew out the candle.

Hernandez handed him one of the mojitos and picked up the other glass. "Cheers, buddy."

They touched glasses, took sips, and sat at the dinette, the air conditioning unit in the window humming loudly in the background.

"I'm gonna miss you, Mike, you lucky dog. Know where you'll be posted next?"

"Nope."

"Figures. Gotta be better than here." He held the glass to his forehead. "Hot and humid all year and rainy for half of it. And no support."

Their safe house apartment had been established before the US closed its embassy in 2019. A number of CIA agents had called it home over the years. As far as Sosa and Hernandez knew, they were the only agents operating in Caracas.

"You'll be going back soon, Carlos."

"Not soon enough, man."

"Did they say who my replacement is?"

"Not yet. He's supposed to arrive day after tomorrow."

Sosa grinned. "Maybe the he will be a she."

"Jeez, I hope not. Marie would have a shit fit. She didn't mind *our* living arrangement, but a woman? No way."

"Is it serious between you two?"

"I'm not sure, bro. I guess I'll have to face that when I get *my* orders to leave. So, are you going directly—" Hernandez's cell phone chirped, and he looked at the screen before turning to Sosa. "The man Perez picked up is Anton Vashkov, known SVR agent."

"Wonder what he's up to."

Hernandez smiled. "Maybe giving the Policia Nacional tips on how to weed out spies like us."

Their cover was a small photography shop downtown—Hermanos Aguilar, Fotografos—open by appointment only. They didn't advertise, and the phone number on the front window was the apartment's landline. They got the occasional legitimate business, for which they had a real photographer only too happy to get referrals.

"You were going to ask me something," Sosa said.

"Oh, yeah. You getting any time off?"

"Got a week before I have to report in. Gonna spend a few days in Aruba. Ann is flying down to join me." He smiled. "I'm gonna pop the question."

"Congratulations! Another reason to celebrate tonight. You gonna tell her?"

"What?"

Hernandez rolled his eyes. "That you're not a troubleshooter for an oil company, after all."

"Oh, yeah, that. Once we're married, I think I'll have to."

"You got that right." Hernandez looked at his watch. "We should get to the restaurant. We'll have the cake for dessert."

⎯⎯ ❦ ⎯⎯

Aruba

Katarina Petrovic had spent two weeks enjoying the climate and beaches of this Caribbean island as she recovered from her injury.

Her superiors had wisely left her alone. They didn't want to get on the wrong side of a dangerous woman who knew who many of them were and how to find them.

But fully functional now, she itched to get back into action. And because she'd been out of commission as a result of personal business, tying up those loose ends would not likely be tolerated—at the present time, anyway.

She was about to get confirmation of that assumption. As she sipped an Aruba Ariba, looking out at the ocean from a seaside bar, she saw her control agent walking up the beach toward her. Sergei Garin took the empty stool to her left and signaled the bartender.

"Yes, sir?" the woman asked in Dutch-accented English, placing a cocktail napkin in front of him.

He pointed to Petrovic's drink. "That looks good. I'll have one of those."

The bartender nodded and stepped away.

"I thought you'd call first." Petrovic stared ahead at the mirrored back wall of the bar.

"I wanted to see your physical progress in person." His eyes drifted to the pink scar above the top of her swimsuit. "It's healing nicely. Are you ready to end your rehab?"

The bartender placed his drink on the napkin.

"Thank you." Garin took a sip of the concoction and turned to his agent. "There's rum in this."

"Vodka too."

"Ah, that explains it. Quite tasty." His mien turned serious. "So?"

"Yes, I'm ready."

"Good." He took a thick envelope from his cargo shorts and put it on the bar. "New credit card, phone, and a plane ticket to Miami tomorrow. Connection to Heathrow."

"Target?"

"You'll be briefed in London. How many more on your list of Americans?"

"Four."

He nodded. "Once your next mission has been completed, we'll consider letting you continue."

"Thank you."

"Katarina, you are a valuable agent. Perhaps *we* can eliminate the remaining bombers. Everyone looks for you, and all your targets have been warned. You have lost the element of surprise. Two of your attempts have shown this. And the last one could have killed you."

"I understand. Thank you for the offer, but I must do this myself. I will take the necessary precautions to overcome theirs. It can be done. By me."

Garin sighed. "We will discuss this again at an appropriate time."

He stood, withdrew bills from his wallet, and placed them on the bar. "I will see you in London." He left the way he had come.

Hand in hand, Michael Sosa and Ann Favreau stepped through the surf to their umbrella and beach chairs in the sand. As they toweled off, a man passed them on the way to the bar. Sosa had seen the man before, if not in person, then in a photo he'd studied. At Langley.

"You know him?" Ann asked.

"I'm not sure." He watched the man sit next to an attractive blonde. "I could use a drink. How 'bout you?"

"You bet. I want to try one of those Ariba things. Some kind of punch I've heard about."

"Coming right up." He grabbed his wallet and cell phone from the beach bag and went up to the bar.

The man and blonde were sitting at the central section of the staple-shaped bar, parallel to the shore. Sosa took a stool on the right arm of the staple to get a direct view of the bald man's face.

He ordered the drinks and held his iPhone pointed at the man, trying to look casual as he pretended to scroll the screen. When the man turned to the blonde, he snapped a picture.

He paid for the drinks and took the plastic cups to the beach. He handed one to Ann. "Can you hold mine for a sec, hon? I want to lie on my towel to get some rays."

She took his cup. "Want some sunscreen? The tropical sun is strong."

"I'm good." He laid his towel on the sand, took his drink from Ann, and lay down so his head faced the bar. He screwed the bottom of his cup into the sand to secure it upright and waited with his cell phone.

The man left a few minutes later, and Sosa took two more photos of him as he passed. Then the woman moved from her stool to a beach chair about twenty yards away. Sosa snapped two pictures of her.

"You're right, Ann. This sun is brutal." Sosa got up, sat in his chair, and emailed the photos to his boss.

Dee had left two days earlier for parts unknown, leaving me with mixed emotions. I missed her already, and sadness was compounded by not knowing when I would see her again. I was relieved not to be in the assassin's crosshairs, but it meant, frustratingly, that I was no longer a part of the hunt.

While working on an ad for the *Key West Citizen*, I got a call from Truax.

"How're you doin', Alex?"

He was upbeat, and I wondered why. Angela had been exposed and taken down, but she wasn't the assassin. And I assumed he was focused on Dee, whom the CIA had sent somewhere beyond his reach.

"Fair to partly cloudy," I answered.

"Nice work with Angela. She's off the suspect list now."

"Which leaves Dee, right?" *What does he know?*

"Well, that's why I called. Thought you should know, since you got up close and personal with her."

I didn't respond.

"We have a new lead."

"Good."

"An SVR agent was spotted in Aruba. Talking to a woman."

I waited for more then realized he was dragging it out for dramatic effect. I could play that game too. "Don't Russian spies get to go on vacation?"

"We have photos. The woman had a scar on her upper chest. A round one. Consistent with a bullet wound."

We were getting somewhere. "You think she's the assassin?"

"I *know* she is. We sent the photo to General Sizemore in Charleston. He identified her as the bogus real estate agent."

"Great news, Jim."

"It is! Wanted you to know that Dee Norton has been ruled out now as the assassin."

"So who is she then?"

"Are you sitting down?"

Too bad he couldn't see my eye roll. "Just tell me, okay?"

"She's CIA. Has been working on the hunt for the assassin for some time now. That's why she was in New York."

I tried to act surprised. "Wow. That explains a lot."

"It does."

Here we go. "When did you learn this, Jim?"

"Yesterday. Morganthau called me."

"And when did *he* find out?"

He was silent for a moment. "Yesterday."

"Are you okay with that?"

"Look, Alex, I'm pissed, and so is the FBI. But it's not the first time for either of us."

"Christ, man. How can we get anything done when one of the partners withholds information?"

"I hear you. They're not known as spooks for nothing. But we all have bosses, up to and including the president. And that's why the CIA came clean about Dee."

I wondered about the timing. "Why now?"

"She's one of their top agents. The FBI director was about to put Dee on the Most Wanted list. The spooks couldn't afford to have that publicity. Her value to them would be over."

That was all well and good, but my father's killer, though finally identified, remained at large. "I assume you don't have the Aruba woman in custody."

"She'd already left for Miami before we were on to her. From there, she flew to London. We lost her there."

"And Dee is looking for her?"

"Yes."

"Looks like I'm completely out of it now."

"I'll make sure you're kept in the loop, Alex. When we get her, you'll know."

"Thanks for that."

"The least I can do now. Take care."

I put the cell phone on the desk and picked up my pen to resume working on the ad. But I tossed it down, my mind elsewhere. I hadn't heard from Dee since she left. And now I knew she was in Europe, hunting for the dangerous killer supported by the spy apparatus of the Russian Federation.

I still had skin in the game.

Chapter 16

Prague, Czech Republic
January

Unlike Alexi Navalny, and most likely because of that outspoken dissident's treatment when he returned to Russia, Anatoly Morosov expressed his objections of the Putin regime from afar. But not far enough. No place, actually, was beyond the reach of the SVR and its lethal weapon of retribution, Katarina Petrovic.

Two years earlier, while a professor of history at Moscow State University, Morosov left Russia with his wife—ostensibly to visit his brother living in Prague. He never returned. Instead, he found employment at Prague's prestigious Charles University, which was only too happy to add the renowned professor to its faculty.

The brother, Fyodor, was also a professor there, teaching a class in International Security Studies. In years past, such a course would have taught military strategy, but it had expanded its coverage into the social studies realm to include the geopolitical concerns and origins of armed conflict. As a former soldier in a special forces unit of the Czech army, Fyodor had the qualifications for the position.

Anatoly had no bodyguards per se, but his brother accompanied him whenever he ventured beyond the confines of the apartment building in which they both lived. Katarina assumed that Fyodor, at least, was always armed.

Each weekday morning, the brothers took the Prague Metro, which had an access only a block away from the apartment building, and emerged at a subway stop that was a ten-minute walk from the university.

That hour of the day, the downtown station was busy, with crowds of people heading for their workplaces. Wearing different disguises, Katarina had followed the brothers on their commute for several days and devised a plan.

Anatoly would be wearing a winter coat, and that increased the level of difficulty, but she'd had hours of training on the ballistic gel dummy and knew anatomy well. Her main concern was ensuring she was directly behind the target as he left the train with the rush of passengers. Once he was on the escalator to the street, it would be too late.

Key West
Trish and I agreed that Troy Ingram, aged fifty-five, was a good candidate for the manager of our Key West project. He had called us in response to our ad, first speaking to Trish, who then buzzed me on the intercom so that I could join the conversation. He'd been living in Key West for thirty-four years, ran fishing charters with his own boat, and certainly knew his way around the island.

I wanted to see Key West again after my one brief visit two months earlier, especially to gauge the popularity of ocean-related activities in the heart of winter. Google and travel ads couldn't beat firsthand experience. So I set up the interview on his home turf.

Ingram picked me up at Key West International Airport and drove me to a marina where he berthed his boat. He was medium-tall, fit, and deeply tanned. He sported a salt-and-pepper beard that matched his hair. I took his resemblance to photos I'd seen of Hemingway as a good sign.

I didn't know squat about deep-sea fishing, but his large boat looked clean and capable. And it had a spacious enclosed cabin topside for passengers who wanted to get out of the hot sun for a cool drink. This is where we sat to discuss my ideas.

"What's the passenger capacity?" I asked.

"For fishing?"

"Yeah."

"I've had ten clients comfortably. Could do twelve in a pinch."

"Business good?"

"Can't complain. Got a 4.7 average on Yelp with over five hundred reviews."

I smiled. He'd come prepared. "Impressive."

"Would've been closer to a 5, except some folks got seasick and blamed me."

I liked him already. "Could you do snorkeling tours with this boat?"

"No problem. I've got a swim platform off the back."

"And the trip to the Dry Tortugas?"

"You gonna hire a bartender?"

"Wasn't thinking of it."

"Well, I gotta be driving most of the time." He pointed to the front of the cabin and an old-fashioned Coca-Cola ice chest, the kind that used to be outside gas stations back in the day, according to what I'd seen on *American Pickers*. "You mentioned a cocktail cruise, but I suggest wine and beer only."

"Makes sense. Is snorkeling doable in January and February?"

He shrugged. "Water never gets too cold. Low seventies this time of year. Coral peepers come here in the winter too."

"So this could be a year-round operation, then. You okay with that?"

He grinned. "Let's get a beer, and we'll talk business."

He took me to the Green Parrot Bar, obviously a popular watering hole with a funky décor. A white, orange, and green parachute hung from the ceiling in the main section of the place. A pool table sat tucked away in another section. An eclectic array of posters, signs, photographs, and other mementos crammed the walls. I saw no tables, only different areas of bar seating. He took me to a relatively quiet one, and we ordered drafts of Green Parrot Session Ale.

"You never mentioned scuba diving," Ingram said and took a drink from his glass.

"Think we should offer that?"

"If you're gonna do snorkeling, you can't ignore scuba diving." He chuckled. "We're sitting in what's called a dive bar. Some say it's the best in town. Now I don't know if it's a play on words, but lots of divers come here after going down to the shipwrecks in the area. The Keys are an attraction for serious divers. You could make it a focus for a tour. Dive during the day, hit the Green Parrot or other places like it at night."

"You could do that too?"

He chuckled again. "When I got out of the U—"

"The U?"

"University of Miami. I had this crazy idea I could make a fortune diving on wrecks for artifacts, and I came here. Hundreds of them around the island, some dating back centuries. I know where many are in water not too deep. Sure, I could do that. I'm doing a little of it now."

I couldn't think of anything else to ask. He seemed perfect for the position. "So what do you think about the job?"

"With a few tweaks here and there, I think the tours would work."

"And you'd be willing to manage them?"

He squinted at me. "That'll depend on what the job pays, of course."

"This is a new project for us, and I appreciate your input, but we'll have to see if it works out. I'm willing to guarantee six months. What's your net during that time frame, on average?"

He rubbed his bearded chin, no doubt thinking about how much he dared to add to the real figure. "About thirty."

More like twenty, I figured. "Okay, I'll guarantee forty. You'll be responsible for the insurance and upkeep for the boat, but we'll pay for the fuel and any extra equipment you'll need. Also the refreshments for the cruises. Send us the invoices. If business warrants, we'll extend an additional six months."

"Health insurance?"

"You have it now?"

"I do." He looked at me questioningly.

I couldn't blame him for trying to up the ante. But I didn't want to test if it was a deal-breaker by hesitating and looking cheap. "We'll pay the premium."

He stuck out a hand, and I shook it.

"I'll send you a contract, starting time to be determined. Meanwhile, start thinking about places you'll be taking our tourists on their fun vacations."

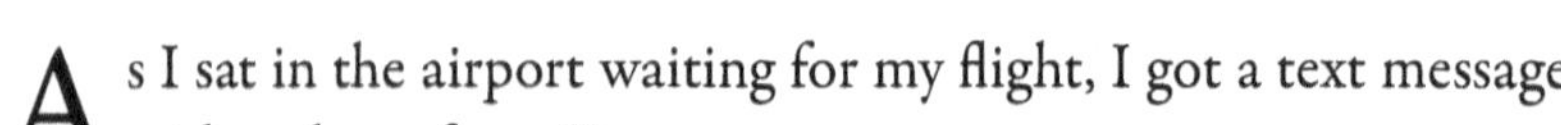

As I sat in the airport waiting for my flight, I got a text message with a photo from Dee.

I'm still looking for you know who. But now I have a photo to work with. Thought you should have it. Just in case, love. Don't know when I'll be coming back to the States, but I hope it will be soon!

The woman in the picture didn't look familiar. I texted back, *Thanks! Truax told me about the photo, but I hadn't seen it. I'll keep my eyes peeled. Miss you!*

Joy from Dee's contact competed with regret that it was from far away. Seeing her again was certainly not guaranteed. She faced a formidable opponent who had heavy support. I hoped *her* support was up to the challenge.

I'd planned on combining my business trip to Key West with a visit to my mother in Denver. Connie had been out to see her twice and related she was adjusting as well as could be expected and had made friends with her neighbors. But it was the dead of winter, so it would be a good time to feel her out about perhaps moving to a warmer clime. And I wanted to tell her about the progress being made to bring Dad's killer to justice.

I hoped the passenger sitting next to me on the plane would be a skier headed for the Colorado slopes so I could plug my Vermont ski packages.

Berlin

The CIA had received a tip from a source inside the SVR that Professor Morosov had been targeted for assassination. Now that they knew what AOD looked like and had a credible and actionable threat, it was decided to give Petra Nikolic a partner. And the agent who had taken the photo was the perfect choice.

Petra had been in Berlin when she was informed of the threat and introduced to Michael Sosa by the Chief of Station, Edwin Farley.

She eyed the good-looking, swarthy Hispanic man and immediately thought Cuban lineage. "No offense, Michael, but I'm used to working alone."

He spread his hands. "Not my call, Petra. Langley sent me here. And you can call me Mike."

"Sit down, both of you," Farley said.

They took chairs facing the chief's desk.

"Petra, Mike is the agent who took that photo of AOD, presumably Katarina Petrovic. He was on vacation in Aruba when he saw her meet with an SVR agent. So with Mike, you have more than a photo to go by. He's seen her up close."

"I understand, Chief, but—"

"It's a done deal. I'm just passing it along. Only for this assignment as far as I know, though."

She sighed. "Yes, sir."

"Your control agent will contact you when you get to Prague. Professor Morosov is aware of a potential threat but not this actionable one. Your job will be to inform him and get his cooperation."

Farley shoved a folder across his desk to her. "His particulars. In brief, he never travels outside his apartment without being accompanied by his brother, also a professor, but a former special forces officer in the Czech army. A de facto bodyguard.

"A team is in Prague now, setting up a trap for AOD if Morosov and his brother are willing to work with us."

"If not?"

"You'll have to babysit him. Luckily, he's taken most of the variables out of play with his safety precautions. It's our hope he'll at least agree to contact you if he changes his normal schedule."

⎯⎯ ❧ ⎯⎯

P rague
As luck would have it, fog hugged the streets on the Friday morning Katarina had chosen to complete the mission. She took that as a favorable omen.

She stood on the subway platform of the Metro station among a crowd of commuters, keeping an eye on the escalator. Her attire and makeup bespoke an older woman likely going to or coming from a menial job of some sort. A drab cloth coat hung over baggy slacks and beat-up athletic shoes. A scarf tied around her chin covered medium-length gray hair. She wore cheap cotton gloves.

The classic Moscow babushka, she thought and smiled.

As the sound of the oncoming train echoed on the tunnel walls, the Morosov brothers appeared. On time, as usual.

She slowly made her way to them. The crowd parted eagerly to give the slattern space, for fear she carried some nasty bug that might decide on a new host.

The train arrived, the doors opened, and a few passengers exited. Those waiting on the platform made their way into the cars in an orderly fashion. Katarina kept close behind the Morosovs.

Few empty seats remained. Anatoly approached one, looked behind him, and waved Katarina to it. She smiled, nodded her thanks, and sat. The brothers stood nearby, holding onto an overhead bar as the train left the station.

The train arrived at the Morosovs' downtown stop. Katarina stood quickly when the doors opened. She reached into the left sleeve of her coat for the stiletto and held it to her side as she shuffled behind the target. A two-shot derringer in her right coat pocket was available if needed.

As the crowd approached the escalator, she struck. The blade entered Anatoly's back below the rib cage to the right of the spine, angled upward and toward the midline, the abdominal aorta in its path.

Her victim reflexively arched backward with a loud groan. Katarina gave him room to fall to the pavement, the hilt of the knife concealed by his body.

"Anatoly!" Fyodor shouted and bent over his brother after looking around frantically. Some of the commuters in the immediate area stood staring at the dying man. One pulled out a cell phone to call for an ambulance. The other passengers, Katarina among them, moved quickly to the escalator to make their escape from a scene that would soon be complicated.

Petra and Mike had arrived in Prague the night before. They now stood outside the Metro access, eyeing the first rush of commuters coming from Morosov's train. The passengers seemed disturbed about something. As two women passed her, one of them said to her companion, "I hope he's all right."

Her gut clenching, Petra approached an apparent businessman and asked in Czech, "Did something happen down there?"

"A man collapsed. Looked like a heart attack."

No! Petra gave Mike a startled look then hurried down the escalator, Mike following on her heels.

Chapter 17

Troy Ingram sat at the counter with his good friend, Victor Mc-Nally, winding down after both had finished their fishing charters.

"Who was that guy you were talking to in here the other day?" McNally asked.

"My new employer."

"No shit? You got another job?"

Ingram smiled. "Not really. I'll be doing what I always do, but my customers will be set up for me. A travel agency in New York wants to start Key West tours and was looking for a local to manage them."

"Fishing and scuba diving?"

"Yeah. And snorkeling and cruises to Fort Jefferson."

"Never figured you for the type who would work for somebody. It must pay well."

"About double what I'm making now."

"Sweet." McNally looked straight ahead as he took a sip of his ale. "Good for you, man."

His friend's insincerity was painfully obvious. *He's jealous.* "You know, Vic, I've been thinking they need a backup. I get sick or injured and can't do a charter, those tourists would be left high and dry." He grinned. "As the second-best charter boat captain in Key West, you could fill in for me."

McNally turned to face him with a smile. "Second best, my ass."

"I can talk to Baker if you're interested."

"Baker?"

"Alex Baker. He was the guy you saw talking with me. He owns the travel agency."

McNally frowned. "Was he in the Air Force?"

"He didn't say. Why?"

"When I wore the uniform, I flew missions with a Patterson Baker. He had a son who went into the Air Force too. I remember Pat talking about him. His name was Alex."

"Small world."

"Pat was a helluva nice guy. He was murdered last year on the day he retired."

"Oh, man." Ingram reached for the bowl of peanuts. "Did they catch the guy?"

"It was a woman. Not as far as I know. And they think it was an assassination—revenge for the bombing we did for NATO during the Kosovo War in '99. After Pat got it, we were all warned to be on the lookout."

"Jesus. Were there any more murders?"

"Two that I know about. Haven't heard anything lately."

"Did you tell Linda?"

"Yeah." McNally shook his head.

"What?"

"She didn't know the other victims, but the Bakers were friends of ours. Linda's scared. She's talking about changing our name and moving."

"Wow. That's some serious shit."

"Tell me about it. I have a shotgun at the house, and"—he pointed to the gym bag at his feet—"I take that wherever I go. I've got a .44 Magnum in there."

"Man, I had no idea."

McNally chuckled. "On the positive side, Linda won't have to worry about me cheating on her with a woman she doesn't know."

"So, you gonna pull up stakes and leave?"

"Where would I go? And do what? I've got a decent business here. Took years to build it up. No, I'm staying. They'll catch the killer. The Air Force, FBI, and the CIA are all looking for her. And if she comes after me, I'll make sure she has a bad hair day."

"I'll drink to that, buddy." Ingram held up his glass to McNally, and they clinked.

"They know what she looks like?"

"They emailed me a photo. I look at it every day."

"Send it to me. I'll be on the lookout too."

McNally pulled out his cell phone and fingered it for a few seconds. "Done."

"As long as you're staying, what about the idea of being my tour backup?"

"I'm interested."

"I'll talk to Baker."

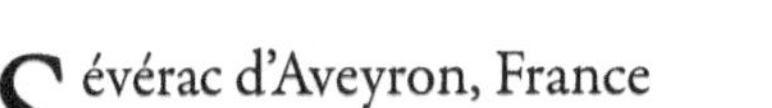

Sévérac d'Aveyron, France
    Hôtel de la Gare

Katarina sipped sauvignon blanc on the terrace of the hotel's restaurant. Though only eighteen degrees Celsius, there was no breeze, and she was comfortable in a light sweater.

She had followed Phillipe Didier north from Montpellier, near the Mediterranean coast, to the quaint and historic village. He would die there, one way or another. So far, it looked like her Plan A had a good chance of working.

In his midfifties, he had been a widower for almost a year. Didier was a retired officer in the action division of the DSGE, France's version of the American CIA. As such, he had led a joint mission with the AIVD—the Dutch intelligence and security agency—to infiltrate the SVR's Cyber Operations Center and plant hidden cameras. The operation had exposed Cozy Bear, a Russian hacker group. And in 2017, his unit uncovered evidence of Russia's attempt to interfere with France's presidential election. Didier's part in those operations had been obtained through the torture of a DSGE agent captured in Algeria.

Though Didier was no longer active against the Motherland, Putin couldn't stomach the thought that the thorn in his side was basking happily in the sunshine of the French Riviera. As far as enemies of the state went, Didier was small potatoes and obviously not a current threat. But Putin wanted him gone.

Didier had a part interest in a nearby vineyard, so he knew the area well. His sister and brother-in-law were visiting from Brussels, and he was entertaining them with a tour of his winery and showing them the local attractions.

Katarina had caught his eye earlier in the day as the threesome toured La Maison de Jeanne, a house that dated from the fourteenth century. And later, as they ambled along the narrow cobblestone streets of the old town, she made sure he saw her again—first at Chateau d'Sévérac, the ruins of a centuries-old castle, then at a café. The fish had exhibited interest in the comely stranger's bait, and she was about to reel him in.

Didier and company were staying at her hotel. They had returned ten minutes earlier from their sightseeing and had to pass her on the way to the entrance. Again, she and Didier had shared a glance.

She played an over-under game with herself using five minutes as the mark. She took the under—and won. Two minutes later, Didier appeared on the terrace and approached her table.

His dark hair was freshly combed, and he had substituted a white dress shirt and navy blazer for the T-shirt and windbreaker he had worn. She caught a whiff of cologne. He flashed a smile of perfect white teeth. "*Bonjour, mademoiselle. Je voyais—*"

She held up a hand. "*S'il vous plaît.* My French is not very good. Do you speak English?"

"*Certainement.*" He smiled again. "I mean, certainly. I saw you touring the town today."

She gave him a slight smirk. "And I saw you."

"I am showing my sister and her husband the sights in this part of France. May I join you?"

"*Certainement.*" She grinned.

He caught the attention of a waiter and sat. The waiter hurried over.

"*Oui, monsieur?*"

"A Pernod, please, Jean." He looked at Katarina. "And another wine for the lady?"

She nodded. "Thank you."

After the waiter left, he asked, "So, what are you doing in France?"

"I'm studying art in Paris."

"Ah, you're an artist."

She chuckled. "I hope to be." She offered her hand. "I'm Libby, from New York."

He grasped it. "My apologies. I'm Phillipe, from Montpellier."

She wrinkled her brow. "Vermont?"

"No." He laughed. "Your Montpelier was named for the original Montpellier, a city south of here near the coast." He released her hand as the waiter returned with their drinks.

"Merci, Jean. Charge to room 210, please."

"Yes, sir," Jean responded in English to match the guest's language and left them alone again.

"So, are you on holiday, Libby?"

"Only for the weekend. I heard about the old buildings and history here. I came to see and to sketch."

"You have done some sketches?"

"A few."

"I would like to see them."

Yes! She gave him her coy look. "They're in my room."

They locked eyes for a moment before he broke away to check his watch. "My party and I will be going out to dinner soon. Perhaps later this evening you can show me your artistic skill?"

"I'm in 220, at the end of the hall."

He downed the rest of his aperitif and stood. "Until then. Say about nine?"

She smiled and winked. "I'll have it on display for you, Phillipe."

"Looking forward to it." He turned and left quickly.

The next morning, before dawn, Katarina drove her rental car to Toulouse, where she ditched it and took the high-speed TGV train to Paris.

While waiting for her flight from Orly to Heathrow, she checked the news on her cell phone to see if the story had broken yet. It had. Contrary to what she'd told Didier, she was fluent in French.

The body of Montpellier businessman Phillipe Didier was found in a room at the Hôtel de la Gare in Sévérac d'Aveyron this morning. He was the victim of a shooting sometime during the night. He had been visiting the village with his sister and her husband. The room in which his body was discovered by housekeeping staff belonged to a Libby Perkins. According to the hotel manager, Perkins claimed to be an art student from New York studying in Paris. She is wanted by the authorities for questioning.

Chelsea, London

This time, Petra and Michael Sosa were in London when they received the news. And this time, they were briefed *after* the fact. They were called to a nondescript row house on Bramerton Street by the CIA's chief of station for London, Malcom Eddington.

Petra had to remind herself that the Peter O'Toole lookalike was an American CIA officer rather than an agent of MI6. Having spent his childhood in the UK before his family emigrated to the United States, Eddington still had a British accent and a voice that even sounded like the famous actor.

Her handler, Norman, and a younger man Eddington didn't introduce were also present at the meeting.

"Didier wasn't on our radar, Petra," Eddington said. "He'd been retired for two years from DSGE and had no public anti-Putin platform. Our SVR source had no clue."

"You're sure it was AOD?"

"Hotel staff identified her photo. A car rented to Libby Perkins at Orly was found abandoned in Toulouse. We figure she took the bullet train to Paris from there."

"And then?" Sosa asked.

"We don't know. She might even be in London as we speak."

Petra sighed. "We were so close in Prague."

"I know." Eddington folded his hands on the conference table. "We want you and Mike to sit tight in London until we get another lead."

"But she has another agenda not involving Moscow. There are still targets in the States."

Eddington nodded. "It's my understanding that all those who have been located have been warned."

"Tereschenko and Morosov knew of the danger too, Chief. And we had advanced warning about the active threats to them, thanks to our mole. But this source we have likely won't know anything about AOD's personal targets."

Eddington leaned back in his chair and interlocked his fingers beneath his chin. "I take your point. You think we should focus on the Belgrade fliers."

"It makes sense," Mike said. "It's a small, finite number we know about. And AOD probably won't have the level of support going after them that she enjoys when she pursues Putin's enemies."

Eddington eyed Norman. "What do you think?"

"I agree, sir."

"All right. I'll see if I can clear it with Langley."

New York

Troy Ingram called me with his proposal as I coincidentally had just finished writing up his contract.

He had an excellent point. It hadn't happened yet in our tours, but Trish and I were prepared to fill in for our managers in a pinch. Neither of us knew beans about running a fishing boat, though.

Troy's friend seemed to be qualified to back him up, and I already trusted Troy's judgment. I told him I would adjust the contract accordingly and add a per diem for McNally should he have to take over temporarily.

The other part of our conversation was a lot more interesting.

"Were you in the Air Force, Alex?" he asked.

"Yeah. Why?"

"Was Patterson Baker your father?"

That took me by surprise. "Yes. What's this about, Troy?"

He told me McNally had flown with Dad's unit over Belgrade, knew about the assassin, and had taken precautions. I thanked him for the information and said I would make sure the OSI remained aware of McNally's situation. I hung up, strangely excited. I now knew of a potential target of my father's killer.

I called Truax immediately. "Jim, is Victor McNally on your Belgrade list?"

"Hold on a sec." After a few moments, he responded. "Yes. You know him?"

"Haven't met him yet. He's a friend of a charter boat captain I'm hiring for our Key West tours."

"So you're going through with that idea. I like it."

"Thanks. How many on that list?"

"Four that we've been able to contact. Not counting the two she already got and the two she tried to hit."

An obvious tactic suddenly occurred to me. "Anyone watching McNally?"

"I doubt it, but I can check. That's the FBI's deal."

"I think we should, Jim."

"We?"

"You know what I mean. There are only four of them. Four chances to nail the assassin. We're not talking about massive manpower here."

He didn't respond for a couple of seconds. "I'll see what I can do."

"Thanks."

An hour later, I got a text message from Dee: *I'm coming to New York tomorrow! I'll call you after I get settled.*

I texted her back. *You can get settled in my condo.*

Would love to, but I have a partner now. We can still get together though!

Me: *Can't wait!*

Chapter 18

SVR Headquarters
Yasenevo District, Moscow

When Deputy Director Dmitriy Koslov entered his office on Thursday morning, his secretary told him of a waiting call. His counterpart in the FSB, the Federal Security Service, had an urgent message for him.

Koslov hung up after hearing the report and immediately called the office of his boss in Directorate S of the Foreign Intelligence Service—the SVR division responsible for Russian espionage.

"Does the director have a few minutes for me, Anya?" he asked the secretary.

"One moment, Dmitriy." A few seconds later, she said, "He can see you now."

"Thank you."

Koslov took his notepad and walked down the hallway to Mikhail Ilyin's office.

"He's here, sir," Anya said into the intercom.

"Send him in."

She nodded at Koslov, who went through the door behind her desk and closed it after him.

Ilyin was seated at his desk. Behind him, a picture window looked out at the skyline of central Moscow in the distance. He gestured at a visitor's chair. "What's on your mind, Dmitriy?"

Koslov sat and opened his notepad. "It seems we have a traitor in the organization."

Ilyin leaned forward. "Who?"

"One of our analysts. Nikolai Zaitsev."

"Don't know him. What do you have?"

"As you're aware, we periodically put our employees under surveillance. Zaitsev came to my attention when he was seen entering an apartment building in the Severny District. We determined he had rented an apartment there under his own name."

"He has another residence?"

"Yes. A house where he lives with a wife and two children. He goes to the apartment on Wednesday evenings at seven p.m. Not every Wednesday, but on no other day. Each time, a young woman arrives shortly thereafter." Koslov checked his notes. "Katya Solovyova, a clerk in the GUM store."

"Your man has a lover's hideaway, perhaps?"

"That was our initial thought, Mikhail. Per protocol, I engaged the FSB to follow up. They arranged for a coworker to ask Zaitsev about it, having supposedly driven by and spotted him. Zaitsev admitted he met his girlfriend there for trysts."

"But?"

"The woman stays for an hour and leaves. Each time, she then goes to a McDonald's on Krasnaya Presnya Street. She orders a sandwich, puts it in her handbag, and goes to the restroom. When she comes out, she leaves McDonald's and goes home to her own apartment."

Ilyin nodded. "The exchange is done in the restroom."

"That's what we think. At first, the FSB officers following her were male. Last night, they stationed a female officer in the restroom. She found another woman already there, taking her time applying makeup. When Solovyova came in, she looked at both women then quickly used the facilities and left."

"The exchange was aborted."

"Most likely."

"There must be a fallback plan."

Koslov smiled. "There is. Last evening, Solovyova went from the McDonald's to a Dunkin' Donuts on Leninsky Prospekt and followed the same routine, except this time, she bought a jelly donut. Naturally, FSB had no one in place there."

"Your suspicions appear well-founded, Dmitriy."

"There's more. They followed the other woman in the restroom to the American embassy. And on those Wednesdays, Zaitsev visits a different McDonald's and a different Dunkin' Donuts before going to the apartment."

"The information is obviously concealed in the food somehow." Ilyin, a former covert agent himself, nodded slowly. "So, Zaitsev somehow signals the GUM clerk he has information to pass on to the Americans. Always on a Wednesday, for efficiency. A phone call would be too risky. It could be something he does to the front of his house that an interested observer would spot when driving by. A closed drape, a moved flower pot, something. Then they meet at the apartment, where the clerk is given a McDonald's sandwich and a jelly donut, both containing the secret message. The bag is left in the restroom to be picked up by a CIA agent from the embassy. Either at the McDonald's or the Dunkin' Donuts."

"That's how we see it, Mikhail."

"What kind of classified data is available to Zaitsev?"

Koslov shrugged. "Specifically, not much. He doesn't have the security clearance for actual operations. He only does research. But he's smart. When asked to focus on certain areas, he might be able to figure out why."

"He doesn't know who our agents are, then."

"No. But it's an open secret in the directorate that we have a woman agent who assassinates enemies of the state." Koslov raised his eyebrows. "Even I don't know who she is."

"The president insists on keeping her identity closely held, for obvious reasons, Dmitriy."

"I understand. But a smart analyst could ascertain her missions without knowing who she is. And I have learned from a source of mine that a woman is being sought by the Americans because she has killed some of their own. They're of the mind that this woman and our assassin are the same person. Are they?"

Ilyin stared at his deputy—and friend—for a moment before he removed his glasses and rubbed his eyes. "Yes."

"Then she is taking unnecessary risks by operating on American soil, Mikhail. Perhaps we should put her on hiatus. If she's captured..."

"It would be a propaganda disaster."

"That's my concern."

Ilyin sighed. "I'll discuss this with the president."

"Zaitsev and Solovyova?"

"You have them in custody?"

"Not yet. When I received the report from FSB, I came directly to you."

"Arrest them at once."

Katya Solovyova did not consider herself a traitor. At least not to the true Russia she had learned about in Professor Morosov's class at Moscow State University. And Morosov had been killed for speaking out, exhorting the citizens of Mother Russia to fight for her and the greatness she had almost achieved. She was no longer the nation that had overthrown the tsar to establish a country for the benefit of the common people.

The hopes invested in early communism had been dashed. War had contributed, of course, but it was mostly greed and the power to satisfy it that had doomed the idealism of over a century ago. Russia was now ruled by rich oligarchs for their own benefit—Romanovs 2.0. And she had to admit, she had a selfish reason for opposing the current regime: her degree from the university amounted to nothing in her quest for a decent, fulfilling job. Russia was hardly the land of opportunity.

She shared her discontent with the good-looking customer as they chatted while she rung up his jeans purchase. He asked how long she had worked there, and she eagerly told him, "Since I graduated from Moscow State," in order to establish herself as someone other than a common salesperson. "Not what I thought I'd be doing," she said, rolling her eyes, and he commiserated with her. Like many in her age group—he didn't look older than thirty—he was similarly disillusioned with the power structure of the country, which she learned that evening after work. She was receptive to the progressive ideas he talked about during their get-acquainted-over-a-beer date. He was friendly and all, but he seemed more interested in discussing geopolitics than personal topics.

During the second date, dinner at a restaurant, she still hadn't sensed he had any sexual interest in her. Not even a goodnight kiss on parting. She was attractive and had hinted she was available. She was beginning to think he might be gay.

The answer came when she invited him to her apartment for dinner. It was going to be his last chance to put up or shut up. Life was too short for games.

As they sat in her living room, having glasses of wine, he came clean. "Katya," he began in the Russian he had always used with her, "I am not a citizen of Russia. In fact, I'm an American CIA agent."

Rendered speechless, she could only stare at him wide-eyed as he gave her a proposition. The man she knew as Ivan Semenov offered to pay her an amount more than she currently earned to be a go-between in the passing of classified information.

"That sounds dangerous," she said, the thought of all that money having overcome her initial shock.

"We have assessed the chance of discovery to be almost nonexistent."

"Almost?"

"Nothing is absolutely foolproof, Katya. The risk would be minimal because we know what we're doing. But if you're afraid to help us in our fight against the illegal and immoral activities of the Russian leadership, I understand. And we can forget the whole thing."

The hope for romance was gone. "You were feeling me out all this time, to see if you could recruit me as a spy."

"Yes."

"Are you married?"

He frowned. "No. Why?"

"Just curious. Tell me how it would work."

He did, though he withheld the mole's identity and the addresses she would need.

"Wouldn't the note get all messy?"

"It will be written on specially treated paper."

"Only on Wednesdays?"

"Yes," said the man who now called himself Tolstoy. She thought that was cute.

"Is he a nice man, this spy of yours?"

Tolstoy smiled. "He is. He wants the same things for his country that we do."

"Are you paying him too?"

"Katya, he's a patriot, like you. If he did it only for the money, we wouldn't trust him. But he deserves to be paid for his efforts."

"How do you pay him?"

"You don't need to know that."

"How will *I* get paid?"

"He'll give you cash when you meet at the apartment."

She sipped from her glass. "Do you trust me?"

He smiled. "Isn't that obvious?"

"But you haven't given me all the details yet."

"If you agree to help us, I will."

"Okay, I'll do it."

His smile disappeared. "If you betray any part of the operation to the authorities, we will find you."

"Oh, my. You can be quite scary when you want."

"This is serious business, Katya."

"Yes, it is. Can you protect me if something goes wrong?"

Tolstoy pulled a cell phone from inside his sport coat. "This is to be used only in an emergency. It's programmed for sending a text message to one number—our source. He will then notify me, and we will get you both to safety."

"In the United States?"

"Eventually."

A loud buzz emanated from the kitchen.

"Dinner is ready. You can give me all the details while we eat."

Over the course of the next two months, the exchanges occurred without a hitch, and Katya got used to the routine and stopped nervously looking over her shoulder all the time. On a few of the Wednesdays, including the week before last, the porch light at the house had not been lit, which meant she had no spy work to do that night.

She had a coworker at the store who seemed interested in her, so she'd managed to squeeze some romance into the secret life she lived less than once a week. She was able to buy a newer car with the extra money and was happy for the first time in quite a while.

But then an exchange did not proceed as usual. A car stayed behind her shortly after she left the source's apartment all the way to the McDonald's. She kept her eye on the entrance as she waited to order the Big Mac, but no one came in. In the restroom, two women were already there. She recognized one from a previous exchange, but this woman didn't give her the signal—smoothing of the eyebrows while looking in the mirror—so she didn't leave the Big Mac in the stall as planned. Still, that had happened once before, so she didn't panic.

But what looked to be the same car that had followed her to the McDonald's then followed her to the Dunkin' Donuts. A man climbed out of it and stood behind her in the order line. When she went to the restroom, she got the signal from the woman who was already in there, so she left the bag containing the adulterated jelly donut in the stall. Coming back to the seating area, she saw the man was gone and relaxed.

His car was still parked outside, though. Pretending not to notice it, she drove home. Sure enough, the car followed her there and drove slowly past when she entered the building. After locking the door, she removed the two Big Macs and the one jelly donut from her handbag to get at the emergency cell phone.

While his children were getting ready for bed, Nikolai Zaitsev had a late supper with his wife. She had become accustomed to his overtime work on Wednesdays, so she didn't complain. She knew he held an important position in the secretive SVR and knew not to question him about it.

As he went into the living room to watch television, the burner phone that was always kept either on his person or on his nightstand announced a message.

The chill that ran through him became full-blown panic when he read the text.

They know!

With trembling fingers, he responded. *Are you sure?*

I was followed to McDonald's. I didn't get the all-clear signal, so I went to the donut place. The same car followed me there, and then when I went home.

You're there now?

Yes.

I'll call Tolstoy.

"What's wrong, Nikolai?" his wife asked, coming in from the kitchen.

"We're in trouble, Bella."

"What—"

He held up a hand to silence her and texted his contact at the embassy: *S.O.S.*

Zaitsev looked up at his wife. "Get the children dressed. We have to leave."

"What's going on?" Fear widened Bella's eyes.

"I'll explain later! Hurry!"

She rushed out of the room and up the stairs.

He paced around the living room until the message came: *Where are you?*

Home.

Zaitsev grabbed his coat from the hall closet as Bella and the kids came down the stairs.

"Where are we going, Dad?" his oldest, ten-year-old Andrei, asked.

"It's a surprise. Get your coats on." He looked down at the new text.

On the way.

"Sit down, everybody. We're waiting for someone to pick us up."

He peered between the closed curtains of the living room window. Ten minutes later, with the children grumbling and Bella just staring at him, a minivan pulled into the driveway. Tolstoy got out and approached the front door.

Zaitsev opened it.

"Ready?" Tolstoy looked past Zaitsev at his family standing anxiously behind him.

"Yes." Zaitsev turned to his wife. "Let's go."

They climbed into the minivan, Zaitsev taking the front passenger seat. "Katya," he said. "We have to get her too. She's at her apartment."

Tolstoy nodded and backed out of the driveway.

"Katya?" Bella asked. "Where is this man taking us?"

"To the American embassy," Tolstoy answered her Russian in English.

"Why?"

"I will explain when we get there," Zaitsev said.

"Nikolai, are you a spy for the Americans?"

"A spy? That's awesome!" Andrei said, continuing in the English now being spoken by everyone.

"Please, Bella," Zaitsev pleaded. "I'll explain everything when we get there."

"Our house, our belongings... Oh, Nikolai, what have you done to us?"

After collecting Solovyova, Tolstoy drove them all to the safety of the US embassy.

S omewhere over the Atlantic
Katarina relaxed with a Daniel Silva spy novel as the Airbus A350 flew her to Miami from London. Though the sometimes humorous banter between the characters amused her—she had never experienced any such droll conversations with *her* people—she had to admit he knew his stuff about the espionage world. After complet-

ing two missions for her bosses, she'd been given permission to pursue her personal targets. She had left London quickly before they changed their minds.

She decided to do the most difficult one, logistically, first to get that one out of the way. Unless one had a boat, there were only two ways off Key West—by plane from the airport and via the only highway connecting the Keys to the mainland.

The hit would have to remain undiscovered until she had escaped by air. Driving away on Route 1 would leave her vulnerable for too long. And the airport offered direct flights to several large US cities where she could easily disappear.

Her handler, Sergei Garin, had flown to Miami and driven to Key West two days earlier. He would set up a base of operations and scout out the situation. They couldn't afford to be seen together in places like London and Miami, where knowing eyes could recognize them. As her only support for this mission, he would stay until it was over.

She closed the book, shut her eyes, and was soon asleep.

Manhattan

Dee and I lay naked in my bed, content in the afterglow of our physical reunion. Only thirty minutes had elapsed since I had let her into the condo building.

"I've missed you," I said, looking at the ceiling.

She chuckled. "I could tell!"

"How long will I have you this time?"

She turned onto her side and ran a fingernail through my chest hairs. "As for being in New York, that's open-ended, darling. I'm through traipsing through Europe for the time being. We have a new strategy."

She told me about the focus on the Air Force veterans, and I smiled. "I know one of them."

"Stearns?"

"Nope. One down."

"McNally?"

"Bingo! But it took you two tries out of only four."

She stared at me. "How do you know how many there are?"

"Truax."

"And how do you know McNally?"

I told her.

"He'd be the toughest one for her." She gave me the isolation reason I'd already thought of.

"Maybe that's why she hasn't gone after him by now, but I figure her time is running out. And I don't know about Stearns and the other two, but McNally had personal ties to my father. I like the odds he'll be next."

"There are actually six possible targets, including her two failures. But I'd put those at the bottom. She won't be able to surprise them. I like your thinking."

My cell phone rang. I'd left it in the living room, along with most of my clothes, which were shed soon after we stepped into the condo.

"I'll be back!" I said in a poor Schwarzenegger impression then climbed out of bed.

It was Truax.

"Speaking of the devil," I answered.

"What?"

"Nothing. What's up?"

"The Belgrade bombers are now covered."

"Good news."

"It helped that the CIA decided to focus on them, and the FBI agreed."

"Because of little old me?"

He laughed. "No. Thanks to Dee Norton, actually. It was her idea."

"That's cool."

"Yeah. Anyway, I have it on good authority that she's headed to New York."

"Really? Do tell."

"Wait a second. You've already seen her?"

"Sorry, Jim. Need-to-know applies. Thanks for calling, buddy." I hung up, padded back to the bedroom, and crawled into bed next to Dee. "That was Truax. Wanted me to know that Dee Norton is coming to New York. Giving me a real heads-up for a change."

"Good for him. But he—and the FBI—were kept out of the loop by us. Not his fault, really."

"Yeah, I know. He's one of the good guys." My fingers stroked her inner thigh.

Her breath quickened. "Alex, before you go any further, there's something else I'd like to tell you about Dee Norton."

My fingers crept higher. "And what would that be, my lady of mystery?"

She gasped. "My real name is Petra Nikolic."

"Nice to meet you, Petra. Do you come here often?"

She grabbed my hand and placed it on her mound. "Not nearly enough!"

Chapter 19

While Petra still slept, I quietly climbed out of bed, slipped on my boxers and a T-shirt, and did my rise-and-shine duties in the bathroom. Then I closed the bedroom door behind me and headed to the kitchen.

I had no idea what my lover's tastes were in regard to breakfast because we hadn't been that far in our relationship yet, but I planned to surprise her with a cheese-and-mushroom omelet. If she demurred, well, there would be more for me.

After setting up the coffeemaker, I turned it on and stepped to the fridge. I knew I had at least four eggs, OJ, and deli-sliced American cheese. The white button mushrooms I'd bought a few days ago were starting to turn brown, but they would do.

As I was cleaning them, Petra came into the kitchen, dressed in my bathrobe again. Considering the total amount of time she'd spent in my condo, the bathrobe was the garment she had worn the most. Well, actually, it was her birthday suit, but that didn't really count. She looked at the gurgling Mr. Coffee on the counter.

"Good morning, Ms. Nikolic. Sleep well?"

"When you finally let me." She yawned.

"Coffee'll be ready soon. Want some orange juice?"

"Yes, please."

She sat at the island, and I poured her a glass. She took a sip and eyed my gathered breakfast ingredients. "What are you creating?"

"A cheese-and-mushroom omelet. Hungry?"

"Ravenous."

"Good. And I've got English muffins and jam." I went to the now-quiet coffeemaker, poured mugs of the brew for both of us, and resumed my mushroom prep at the sink. "Do they pay you when you're not chasing Russian spies?"

"I get a salary for a GS-13, if that's what you mean. Why?"

"I was thinking you might not have to do much now if you're focused on former Air Force pilots."

"Why not?"

"I didn't tell you everything Truax said last night. The FBI has put those people under surveillance."

She sipped her coffee then smiled. "Like when they were watching over you? How did that work out?"

I reached into a cabinet below the island's cooktop for a frying pan. "I'm still alive."

"Because you were dealing with Angela, not AOD."

"AOD?" I melted butter in the pan.

"Angel of Death. That's the name we gave the assassin. I know, it's a little theatrical, but it beats referring to her as 'the woman assassin' all the time."

"Yeah, AOD just rolls off the tongue."

"The way her victims roll off her knife."

"Yikes!" I tossed the sliced mushrooms into the melted butter. "Thanks for the image."

"My point is she's very good at what she does. It's great the FBI is watching over those pilots, but I guess there's a maximum of two agents per target. They could use some help."

I whisked the eggs in a bowl. "So you and... What's your partner's name?"

"Mike Sosa."

"You and Mike will be going to Key West?"

"I'll talk it over with him, but I agree McNally is the most likely next attempt."

I took the mushrooms out, put them in a dish, and poured the eggs into the pan.

The muffled hum of a cell phone was barely distinguishable from the noise I was making. I knew it wasn't mine, which was still in the living room from the night before. Petra pulled hers from a robe pocket. After looking at the screen, she took the phone into the bedroom and closed the door.

At least I wouldn't have critical eyes on my preparations as I seasoned the eggs and cut the cheese into little pieces. While waiting for the eggs to cook, I popped two English muffins into the toaster, ready to go, and took a jar of strawberry jam from the fridge.

Finding the right moment to flip an omelet was a tricky timing thing, at least for me. After messing up a few times—too soon and too late—I got the hang of it. Still, I wanted to impress Petra with my culinary skill, so I was a bit nervous.

She came back into the kitchen just as I added the mushrooms and cheese to the egg firming up in the pan.

"That was Mike," she announced.

I nodded, concentrating intently on my creation. *Time to flip,* I decided. I grabbed my widest spatula and turned the circle of egg into a half moon. Then I rushed to the toaster to send the muffins down.

"So busy," Petra said. "I'm impressed."

I smiled and waited impatiently for the muffins to pop up. When they did, I put them on a plate then removed the omelet from the pan. After dividing it into two equal portions, I placed one of them and a muffin on two separate plates. "Breakfast is ready!"

I set the plates next to each other, grabbed knives and forks from a drawer and paper napkins from a holder on the island. The butter and jam went between us. "Hope you like it."

She took a bite. "Yum!"

"Need any salt or pepper?"

"It's perfect." She started to butter her muffin.

I tasted the omelet. It *was* perfect, and I relaxed. "So what did Mike want?"

"To know when I'll be coming back to the hotel. I think he misses me."

"Too bad!" I bit into my muffin.

She chuckled. "Just kidding, Alex. He's newly married. In fact, he was in Aruba with his fiancée when he happened to spot AOD." She told me the story of how he took her picture.

"Okay, what did Mike really want, if I may ask?"

"We lost a source we had concerning AOD's missions for Putin. He had no knowledge about pilot targets, though, so he couldn't help us with them anyway."

"Good thing you changed your strategy then."

"I suppose. It's all we've got to go on now." I poured coffee refills for us. "So when will you and Mike be leaving for Key West if that assignment is approved?"

"If the FBI has agents covering everyone now, it would be more efficient if Mike and I split up, I think. Cover two instead of just one. We could be wrong about McNally being next, after all. I'll talk to my people about that."

"Be sure you put dibs in for Key West, though."

She grinned. "Of course! Stearns is in Minneapolis, Clancy's in Topeka, and Romano lives in Billings. Brr!"

"Where do *you* live? Your home base."

"I have an apartment in Arlington, Virginia, where I'm known as a flight attendant. And that reminds me. I'll need to get some clothes appropriate for Key West."

"New York has plenty of stores that sell that stuff this time of year for folks going on cruises and the like."

"I should really go to Arlington, to check the place out, show my face. Haven't been there in almost a month, and I don't want neighbors to think something happened to me and get the police involved. And it'll give Mike some time to be with his wife."

"I could go with you. And then we could fly together to Key West. I need to get down there too. If McNally is going to be my tour manager's backup, I think I should at least meet him."

She leaned in for a kiss. "Sounds like a wonderful plan."

Key West

Sergei picked Katarina up from the airport and took her to a bungalow with aqua-colored vinyl siding on Olivia Street. A white picket fence surrounded a front yard dominated by a single palm tree. He drove the SUV down an oyster-shell driveway to a detached single-car garage at the back.

A concrete patio at the rear of the house featured a propane grill. They entered through a door off a back porch barely large enough for the two wicker rockers and small table between them.

To the right was a galley kitchen with gray-and-black-veined granite countertops, stainless steel appliances, and a gas range. To the left sat a round whitewashed table surrounded by four matching wooden chairs. Beyond was a living room with seacoast-motif wall hangings. A large flat-screen TV perched on an antique-white cabinet faced a sofa upholstered with a coral and green floral-patterned fabric, a matching love seat, and a white leather recliner.

"This'll do," Katarina said. "Better than I expected, really."

Sergei put the duffel bag he'd brought in from the car on the dinette. "One bedroom, but the love seat opens out into a bed. The plus is the garage to conceal the car if need be. Weekly rental. So we have five days left. We're Mr. and Mrs. Erwin Neumeister from

Philadelphia, by the way." He reached into the duffel and withdrew a billfold, which he handed to her. "Your new ID and a credit card."

She chuckled as she looked at the driver's license. "Neumeister? To deflect from your accent, I suppose."

"Yes." He smiled. "As long as we don't run into any Russians here, it should work. Are you hungry?"

"No."

"How about a vodka tonic?"

"That, I could use."

"Why don't you freshen up while I make the drinks? The bathroom is across from the bedroom. Down the hall to the right."

She wheeled her carry-on into the living room and around a corner.

When she returned, she sat next to Sergei on the couch and picked up her glass from a hatch-cover coffee table. "Thank you." She took a sip.

"Do you have a plan yet?" he asked. "Because I encountered a problem."

She stared at him, waiting.

"McNally has a watcher. Two, actually."

That *was* a problem. "You're sure?" she asked even as she knew there could be no doubt.

"No mistaking it. A man and a woman follow him to his boat in the morning, then wherever he goes when he returns from the fishing charter. They take turns staking out the house at night in their car. We should have thought of this, Kat."

She nodded. "Yes, it's the obvious—and easier—path to me."

Taking another drink, she stared at a framed print on the wall above the television. It featured a fishing boat coming into harbor, the setting sun behind it.

"Are you a fisherman, Sergei?"

"Like that?" He pointed at the picture that had captured her gaze.

"Not commercial, but like what people McNally takes on his boat do."

He shrugged. "I did some of that on the Black Sea years ago. Why?" His eyes suddenly got big. "No, you can't do him on the boat."

"Why not?"

"It's obvious. No escape. Witnesses, and the FBI waiting for us. Unless we jump overboard after and swim to a waiting speedboat—that we don't have. Forget about it."

"It will take some planning, but there is a way."

Chapter 20

Key West

Katarina outlined her idea to Sergei while they dined at a seafood restaurant that evening.

He nodded slowly as he chewed a flounder morsel dabbed in lemon crème sauce. After swallowing, he drank from his glass of chardonnay. "A little complicated, but it can be done."

"It will depend on your captain's skills."

"A boat is a boat. Doubt they've changed much since I last operated one. Shouldn't be a problem, but it would be nice to have a look beforehand."

"You don't know the area. Won't we need GPS?"

He cut into his asparagus. "Most come equipped with it now. But again, it would be nice to know."

"So how do we do that?"

"I'll sign up for one of his charters." He smiled at her. "As a test run to see if my mother would enjoy the experience too. I bet he'd be happy to show off his pride and joy to me."

She frowned as she twirled the shrimp scampi linguini with her fork. "Mother?"

"You're disguised now, right? I like the curly black hair, by the way. You look like Cher in *Moonstruck*. And you were an old woman for Morosov. They're on the lookout for a young, attractive woman, Kat. I told you this in Aruba. We have to assume all the targets have been warned. Your two failures suggest that's the case, and let's not forget about those two watchers here."

"You think they're FBI?"

He shrugged. "Or CIA. If they hadn't figured it out before, they know now."

"What happened?"

"Everyone in the SVR has heard the rumor about a young woman assassinating dissidents. An analyst in Directorate S defected."

"But only you, the director, and the president know who I am."

"As far as the identity of Katarina Petrovic is concerned, you're correct. But the CIA has to know *about* you now. And your operations in the US against the Air Force people suggest the SVR assassin is the same woman who is getting revenge for Belgrade. This Florida mission—" He stopped, shook his head, and reached for the wine bottle.

"What about it?"

"Nothing." He refilled their glasses.

"Tell me."

He sighed. "Director Ilyin almost canceled this mission. Putin overruled him. But I got the impression that if you fail here, this will be your last sanctioned operation in the US."

"I see. Do or die, huh?"

"Let's just say you're on probation."

She looked down at her plate and sighed. "Okay, I understand." She met his gaze. "Let's get back to the plan and work it out so we *don't* fail. You will check out the boat. Meanwhile, I'll find those locations we need and get the second car."

"I need to do those things, Kat. You have to keep your exposure to a minimum. We took a small chance tonight, but I figured the watchers were covering the fisherman and not wandering about town. Your wig is great, but you didn't change your facial appearance. Someone who knows what you look like might not be fooled."

"But how—" She stopped as the realization of what he was saying hit her. "They have my photo?"

"Remember that old guy on the Isle of Palms?"

"Sizemore."

"Do you think every time he hears his doorbell ring he grabs his shotgun and sneaks around the house to see who's at his front door?"

She didn't respond as she stared at him.

"Security cameras. Lots of homeowners have them so their Amazon deliveries don't get stolen off the front porch or to see if they want to answer the doorbell. In Sizemore's case, maybe it was a precaution because he'd been warned about you. You could have been caught, full face, on tape."

"You didn't ever mention that."

He shrugged. "It occurred to me on the flight from London. I'm surprised you didn't think of it."

She remembered the funny-looking doorbell. "I should have."

"To sum up, we have to assume that not only are the FBI, the CIA, and the targets on the alert for a woman assassin, they know what she looks like. This mission is high-risk. As I told you in Aruba, we have other agents who could complete the revenge for you."

"If I'm out of the picture, I doubt it would be approved. *I'm* what matters to Directorate S, not my vendetta." She looked away. "My other assignments, they're just jobs to me, Sergei. There's a sense of pride involved, and I'm glad I can answer Russia's call when she needs me, but I have no emotional investment in them." She faced him again, her eyes moist. "But Belgrade is personal. For over twenty years, I've thought of those bombs and the men who dropped them on my parents. I have to do this."

"And I'll help you any way I can. We just have to be careful." He smiled. "I like these assignments in America too much to see them end."

Arlington, Virginia/Washington, DC

Petra eased her neighbors' concerns by explaining she'd taken a temporary job for a time-share jet company in Europe. She didn't explain me, and I was fine with it. *Let them wonder.*

She got the go-ahead for Key West, and Mike would cover the Minneapolis target. She paid bills and touched base with her friends in the area. During one such visit of hers, I arranged to meet Truax.

He was already sitting at the bar in an Irish-themed pub near Washington's K Street when I walked in.

Despite the neighborhood charm of the place, at that hour patrons in business attire were in the vast majority. Because of the watering hole's location near the heart of American government, I imagined these folks to be lobbyists bending the ears of congresspersons, lawyers meeting with nervous clients, and Hill staffers seeking respite from demanding bosses after a day in the trenches.

Truax wore civilian clothes—a navy crewneck sweater and gray slacks. He waved me over, and I took the empty stool next to him. He eyed my New York Yankees sweatshirt. "Not a good choice for this town, Alex."

I laughed. "Yeah, what was I thinking?"

The bartender took my Manhattan order, and Truax said, "On my tab."

"Thanks."

Truax smiled. "I'll be getting a raise soon."

I raised my eyebrows.

"I'll explain later." He looked around. A table had just become vacant, and he pointed at it. "Let's get some privacy."

He grabbed the chit and his drink of bourbon or scotch over ice and headed to the table. I joined him moments later, after my Manhattan was put in front of me. We waited while a server cleared the evidence of the previous customers from the table.

"So what brings you to my neck of the woods?"

"Visiting a friend." I took a sip.

He did likewise and nodded. "In Arlington?"

I should have known. "As a matter of fact, yes."

"Will you be going with her to Key West?"

"You know that too?"

"The CIA is working with the FBI now, and I'm still in the loop."

"That's good to know, because I no longer am. Yeah, I'm going with her. I haven't met McNally yet, so I should check him out."

"The two agents there know she's coming. I agree with her assessment, by the way. McNally would be the toughest nut to crack, and I think that would be an attractive challenge for AOD." He peered at me, to see if I knew the nickname, I figured.

"We talked about that. And an additional fact favors McNally being AOD's next target. He and his wife were friends with my parents."

"I didn't know that."

"Has McNally been informed of what we're thinking?"

"I don't think so. You going to tell him?" He sipped his drink.

"Wouldn't that be wise? Put him on extra alert?"

"Well, I can't stop you." His expression told me he had no problem with it.

"Thanks." I sipped my Manhattan. Icy cold, just as I liked it. "How's the career going? You mentioned getting a raise. Did you land a good job after retirement?"

He laughed. "How old do you think I am? No, I have a few years left in uniform, God willing. I'm on the generals list."

"Congratulations!"

"Thanks. My position actually calls for a one-star. But the Air Force let me take over after General Woodford retired because I was the highest rank with the experience."

I held up my glass to him for a clink. "Good for you, Jim. The OSI will stay in good hands."

"I appreciate that."

We drank in silence for a few moments before he said, "This thing with you and Dee. Does it have legs?"

"Who knows?" I ate the maraschino cherry. "I like her; she likes me."

"I don't know her, of course, but she's obviously smart."

I grinned. "Because she's with me?"

"That too," he said and laughed. "Anyway, I wish you luck. A relationship with a CIA operative can't be easy."

"We'll just have to see where it goes. I'm not making any plans yet." I finished my drink. "I better get back. Dee will be anxious to know what we talked about."

"You know that's not her real name, right?"

I stared at him for a moment. "I do."

"Whew!" He made a show of wiping his forehead with a hand. "That's a relief."

"What?"

He winked at me. "I knew her real name since last week. But I wasn't sure you did. Makes me feel better about you two."

I chuckled and stood. "Yeah, getting our names straight is a good start. Thanks for the drink and the conversation. I hope we can do it again."

"Me too." He rose from the table, and we shook hands.

"Did you use the garage up the block?" he asked.

"Yeah."

"Let me settle up, and I'll go with you."

Key West
          The next afternoon, Petra and I flew to Key West out of Reagan National and checked into a suite at the Fairfield Inn on North Roosevelt Boulevard. Because of Florida's gun laws, my New York concealed carry permit wasn't accepted by the Sunshine State. Petra, though, as a federal officer, had no problem, so I used her luggage for my Beretta.

After settling in, I called Ingram.

"Howdy, Alex."

I liked the upbeat tone of his voice.

"Did you get the contract?"

"Yup. Looks good. Vic's onboard too. I'll send it to you tomorrow."

"Actually, you can give it to me in person. I'm here, just arrived. Wanted to have a face-to-face with your buddy."

"Sure."

"Where would I find him?"

He gave me the address, which I wrote down on hotel stationery.

"Like me, though, he's probably out on his boat now."

"Give me his cell number."

He did. "Maybe we can all have a drink later?"

"Good idea. I'll let you know after I get hold of him."

"Okay."

I disconnected and called McNally.

"Hello?"

"Victor McNally?"

"That's me."

"This is Alex Baker."

"Oh, hi. I signed the contract today. Thanks."

"Good to have you. I just flew into Key West and would like to meet you."

"Same here! I'm doing a charter now but should be getting in soon."

Like Ingram, McNally sounded enthusiastic. That was encouraging.

"Where would that be? I can meet you there."

"The Green Flash Marina on Caroline Street. A restaurant, Benny's, overlooks the docks. I'll meet you at the entrance. I'll be wearing a Florida State T-shirt and a LandShark ball cap."

"Okay, see you then."

"And you?" he asked before I could end the call.

"What?"

"How will I recognize *you*? Can't be too careful these days."

He's on alert. Good. "Gotcha." I looked down at the sweater vest I wore from still-wintry Virginia and thought of what I'd brought with me. "Statue of Liberty T-shirt."

"See you in about an hour."

I drove Petra to the marina and parked in the restaurant's lot. I hadn't mentioned her to McNally, not wanting to worry him enough to risk his cancelling the meet-and-greet.

We climbed out and went through the row of cars in front of us. They were all empty except for a Chevy sedan that had a man in the driver's seat and a woman next to him, just sitting there. They both eyed us as we walked past to the restaurant entrance.

We waited outside and looked out at the myriad boats of various types and sizes in their slips—masted yachts, day-trip sailboats, cabin cruisers, and fishing boats. The sun was low in the west, and I wondered if I would have the chance to see the flash of green that supposedly occurs just as the sun sinks beneath the horizon.

A group of men came up the gangway from the berths and through the security gate carrying coolers—the day's catches, I assumed.

Ten minutes later, a beefy man wearing a T-shirt and ball cap and carrying a gym bag appeared alone on the gangway. When he came through the gate, I recognized the Florida State logo. As he neared the restaurant, his eyes fell on me, and he approached.

"Alex?" he asked and looked warily at Petra.

"Yes." We shook hands. "This is Dee Norton. She works for the government."

When he shook her hand, he said, "Government, like the two following me around?"

"You know about them?" she asked.

He chuckled. "Hard to miss. Why don't we go inside and get acquainted over a beer?"

"Sounds good." I took out my cell phone. "Troy wanted to meet with us. Go on in, and I'll call him."

"After you, Dee," McNally said, opening the door. Before he followed her in, he waved at the Chevy. The two in the car didn't wave back.

Ingram picked up after three rings. "You get hold of Vic?"

"We're at the marina's restaurant."

"Benny's?"

"Yeah."

"I just got in. See you in about thirty."

I entered the restaurant and saw they'd secured a table. McNally's chair faced the front door. I joined them and sat to his left.

"There they are," he said, and I followed his gaze. The couple in the sedan had come in and were headed to the bar. *Feds.*

A waitress took our orders—draft beers all around—as McNally stared at the agents, causing Petra to look at them too.

"Those the ones?" she asked.

"Yup. They never say anything, though I've tried to get a rise out of them. They know I know they're there, but they keep pretending they're not watching me. Kinda creepy, actually."

The server, a thin forty-something brunette with a pleasant smile, brought the beers. "Would you like menus?" she asked.

"Maybe later, Carol," McNally said, and she left.

After we mutually agreed to be on a first-name basis, McNally took a long pull from his glass and eyed me then Petra. "Which one of you is going to tell me what this is about? Why are you two meeting me as a team?"

I glanced at Petra. "We're here for two different reasons, Vic. I'm here for the travel agency, like I told you." Mostly true. "And Dee is here to assist in the surveillance you've already noticed. We met during the investigation of my father's murder."

He nodded. "Your dad was a good man. One of the best. I'd like to get my hands on that woman before they lock her up."

Petra said, "Do the watchers follow you to the marina and pick you up again when you're done for the day?"

"Yeah. I don't know what they do in between, but they're always there when I get back. At first, they spooked me. One of them was a woman, after all. But when they camped out every night by my house and didn't make any moves against me, I figured they had to be cops of some sort. Are they FBI?"

"Yes. They never go on your boat then?"

"No." He suddenly smiled and looked sideways at Petra. "I see where you're going. The assassin could pretend she's one of my charter people, right?"

"That was my thought."

"But I know what she looks like. I carry her photo with me. She wouldn't be able to do that."

"She could be in disguise."

"Maybe. But I can protect myself if that happens. See that gym bag on the floor? I've got a .44 Magnum in there. That goes everywhere with me too. And besides, how could she kill me at sea with a boatload of people and hope to get away?"

"That was my next question."

"Here's Troy," he said and waved.

Ingram came over and pulled up a chair. Carol hustled over and took his order.

I introduced Petra and explained her presence as I'd done with McNally.

"We were discussing a flaw in Vic's security," I said. "What if the killer manages to get on his boat posing as one of his clients?"

"I thought of that," Ingram said. "But how could she get away with it? They're out on the ocean with other people on board."

"That's what I said."

Carol brought Ingram his beer. After she left, I said, "Think this through, guys. You're the boat captains. Let's assume she comes to Key West—"

Petra interrupted with "And we think there's a good chance Vic will be her next target."

"That's right," I went on. "So she comes here, stakes Vic out, sees the feds are always around. But not on the boat. That's their blind spot. How could she use that, hypothetically?"

"She'd have to get on board without me recognizing her, first of all," McNally said. "Then she'd have to know how to operate the boat."

"Is that difficult?" Petra asked.

"Not really, if she knows boats. The controls are straightforward."

Ingram said, "So she could kill Vic, maybe all the witnesses too, then take the boat to a prearranged location where another boat will be waiting. She leaves Vic's boat to drift in the Gulf."

"Your boat has GPS?" Petra asked.

"Sure does. But I thought this woman works alone."

"We know she has support," Petra said.

"Damn! Troy's hypothetical could work. I have to make sure she never comes aboard then. And there's only one way to do that. No woman will be allowed on my boat!" McNally's outburst attracted the attention of nearby patrons, and he lowered his voice. "There, that should do it."

"What if she disguises herself as a man?" Petra persisted.

"Oh, jeez, I give up." McNally covered his face with his hands.

"There's another option," Petra said.

He peeked out between his fingers. "I'm all ears."

"I go on the boat as one of your customers."

"Me too," I blurted out. I'd already thought of that.

Petra scowled at me.

"It makes sense, Dee. Two of us to prevent anyone getting the drop on Vic. He'll be busy running the charter and can't go around with his Dirty Harry pistol on his hip." I looked at him. "Or can you?"

"Not with Florida's law. Concealed carry only."

I continued. "She won't expect two of her fellow customers to be armed. And dangerous."

"Alex, it's not your job. One of the FBI agents can do it."

"I've had the training. I used to be a cop, remember? And I've got a stake in keeping Vic alive."

She narrowed her eyes. "I can't approve that."

What the hell? Her attitude surprised me. I thought we were working together, but apparently that wasn't the case. She had her CIA hat on, and it wasn't big enough to include a civilian, even if he was her lover. But if I wasn't in the club, she couldn't give me orders.

"Well, it's not really up to you. If you want to work your plan by yourself, so be it. But I'll be on the boat too. I have a personal interest in catching this woman. She killed my father, okay?"

She glared at me, no doubt considering her options. She knew, short of having me arrested or killed, she couldn't stop me. I wished it hadn't come to a confrontation, but there it was.

She held my gaze for a moment before turning to McNally. "That okay with you, Vic? You've probably felt safe on your boat until we butted in and spoiled that. You can always go on vacation."

"But I'd have to come back sometime. I want this to be over. Whatever it takes." He grinned. "But since you two will be taking the place of paying customers, you don't get to keep any fish you catch."

Chapter 21

There was no lovemaking that night at the hotel. Petra was pissed I had inserted myself into a federal operation. But I thought it was naïve of her to expect my only role to be introducing her to the potential target. She hadn't thought it through beforehand, obviously. Or maybe she'd just assumed, without sufficient reason to do so, that I would meekly let her call the shots. I had hitched myself to her spy wagon, thinking it to be a great way for me to be in on AOD's capture, and I wasn't getting off now, no matter what Petra wanted me to do.

After a sometimes heated discussion, she grudgingly decided it would be better if we were a team to prevent working at cross-purposes.

The next morning, before going aboard McNally's boat— the *Bounty of the Sea*—Petra and I sauntered over to the FBI car and introduced ourselves to the agents.

Tom Blankenship and Gwen Michaels, who both appeared to be in their thirties, were stationed in Miami.

Blankenship had worked in Manhattan but had requested a transfer a year earlier to be near his ailing mother, who had since passed. He knew Special Agent Reinhardt.

"Pete told me about you," he said. "You've been involved with this since the beginning."

"Wish it could've been otherwise," I said.

He realized his faux pas. "I'm sorry. Put my foot in that one."

"It's okay. But yeah, I've got the motivation to see AOD gets what she deserves."

"So, why are you here this morning?" Michaels asked.

"We're going on the boat," Petra said.

Michaels glanced briefly at her partner before saying, "We thought about doing that. It's a blind spot in our surveillance."

Petra said, "It ups the risk factor for her, but you guys have everything else covered, so she doesn't have much choice."

"You think she's already in Key West?" Blankenship asked.

"Could be," I said. "We're only guessing McNally is her next target. As far as we know, she could have been here for days, observed his routine, spotted your surveillance, and will now show up on his boat. That's why we'll be on it."

Blankenship chuckled. "We have a bet going. A one in four chance to win. Each team ponies up a hundred bucks. If AOD goes after their target first, they win the pot. With you here, Dee, it looks like the odds favor us."

"How about a bonus to the team that actually captures her?" I asked.

Michaels smiled. "I hope that prize will be a bump up in our pay grade at least."

We shared cell phone numbers, then Petra and I headed to the boat.

McNally's boat was a little smaller than Ingram's, but it also had a central cabin, where we stowed our cooler. We were the first of the passengers to board, and over the next twenty minutes, the paying customers arrived. Six in all, they ranged in age from the early twenties to the late sixties. We checked them out carefully. No doubt about it, they were all men.

Vic did a headcount and called everyone to the rear of the boat, where he stood in front of the transom. "I'm Victor McNally, and I'll be managing this charter. I have a few announcements before we head out to sea. Behind me is a bin containing life jackets. While fishing, each of you must wear one. Number two—we'll be using live bait." He pointed to a bucket near his feet. "If you are unfamiliar with the equipment or how to properly bait the hook, I'll assist you when we reach the fishing ground.

"We'll be going after food fish, not game fish, but some can be quite large and put up a fight. And there's always the possibility you'll hook a shark or a game fish like the tarpon. If you're having trouble reeling your catch in—and that's where the importance of the life jacket comes in—give me a holler. Any questions?"

"Does the boat have GPS?" a tall man in a ball cap and windbreaker asked in an accent that sounded Eastern European.

Vic smiled. "Yes. Don't worry, people. We won't get lost. Any other questions?"

Hearing no further responses, Vic said, "Let's catch us some fish!" He went forward to the pilot's cabin to start the engine then threw off the mooring lines. After backing out of the slip, he motored slowly toward open water. The sun was rising on the starboard side, gulls flew overhead, and the breeze coming off the ocean was refreshing. With no assassin on board, I could relax and enjoy a pleasant day at sea. I might even catch a fish or two for Vic's freezer.

Petra's expression did not match my feeling of contentment, though. She frowned as she stared at something.

"What's wrong?" I asked.

"That man who asked the question. He's up there with Vic. I need a better look at him."

She went forward, and I followed her.

The man was talking with Vic and turned as we approached the pilot's cabin, essentially an enclosed cockpit, giving Petra a full-frontal view of his face. She kept going toward the bow, but he stopped us.

"Hi, folks. You should see the equipment Captain McNally has for his boat. Amazing. He has a fish finder, depth gauge, and a radio he can use to call for help."

"And a GPS," I said, smiling. I still couldn't pin down the accent, but in light of our task, I immediately considered Russian.

"Yes, that also." He gave us a sheepish look. "As you might have noticed, I am a little nervous, as I have never been out on the ocean before."

"The captain comes highly recommended," I said, giving Vic a plug.

"This, I know. But still, I am nervous, and Captain McNally has been kind to show me his safety measures."

"Haven't lost a customer yet," Vic said as he steered past a buoy.

"A good record, yes?" The man smiled. "I hope we catch many fish." He stepped past us and headed aft.

Petra took out her cell phone, found the photo, and showed it to me. It was the man we had just talked to. "Sergei Garin. A known SVR agent, and we think he's AOD's handler."

"She's not on the boat."

"No, but if Garin is here, she must be around, or will be soon."

"What're you guys talking about?" Vic asked and opened up the throttle.

"That man who was just here is a Russian agent." Petra showed him the photo. "He works with the assassin."

"He was checking out my boat, then, to see if he could handle it. So now we have two of them to worry about."

"Looks like we guessed right, though," I said, excited.

"She's not on board now, is she? Disguised as a man?" Vic looked down at the gym bag by his feet.

"No. This must be a dry run to see if taking over the boat is doable." Petra put away the phone.

"He signed on as Erwin Neumeister, on vacation from Philadelphia. He asked me if a charter would be safe for his mother, who's in her sixties."

"That's how she'll be disguised," Petra said. "As his mother."

"We got her." I couldn't hide my exuberance. Our hypotheses had proved to be correct: AOD would strike in Key West next, and she planned on killing her target on his boat. *Damn, we're good! Or just lucky. But either way, we have her.*

"Yes. When Neumeister and his mother come on board, we'll arrest them." Petra smiled. "Actually, Tom and Gwen will. The CIA doesn't arrest people."

"Who are Tom and Gwen?" Vic asked.

"Those two FBI agents following you around," I said. "We met them this morning."

"So I can relax for at least one more day?"

"Business as usual, Vic."

The way the woman had looked at him sounded an alarm bell. He saw recognition in her eyes. Just for a second, but it was there. And as he watched them from the rear of the boat, she showed her phone to her companion then to McNally. The CIA likely had a file on him. They might not know he was Katarina's handler, but his presence in Key West would lead to that conclusion. If those two were CIA operatives, knew Katarina was here, and were waiting for her to show up on the boat, they deduced her plan.

Those were a lot of suppositions, and he could be jumping to conclusions based only on a momentary glance. But they couldn't afford to proceed as if it were all innocent. He trusted his instinct, which had saved his ass on more than one occasion, so the answer was no. Surviving to fight another day was the prudent option to take.

They had to leave Key West immediately.

Petra called Blankenship. "Tom, AOD's handler is on the boat... He must be checking it out for when they take it over... He's tall, wearing a black ball cap, black windbreaker, and jeans. In case he ditches the hat, he's bald. Follow him when he comes off the boat. We'll cover McNally."

She looked at me, and I nodded.

"I don't know, but he might have made you and Gwen from surveillance... Good. If he doesn't spot the tail, he should lead us to AOD... Well, if he has made Alex and me, he's got a big problem to work out."

She disconnected. "Tom and Gwen will follow him in separate cars, and we'll babysit Vic."

"Good." I was glad we were a team again.

Garin stood at the railing, staring out at the sea as if he were thinking of what had to be done. He had to warn Katarina, and he couldn't return to the house.

They will follow me.

He pulled out his cell phone.

"He's on his cell," I said to Petra. "And I don't think he's calling his mother. Could he have made us?"

She sighed. "He's an experienced agent. We have to assume he did. Damn it! I should've waited for a better opportunity to get a look at him."

"What can we do?"

"See what he does. I know what *I'd* do if I were him and thought the CIA was on the boat. Get out of town."

"And abandon AOD?"

She shook her head. "He'll act as a decoy. Pretend he was here as an advance man to scout out the situation and report back to AOD, who's somewhere else waiting for him. The watchers will follow him, and his agent can slip away unnoticed."

"Not by plane."

"No. The airport will be covered. She'll just get in her car and drive to Miami."

"Roadblock?"

"When do we do that, Alex? Right after Garin leaves? And how long do we maintain it? Days? Weeks? On the only route through the Keys?" She shook her head. "Nobody's going to authorize that."

"So she holes up until everything quiets down."

"You got it."

My earlier excitement had become frustrating despair. We were so close, only to let her slip through our fingers. Petra's reasoning was solid, though the what-if game couldn't lead to a definite conclusion. There had to be a way to salvage the operation.

"Maybe he didn't make us," I said.

"We'll know when he leaves the marina. If he heads to Route 1, we're screwed."

"Unless he isn't a decoy but is actually going to report to AOD what he's learned. We wait for them to return."

"Back to square one?"

"Possible, right?"

She looked out to sea. "I guess. But she's here in Key West now. I just know it."

"How about we arrest *him*? That would leave AOD high and dry, alone without support."

"On what charge?"

I forced a smile. "Being a spy?"

She laughed. "Nice try. We *know* he's a spy. That's why we have his photo. But he has to be caught doing spy stuff. Besides, he probably has a diplomatic passport. And there are more Sergei Garins out there who could come to her aid."

The boat throttled down and soon stopped. We rocked gently in ocean swells.

"We might as well catch some fish," I said as Vic started distributing the gear. "Nothing's going to happen until we get back to the marina."

Though what I said was true—Garin's move wouldn't be made until we got back—it couldn't hurt to think of options we had now.

I halfheartedly held the rod over the railing as I searched for something we hadn't considered yet. I ran through what we knew, which wasn't much, and what we were only guessing about. The unknowns were the key, and I ticked them off in my head. That was when the idea burst into full bloom from the bud of a thought we'd already discussed.

But I was distracted by a slight tug on my line. I reeled it in to discover my bait gone. That was just as well, because I had something else to do. I glanced down the line of fishermen and saw Vic netting a fish Garin had caught. Vic removed the hook from the flopping fish in the net and headed to the ice chest at the rear of the boat. He'd explained to us he would tag the catches so we would know which belonged to whom when we docked. Garin went into the cabin.

I put my rod down on the deck against the railing and turned to Petra. "I have an idea."

After I'd outlined the ploy, she said, "Worth a try."

"Either he buys it, or he doesn't. Or he doesn't care because he never made us to begin with. He's alone in the cabin now. Give me five minutes, then make your appearance."

Garin was sitting on a bench, a can of Budweiser in his hand.

"Any luck?" I asked as I went to our cooler.

He smiled. "I caught a little one." He spread his hands to a span of about two feet. "Captain says it's a yellowtail snapper. Good eating, he says."

I popped the top of my Yuengling and held out my hand. "I'm Brad."

He shook it. "Erwin."

I sat across from him. "Where're you from, Erwin?"

"Philadelphia."

"I mean originally."

He smiled again. "Oh, the accent, right? Germany. Heidelberg. But I've lived in the US for the last three years."

"My fiancée thought you looked familiar."

"I did not recognize her."

"Then she heard your accent and knew you weren't the professor she had at Hunter College."

"I see. These things happen. You, Brad, look like my cousin Karl."

I grinned. "He must be a handsome man."

Garin laughed. "He is!"

"The captain said you were asking if your mother would be safe going out on the boat."

He took a sip of beer and squinted at me. "You know Captain McNally?"

I nodded. "Victor is my brother-in-law. I live in New York, and he's been after me for years to go fishing on his boat. I get seasick easily, so I always begged off. But my fiancée wanted a vacation in Key West, and I finally gave in." I smiled. "And if *I* can do it, your mother can."

"I will think about that. Thank you. Did you catch a fish?"

"Not yet." I chuckled. "I'm taking a break from the stress."

Petra walked in. "There you are! I was looking for you."

"I was thirsty." I stood. "Dee, I'd like you to meet Erwin. He's from Philadelphia."

Garin rose from the bench. "A pleasure, Dee." He held out his hand, and she shook it.

"I was telling him you thought at first he might be that college professor."

"I'm sorry if I stared, Erwin. It is a striking resemblance, though."

"I understand. I told Brad that he looked like my cousin."

"He must be good-looking, then."

I laughed. "That's what I said! So, my love, did you catch anything?"

"I did!" She beamed. "I brought it in all by myself. Vic said it's a red grouper. How about you?"

I shook my head. "Nada."

"Poor baby. But what I caught is enough for both of us."

"Enough for four? We're eating at Vic's house tonight, remember?"

"He said we'll all be having that grouper this evening."

"Great. We'll pick up a bottle of wine. Why don't you take a load off and have a beer with me?"

"Sure."

She sat on my bench, and I grabbed a beer for her from the cooler.

Garin looked a little bored with our happy talk, which was encouraging. "Nice to meet you folks," he said and tossed his beer can into a trash bin. "I will try to catch another fish."

"Good luck," I said, and he left. I looked at Petra. "What do you think? Did we lay it on too thick?"

"I didn't detect any suspicion. Maybe it worked."

"We'll see."

Katarina fumed following Sergei's call. The FBI, she could understand. Only six Belgrade bombers remained, and it didn't take a genius to figure out they were all targets—especially after the failure in Brooklyn. They were easy to cover with minimal manpower.

But the CIA was a different story. And not only that, but an agent had recognized Sergei. *On the boat!* A feeling of doom threatened to engulf her. Forces that wanted to destroy her were closing in. Because of blind luck or tactical analysis, it didn't matter now. They were in Key West, knew her plan, and would catch her—only if she continued with the mission. Sergei's idea would let her escape. But that would mean abandoning her quest to avenge her parents' deaths. She might not get this chance again. Director Ilyin could see to that.

No. Despite the risk, she had to continue. If she died trying, so be it.

With a new sense of resolve, she sat at the dinette to devise a new plan that would not involve Sergei. And that was when he called again.

Chapter 22

I finally caught a fish—a cobia, according to Vic. It was larger than Petra's grouper, and that massaged my ego a bit. But Vic said that, though the cobia was good fare, the red grouper had it beat on the dinner table. Not that we cared one way or another. Both fish were destined for Vic's freezer anyway. And after hours of fish odors in the air, I was hankering for a good old-fashioned hamburger.

Vic had some housekeeping to do after we docked, so Petra and I waited while he hosed off the deck, stowed the fishing gear, and transferred the remaining live bait from the bucket to a wire mesh cage, which he lowered into the water next to the boat.

As we were walking up the gangway, Petra got a call from Blankenship. She listened for a couple of minutes and said, "Thanks, Tom. Stay with him." She disconnected.

"Garin went to Route 1," she explained, "but then he turned off at Stock Island, just east of here, where he checked into the Perry Hotel. He changed his clothes and is now at one of the hotel's restaurants. Oh, and along the way, he ditched the fish he caught."

We reached the parking lot, and Vic looked around. "Seems strange not to see them waiting for me."

"You have us now," Petra said.

"Look, guys, no need to stake out my house at night. I'm safe there. I have security cameras and an alarm, a shotgun, and"—he held up his gym bag—"my .44. But you can follow me to the boat tomorrow if you want. I leave at six."

"Okay," Petra agreed. "And we'll make sure you get home safely now."

He climbed into his pickup and drove out of the lot, and we followed in our SUV.

"He checked into a hotel," I said. "Which means he was staying elsewhere before today."

"With AOD."

"Yeah, probably. And I was thinking that maybe we got the escape order wrong. AOD doesn't have to hole up here if she leaves first. That could be what the call he made was all about. Garin's on the boat, watched by us. Meanwhile, AOD drives to Miami."

"A good point, Alex. It would be the more efficient move. And the hotel gives them separation. She gets to Miami and flies off before he arrives the next day."

"Right. So Garin's still the key. Wherever he goes, that's where AOD will be." After seeing Vic enter his attached garage, we headed to the Fairfield.

"Do you mind if we don't dine on seafood tonight?" I asked.

She laughed. "I'm with you there." She pulled out her cell phone and made a call on speaker. "Tom, there's a chance AOD has already left town, and Garin is using a delaying tactic."

"Yeah, that occurred to us too."

"Can one of you stick with him and the other stay here just in case?"

"We already drew straws. I got the tail duty. And if he goes to Miami, I can get backup from the field office."

"McNally's tucked in for the night."

"Looks like Garin is too. He just went to his room."

"How are you going to cover him?"

Blankenship laughed. "SAIC Johnson won't like it, but we got a room here. This place ain't cheap. We'll take turns watching the parking lot and getting some shut-eye."

"Talk to you tomorrow." Petra hung up as we pulled into the Fairfield's parking lot.

I said, "You think she was here, and we scared her off?"

"No. She was here, all right, and still is."

Ironically, or perhaps understandably, Vic didn't eat seafood very often. He sat down to a dinner of honey-garlic pork chops, mashed potatoes, and broccoli. He finished the beer he'd snagged from the fridge as soon as he entered the kitchen and reached for the bottle of cabernet.

"So she didn't show up today, I take it." His wife Linda sat next to him at the round table.

"No, but another spy did. Alex and Dee think he's her handler, as they call it." He poured a glass of wine, took a sip, then cut into his pork chop.

"There are two of them?"

"Seems so, but now we have a lead to find where the assassin is."

"And that's a good thing?"

"Mm-hmm," he mumbled then swallowed his mouthful. "Where he goes, so does the woman, and it looks like he might leave town, afraid he's been recognized. But she might not even be here, and her partner was only here to check out the situation for her. That's what they're thinking, anyway."

"But they don't really know."

"Yeah, it's a guessing game for sure."

Linda put down her fork and glared at him.

"What?"

"This isn't a game!"

He grabbed her hand. "I'm sorry, honey. I know that. I'm trying to deal with it the best I can. I want it to be over as much as you do."

"It's Stacy's birthday next week. She wants to come home from college. What do we tell her? She can't do it because someone is trying to kill her father?"

"Oh, man." He released her hand and took a gulp of wine. "It should be over by then, Lin."

"What if it isn't? Maybe we should go to Miami and celebrate her birthday there."

"Honey, we wouldn't have the protection in the city we have here, where everything is contained."

She shook her head. "All of this... torment—yes, that's the word—we're going through is because of that damned war you were in. I wish that never happened!"

"Me too. But c'mon, I didn't have any say in the matter. That was my job, and I had to follow orders."

"It wasn't even for your country, Victor. You risked your life for NATO! And you're still doing it."

"It *was* for my country. We're a part of NATO. You know that. Honey, let's not fight about this again. Please? What's done is done. I can't change what happened, so I have to deal with it. And you're not making it any easier."

Linda finished her wine and poured a refill. "Don't they have, like, witness protection or something?"

He rolled his eyes. "That's for gangsters who rat out other gangsters. Situations like mine don't apply. Besides, you don't want to leave Key West, do you?"

"If it'll keep you alive, I do."

"I'm not going to leave, Linda. No one, no matter who it is, is going to make me. This is my home!" He jammed his fork into his mashed potatoes then let the handle fall to the plate. When he looked up, there were tears in his wife's eyes.

"Vic, you don't know how I felt when you went on those missions. I always worried you wouldn't come back to me. And now it's happening again. I thought those days were over."

He got up from his chair and put his arms around her from behind, resting his cheek on hers. "Honey, it'll be over soon. They're going to catch this woman. And chances are she's given up on me because they're closing in. She's worried about her own life now."

He put a finger on her chin to turn her face to his and kissed her.

"Tell you what," he said, going back to his chair. "When this is over, how about we get on a plane and visit our boy in San Diego? We haven't seen Todd in almost a year."

She wiped away a tear and smiled. "First class?"

"Absolutely. I'm not going on that long trip in coach."

"You're not just saying that to make me feel better, are you?"

"I've been thinking about it for a while. And what would be a better time to go? We'll celebrate getting our lives back again."

"You've got a deal. Now finish your dinner before it gets any colder."

Relieved at the temporary reprieve from his wife's angst, he changed the subject. "You have any plans tomorrow?"

"The school called this afternoon. They need a sub for Marilyn's class again. Another chemo treatment."

"That poor woman. I don't know how she does it."

"Compared to what she's going through, our problem doesn't seem so bad. We should count our blessings, Vic. At least we're both healthy."

After we took a shower, during which the soaping-up part was a prelude to the wet-and-wild main event, we got dressed and drove downtown. I found a parking space, and we sauntered along Duval Street, Key West's most popular thoroughfare. We checked out various shops and galleries until we came to Sloppy Joe's, the bar and restaurant even this New Yorker had heard of. Our sightseeing was over. It was time to eat.

We were able to snag a small table. Petra ordered a mojito from the server, and in the spirit of Key West, I chose a Papa Doble—some kind of rum punch—to drink while we perused the menu.

For our meal, I selected the Full Moon cheeseburger with mushrooms and peppers, and Petra chose the Cuban sandwich. We ordered LandShark lagers to accompany the food. First the mojito, then the Cuban. She'd told me about her new partner, and I wondered if Sosa's Cuban origins were rubbing off on her. But I wasn't jealous. Really, I wasn't.

"So, are we going out on the boat again tomorrow?" I asked.

She shrugged. "In for a penny, in for a pound."

For a girl who'd grown up in the Balkans and Russia, her grasp of English idioms surprised me. But then, discovering new things almost daily about Petra was the norm.

"She won't try anything now," I argued. "In fact, she might not even be in Key West."

"Don't jump to conclusions, my love."

I chuckled. "Isn't that what you do as a spy?"

She gave me a smirk. "Reasoned hypotheses. No jumping."

"Okay, so we do the boat thing until we get a feel for what Garin is doing."

"I think so. We'll have a good idea about that tomorrow."

Damn, my burger's good. Messy, but good. "How do you like your Cuban?"

"Excellent."

"As good as Mike makes?" I couldn't help it. *What a dork!*

She wrinkled her brow and tilted her head. "What does that mean?"

"Nothing. Just kidding." I looked down at my burger and took another bite.

I managed to get through the meal without making a fool of myself again and was feeling a little euphoric. I had a beautiful, sexy, and intelligent woman sharing my bed. I had pleasantly experienced two iconic Key West establishments, had gone deep-sea fishing, and was learning how to get around town, so I felt I was getting to know the latest addition to my agency's offerings. Whatever else happened in the next few days, at least I'd accomplished that.

As usual, Linda McNally sent her husband off to work after a hearty breakfast. She peeked through the living room window and saw the white SUV waiting at the curb then following Vic's pickup after he backed out of the garage. She cleaned up the kitchen and went to the bedroom to get ready for her day.

When Katarina drove by the McNally house at five thirty a.m., there were no cars parked on the street. A good sign. It meant Sergei's plan had worked, and the watchers were chasing him.

She parked a block away, where she had a view of McNally's driveway. Fifteen minutes later, with the sky turning from black to gray from the east, she ducked down when she saw headlights in the rearview. A white SUV drove past her and parked in front of the Mc-Nally house.

Another fifteen minutes went by before a pickup backed out of the driveway and headed west. The SUV followed.

So he still has protection.

But his wife didn't. A quick Facebook search had revealed Mc-Nally was married and had two children living outside the home—a daughter attending the University of Miami and a son selling real estate in San Diego.

Linda McNally's page listed "Teaches at Key West High School" in the bio info, so Katarina had a good idea what the wife's schedule would be.

Garin was not among the new set of customers for that day's charter, but we couldn't relax completely. For all we knew, other Russian operatives could be involved with the mission.

I caught another fish, and I didn't care what it was. I never saw the allure of fishing as a sport. The adept angler can research the right bait for a specific fish or fashion an elaborate lure to catch it and know the right places to increase his chances of bagging the elusive creature, and more power to him. But in the end, in my view, the fish catches itself while the fisherman waits for it to happen.

I could tell Petra had also lost her enthusiasm—if she'd ever had any—for the exercise, and I suggested we take an early lunch. It was only eleven a.m., but we'd left too early to get our "free" breakfast at the hotel, and we were both hungry. The only place open when we left for Vic's house was the McDonald's on North Roosevelt, so it had to do. The first time out on Vic's boat, we'd bought already-made sandwiches at a Publix deli, but this time, we hadn't prepared. We put our rods on the deck and headed for the cabin.

"What did you get for us?" Petra asked.

"Their fish sandwich." I tried not to smile as I went to the cooler.

"You didn't!"

I laughed. "Just having some fun with you, love. But salads were the only thing on the menu that could last in the cooler. I got their chicken Caesar."

At that moment, Petra's phone rang. We had the cabin to ourselves, so she put the cell on speaker. "What's up, Tom?"

"Garin got up bright and early and headed to Miami, where he went to the airport. Guess where he's flying to?"

We waited, but the other end of the line remained silent. "Why don't you tell me?"

"Minneapolis! Looks like Gwen and I will lose the bet."

"What's the flight number?"

Blankenship told her.

"Where are you now?"

"At the field office for a debriefing."

"And Gwen?"

"Still at the Perry. With this new development, I think we'll be taken off the Key West duty."

"AOD could still be here, Tom, and Garin's creating a ruse for our benefit. He figured he'd be followed."

"Yeah, well, it won't be up to me. If I don't see you again, it was nice meeting you, Dee. And give my regards to Alex."

"I will. Thanks." Petra disconnected and turned to me. "It could be an elaborate deception."

"And a logical one, to make us think AOD has left, Garin is following, and they both end up in Minneapolis. But if he's trying to fool us, it means he didn't buy *our* deception."

"Or he's just playing it safe. I better call Mike."

She did and relayed the information. They chitchatted for a while before she hung up. "The FBI people there will follow Garin from the airport."

"You know, if Garin's playing us, it can only work so far."

"Meaning?"

"Say he checks into a hotel. Maybe he does some drive-bys of... Who's the target there?"

"Stearns."

"So he makes it look like he's surveilling Stearns. But where's AOD? Like here, he can't meet her anywhere without the FBI knowing. But as a temporary diversion, it works if AOD is still here and hits Vic after we start chasing Garin."

"You're underestimating the way we spies can elude tails. And maybe she has the room right next door to him at that hotel. A connecting room."

"Maybe this, maybe that. Level with me. Do you think AOD is in Minneapolis?"

"No."

Chapter 23

After watching for an hour, Katarina was rewarded when a black sedan backed down the McNally driveway and headed west as McNally's pickup had done earlier. She started the engine and followed.

Ten minutes later, the car pulled into the parking lot of Key West High School, as Katarina had anticipated. She parked near the Honda.

When the woman came out to her car later, she would be confronted with a woman in distress because she'd forgotten her cell phone and her car battery was dead. "May I use your phone?" It would establish that McNally did, indeed, have a cell phone—that was necessary for her plan—and give Katarina the opportunity to abduct her at gunpoint.

As Mrs. McNally headed to the building's entrance, a school bus drove into the lot and disgorged a throng of boisterous students. Another school bus and other cars driven by older students and presumed teaching staff entered the lot over the next fifteen minutes. A bell sounded from within the building, and the kids still congregating outside went into the school, leaving the parking lot quiet.

Katarina checked the dashboard clock and opened her laptop. After a few seconds, she learned that the school day ended at two-thirty, which meant she had a seven-hour wait.

Satisfied she knew where the McNally woman would be, and not wanting to sit in the car all day, Katarina switched on the ignition and drove back to the rental house for breakfast.

Garin smiled as he drove into downtown Minneapolis from the airport. A nondescript dark-blue sedan had stayed behind him the whole way. The feint had been necessary after all. Those two on the boat were, indeed, CIA.

He was glad he hadn't fallen for their act, which, looking back at it, was pretty obvious. They'd pressed all the appropriate buttons if they suspected he'd made them, making the tag team's presentation ring false.

But that left Katarina on her own, which wasn't a new thing for her, but he worried about her being alone without backup in a place so conducive to setting a trap. Key West was like the box canyons cavalry soldiers always seemed to be riding into in the Westerns, only to be ambushed by the Indians they were chasing.

He liked her plan, though. It was the best option left as long as she insisted on completing the job, and it was far less complicated than the plan they'd had to abort.

He pulled up to the entrance of the Hyatt Place Hotel on Seventh Street South. He figured he had two days at the most before the feds caught on to the scheme. By then, Katarina would either have accomplished the mission or be in custody. Or be dead.

When Katarina returned to the school a half hour before classes were over, she was dismayed to find the Honda gone.

Perhaps Mrs. McNally had spotted her on the way to the school. She looked around the lot and didn't see anything suspicious. No law-enforcement types headed her way. A woman in her twenties carrying a briefcase emerged from the school entrance and went to her car. She was too old to be a student, obviously, but likely a teacher leaving early for some reason.

Then she realized there didn't have to be a reason. If a teacher had finished her classes for the day and had no other responsibilities at the school, she could leave.

"*Blyad!*" she said, cursing her error. Avoiding a long stakeout had necessitated doing one after all. The next day was Saturday—no school—and she had no idea what the McNally woman's weekend schedule was and if it involved leaving the house.

She turned around, trying not to think that the obstacles in her way the last two days were warning signs, omens telling her that persistence would result in disaster. There had to be another way.

I was bored. Bored with fishing. Bored with pretending to fish while wearing the uncomfortable life jacket. Bored with nothing else to do on a boat out on the ocean. I should've brought a deck of cards.

Petra and I had chatted it up with the other customers on the charter and concluded no Russian killers were among them. And we had about two hours to go before Vic headed the boat back to the marina. "We're not doing this again tomorrow," I said to Petra. I could tell she shared my ennui.

She looked at me and shook her head. "Not your decision, Alex. I agreed to let you take part because of your personal interest. Please don't make me regret it. I'm going to do what I think is necessary."

I had to admit she was right. I'd been taking advantage of our relationship in my eagerness to bring my father's killer to justice. And without that relationship, Petra likely wouldn't have consented to me tagging along. To her, that's what I was doing—just tagging along.

"So what do you think should be the next step?" I asked.

"Staking out the boat won't lead anywhere. I agree with that. If AOD is still in Key West, she can't go after Vic on the boat now. Her hijack captain has left town."

"At least we accomplished that, whether it's because he thinks we made him or he's just taking a precaution."

"But a precaution he had to tell her about. And if he spots a tail in Minneapolis, he'll know for sure. I'll check with Mike."

She took out her cell phone and walked away, cutting me out.

She joined me at the railing a few minutes later. "Garin checked into a downtown hotel in Minneapolis."

"That's it?"

"For now." She looked up as a gull flew over the boat.

"Petra," I began as Vic approached us.

"Taking a break?" he asked.

I shook my head. "To be honest, no offense, but fishing isn't one of our favorite things."

He slapped a hand on his chest. "I'm shocked!" Then he laughed. "Yeah, I figured as much. So I guess you won't be joining me tomorrow?"

Petra said, "Now that Garin knows that *we* know what they were planning, the boat caper is out. And Garin flew to Minneapolis today."

Vic's eyebrows shot up. "Dave Stearns?"

"You know him?"

"Haven't seen each other in years, but we exchange Christmas cards, and we've talked on the phone a couple of times after this assassin started killing us."

A commotion toward the bow caught our attention.

"Hold on, I'll be back." Vic went to net a large fish for a customer. After taking the catch to the ice chest, he returned. "Is Dave the next target?"

"Garin wants us to think so," Petra said. "But we're betting AOD is still here."

"Will the FBI stick around?"

"We're not sure. Garin might be playing us, but it could be enough for the Miami field office to let Minneapolis take over and pull Tom and Gwen from the protection duty here."

"Which leaves just you two."

"Maybe."

"That's okay. I never thought they were needed anyway. My wife might get nervous, though. She felt safer with them around."

The proverbial light bulb turned on in my head. "Your wife!"

"What about her?"

"That could be what AOD will do next. Use your wife to get at you."

Vic and Petra stared at me.

"My god!" he said. "I never thought of that!"

"Does your wife work?" Petra asked.

He turned and ran to the pilot cabin, and we followed.

He grabbed his cell phone and tapped a number. "Linda, are you home?... I'm just checking in, see how your day went. It's been a little slow today.... No, I'll be home at the usual time.... Sure, I can pick that up on the way. In fact, don't leave the house until I get there.... Because I want to be sure you're home. I have a surprise for you.... It wouldn't be a surprise then, would it?... Love you."

He put the phone down and looked at us. "She's going to have a fit. We had a big argument last night about the threat to me, but I calmed her down. And now this? Shit!" He had a wild look in his eyes. "What am I going to do now?"

"I'll call Gwen," Petra said. "She was still in Key West as of this morning. Maybe she can drive over there to stand guard."

"No. Linda would freak out. She knows the FBI was only there when I was. We have a security camera, and Linda keeps the doors locked when she's alone. She's safe as long as she stays there. But what do I tell her? She has to be a prisoner in her own house?" He ran a hand over his face. "Oh, man. I should call Phil."

"Who's Phil?" I asked as Petra stepped away to make a call.

"Phil Landry. He's the sheriff. A friend of ours. His daughter goes to the U with our daughter. Maybe he'll know what to do."

Petra returned. "Gwen's in Miami now."

"Vic's thinking of getting the sheriff involved," I told her.

"We can't involve local law enforcement."

"I'll involve anyone I want. This is my wife we're talking about! Oh, man. I'm gonna see if everybody's caught something so I can head back."

He started to walk away, but Petra put a hand on his shoulder. "If your wife is safe in the house, there's no hurry. We have the time to work something out."

"Easy for you to say. I gotta get back."

"Okay, but don't contact the sheriff yet."

He left without responding.

"I need to talk with his wife," Petra said. "Get both of them on the same page. I'll get the FBI back here."

"Maybe asking the sheriff for help is a good idea. Move them to someplace safe. Vic's right. Staying a prisoner in the house isn't practical."

"The obvious solution is for the FBI to take them into protective custody. Then we can focus on Stearns and the others."

"And what then, Petra? Take them all into protective custody? That would be the prudent move, because AOD going after them is no longer a hypothetical. Vic was willing to be used as bait. Will the others feel the same way? Has it even been discussed with them?"

She stared at me. The realization of where I was going was clear in her eyes.

"You said you lost your source in Moscow. If you put the Air Force targets out of reach, how would you catch AOD then? You can go to Minneapolis and try your luck there, but I'm staying if Vic and his wife are willing. I'd like to have your help, but I'm doing this regardless."

"Unlike you, I have bosses to answer to, and I'll need to check with them before we get back to the house."

The house. I stared at her as an idea took shape.

She frowned. "What?"

I told her.

Katarina drove by the McNally house on her way back from the school, hoping for an inspiration. The double-wide garage door was closed, and she couldn't tell if anyone was home.

Then it dawned on her. She had turned to the wife as a fallback plan, but it should have been Plan A. While she and Sergei were concocting the complicated boat-hijack scheme, the much simpler solution lay in front of them the whole time.

Sergei had observed the watchers staking out the house—but only when McNally was there. *The FBI missed it too!*

Before the fiasco on the boat, no one knew about Sergei. They'd been waiting for her—only her—to show up. A man ringing the doorbell wouldn't have set off any alarms.

It would have been so easy! She slammed her hand on the steering wheel in frustration. With Sergei out of the picture, it would be much harder. But she would have to find a way.

As she pulled into her driveway, she started thinking of how it could be done.

Chapter 24

We docked in the marina at four, and Vic did a hurry-up job on the boat's cleanup. I'd told him my plan, which would include Sheriff Landry contributing, but Vic couldn't commit to it until we had talked to his wife.

We followed him to his house. He drove into the garage, and I parked out front, where Tom and Gwen would have been. Petra and I walked up to the front door, and Vic quickly ushered us inside. I hoped AOD wasn't lurking around to see this change in the routine established by the FBI agents.

Per our plan, Vic introduced us to his wife. Dee Norton's presence spoke for itself. Though Linda knew of me as Vic's future employer, I needed another reason to be involved in the assassination threat. So I explained that I was a former member of the OSI on temporary duty for the organization by virtue of my inherent interest in the case.

I'd kept my Air Force credentials in my wallet, primarily out of nostalgia. But like the retired cop who keeps his for when he gets stopped for speeding, I thought it might come in handy one day.

Linda McNally frowned at her husband as we stood in the foyer. "Is this my surprise?"

"Uh, yes, honey."

"I'm waiting." She crossed her arms over an ample bosom. She was of medium height, slightly overweight, with short brown hair framing a face that reminded me of the actress Sandra Bullock.

"Can we do this over drinks, Lin?" Vic asked. "We have a lot to talk about."

She sighed. "I guess. I'll put the lasagna in the oven later." She looked at us. "You're welcome to stay for dinner."

"Thank you," I said, "but that won't be necessary."

"Well, we'll have to see how much we have to talk about. Take their orders, Vic. You know what I want."

"White wine if you have it," Petra said.

"That's good for me too," I said, though I would have preferred something stronger.

"Coming right up. Make yourselves comfortable."

Vic left for what I assumed was the kitchen, and Linda led us into the living room. She sat in an armchair and gave us the once-over after we took seats across from her on a sofa fronted by a coffee table.

The room was larger than I expected from my quick appraisal of the ranch house from the outside. Petra and I would do a thorough recon later if our plan got the green light.

"So, that was your car I saw this morning," Linda said.

"Yes," I answered.

"What happened to the FBI people?"

"They were called back to Miami," Petra said, "and we'll get into that. May I call you Linda?"

The woman chuckled. "Considering the situation, I think first names are appropriate, Dee." She looked at me. "Vic told me he knew your father."

I nodded. "I wasn't aware of that until a few days ago. Small world, I guess."

Vic returned bearing a tray of drinks, which he set on the coffee table. He handed wine goblets to Petra and me then what looked like a whisky sour to his wife and took a mug of beer for himself. He sat next to Linda in a matching armchair, a small table between them.

"How much do you know about what's going on, Linda?" Petra asked.

Linda eyed Vic. "I thought I knew everything, but apparently not."

Petra set her glass down on the coffee table. "I'll lay it all out—what we know for sure and what we're guessing about. Then we'll get to why we're sitting in your living room."

Linda stayed silent and calm during the narrative, seemingly taking it all in stride. She impressed me as strong and smart, and I hoped she would remain unruffled when she heard what would be coming next.

"That brings you up to date," Petra said. She picked up her wineglass and looked at me. "Your turn, Alex. It was your idea."

"Okay," I began, "we assume AOD knows where you live. Vic has been guarded by the FBI for the last week, and we also assume she knows that too, including that when Vic leaves for the day, the FBI goes with him—leaving you here without protection. Now that the boat-hijacking scheme has been ruined, we think the only option she has left is to get at Vic through you."

I stopped and waited for her reaction.

She finished her drink and slowly set the glass on the table before turning to me. "That's a logical theory. But it has a flaw. She would have to invade my house, and I don't see that happening. We have security cameras, a burglar alarm, and I won't open the door to anyone unless I know them."

"Don't forget the shotgun," Vic said.

"Yes, we keep a loaded shotgun in the hall closet, and I know how to use it."

"That's all well and good. But you have to leave the house from time to time—for shopping and such. And Vic tells me you teach at the high school."

"I'm only a substitute, and I haven't been notified they'll need me for Monday. Vic can do the shopping when he gets off work. But you're right—this can't go on forever. So how long will it take for you to catch this bitch? Pardon my French."

I glanced at Petra and saw her nod. "Waiting indefinitely for her to make a move is not a practical option. For us or for you. So this is what we'd like to do."

I told her the plan.

Vic, who had heard only the basics on the boat, objected. "This plan of yours doesn't include me. I told you I want to be involved."

I shook my head. "Can't do that. For one thing, you're a civilian, and for another, you have to be the decoy for the plan to work."

"Not necessarily. If Phil comes on board, one of his deputies can be the decoy. And I'm no more a civilian than you are."

He kind of had me there. "But I've been a cop," I responded lamely.

"Years ago, right?"

I didn't answer.

Vic said, "Okay, let's put that aside for the moment. One thing bothers me about the whole deal. The assassin needs to take the bait. Why would she? The house is secure, we know what she looks like, and Linda wouldn't open the door to a stranger. If I were her, I'd just forget about it and leave town."

"Does AOD know all this?" I asked.

"Doesn't she?"

"She might think what you say is possible, but she doesn't *know*. Like us, she has to guess what the other side is doing. So she'll try out her plan to see if it works, and we'll accommodate her."

"But when she sees Dee at the door, she'll know she's being conned. If she's as smart as you say she is, she'll know what Linda looks like. Facebook, man. I'm on it, and so is Linda. And she could have followed her to school today."

"It won't matter. Because as soon as that door opens, she'll be surrounded."

"If Phil goes along. I better call him, see if he can get over here."

"You'll have to pick him up," Petra said. "And he can't be seen in the truck when you come back. She could be watching the house now."

"Yeah, okay. Let's see if he'll agree to talk to us."

He left and I asked Linda, "Do you think he'll hear what we have to say?"

"We're good friends. Phil will listen. But he's a tough sheriff, and regardless of friendship, he'll play by the rules."

Vic returned, a big smile on his face. "I told him enough to get his curiosity in gear. And when I said a CIA agent was sitting in my living room, that did it. I'll pick him up." He headed for the kitchen.

Linda stood. "We have five for dinner now. Alex, can you help me put the leaf in the table?"

I smiled, admiring her matter-of-fact attitude. It could have been an act, but I didn't think so. The woman was tough, and we would need that.

"I'd be happy to."

Katarina drove by the McNally house to see if anything new had developed. The white SUV that had followed McNally in the morning was parked outside again. But empty. *The agents must be inside the house.* But according to Sergei, they hadn't done that in the two days he'd observed them.

Perhaps they were telling McNally they'd been called off the case, thanks to Sergei's gambit. Or perhaps they were new agents introducing themselves to the target. Whatever the reason, something new was happening. She decided to stick around and parked up the street.

A few minutes later, McNally's pickup backed out of the drive-way, and he drove past her. She thought briefly about following him, but what was going on in the house seemed more important. Twen-ty minutes later, he returned. Nothing happened over the next hour, with the SUV remaining unoccupied. Katarina drove back to the rental house. She would return in the morning, her plan in place, to see if the routine at the McNally residence remained the same. If so, she would make her move.

Vic had gone to fetch the sheriff, and Linda was busy in the kitchen, leaving Petra and me alone.

"I'm not comfortable with this," she told me.

"With what?"

"Your involvement. Vic was right. You were a cop, but you're a civilian now. It's not your place to be involved in this operation. I'm sure the sheriff will agree."

I stared at her, giving my best the-hell-you-say expression. "Look, just because you've been cleared to go along with the plan—*my* plan—does not give you the authority to cut me out. Yes, I'm a civil-ian, and I don't have to answer to you. What did your superior have to say about that?"

She sighed. "He said it would be up to the sheriff, if he agrees to participate. The sheriff has law enforcement jurisdiction here."

"Exactly. If he wants me out, I'm out. No choice."

"If Landry wants no part of it, then the FBI will take over. They can kick you out too." Her expression softened. "Alex, I don't want a fight over this. I understand why this is important to you. I hope you can understand my position."

I did, of course. "We made a good team on the boat, didn't we?"

She didn't respond.

"Well, I guess we'll have to wait to hear what the sheriff has to say."

I loved this woman—yes, I believed I did—but she was pissing me off, and the road to a future together had hit a major speed bump. But I wouldn't let that stop me from trying to put an end to AOD.

The rumble of the garage door opening came through the walls.

"They're here," I said.

Muted voices drifted in from the kitchen before Vic and another man entered the living room.

I had a preconceived image of Sheriff Landry, likely formed from stereotyped small-town sheriffs I'd seen in the movies. But Landry was not big and potbellied. Medium height, thin and wiry, with curly dark hair, he wore jeans and a green golf shirt.

We rose and came around the coffee table to greet him.

"Dee Norton and Alex Baker, meet Sheriff Phil Landry," Vic said.

We shook hands.

"Vic's told me a little of what you people are doing here." He glanced at Vic, smiling. "And considering I had to hide in his truck, it must be serious."

"It is, Sheriff," Petra said.

"You're the CIA agent?"

"Yes."

Landry looked at me. "And you're here because you just hired Vic for your travel agency. And, coincidentally, he's a target of this assassin who has already killed your father."

"That sums it up," I said.

"Yeah, well, there're a lot of gaps that need to be filled in. I came here tonight because Vic's a friend of mine, but it's also official business now."

I shot Petra a glance, and she gave me a slight nod.

"I understand," Landry went on, "that you folks are asking for my help in catching this spy. But further involvement of my office will depend on my knowing the whole picture."

"Let's do this over dinner," Linda said from the doorway. "It's ready."

Petra summarized the threat to Vic and his wife.

Phil had no problem accepting Petra's CIA credentials. To back them up, she told him the extension to use if he called Langley and to ask for Norman.

My involvement, though, was a bit trickier to explain.

Phil had just washed down a bite of lasagna with a drink of water when he eyed me. "Dee, I understand. Ditto the FBI agents who were watching over Vic. But you, Alex, don't appear to have any standing in this situation beyond coincidence."

I was ready for it. "Officially, that's true. But it looked for a while that AOD was also targeting me—because I was the son of one of the men who bombed her city. So the FBI used me to smoke her out. A few years ago, I commanded an Air Force criminal investigation unit. The current head of that organization is the lead investigator, due to my father's murder, in the hunt for AOD in the US. He's kept me in the loop."

"The OSI?"

"That's correct." I was surprised he knew the acronym.

"Who's that commander you mentioned?"

"James Truax."

He nodded. "I knew Jim. We worked together on a case at Fort Bragg when I was in the MP there."

That helped. I smiled. "Talk about coincidence." I breathed easier and had started a forkful of ambrosia toward my mouth when he hit me with another zinger.

"But the OSI is not directing the operation here in Key West."

I put down my fork. "As you pointed out, I just hired Vic for my company. But I hadn't met him yet, so that's primarily why I'm here. Dee and I worked together in New York when AOD was active there." That wasn't quite true, but it sounded good. "I knew she was coming to Key West to assist the FBI in their protection detail, so I tagged along. Jim knows I'm here."

Phil looked at Petra then at me and smiled suddenly. "Okay, I get it. Two birds with one stone, huh?"

"Something like that."

Phil tried to hide his grin with a napkin and turned to look at our hostess. "Linda, the lasagna is great. What do you call this side dish?"

"Ambrosia."

"I would never have thought so, but it goes well with the pasta."

"Thank you. Are you satisfied with our guests being who they say they are and why they're here?"

He nodded. "I am."

"Good. Now can we talk about what we're going to do?"

"Absolutely." Phil looked at Dee. "What are you thinking?"

She eyed me briefly before answering. "We carry on as before. Ostensibly. Vic will drive to work in the morning, only it won't be Vic. A car will follow him to the marina as always, only it won't be the FBI agents. And Linda will be alone in the house, but she won't be there. Vic and Linda will be tucked safely away in a place of your choosing."

"So you need my deputies to play these parts."

"That's the plan."

"How long do we keep up this charade?"

I spoke up to solidify my role in the strategy. "Two days at the most. We figure AOD's handler can't maintain his con in Minneapolis longer than that, and the FBI will be back here again. She'll have to leave before that happens."

"But as you conceded earlier, she might not even be here."

"Then we haven't lost anything," Vic said. He'd been quiet until then, but I'd noticed he was getting antsy.

"Linda being safe elsewhere," he continued, "is a great idea, but I'm not going anywhere. I'll wait in the house too. It *is* my house. If you don't go along with that, it's a deal-breaker."

"I'm staying too," Linda said.

"Honey..."

"You're not leaving me again to worry about you, Victor. Besides, somebody has to cook for the troops. Like Clemenza did in *The God-father*. We'll have a similar situation."

"Linda—" her husband began, but Phil raised a hand.

"Okay, you've got me involved, Vic. And you should have. It was the right decision. But now that I am, *I'll* be making the decisions. I like the plan in general, but this is how I want it to go down."

Chapter 25

The sheriff finished laying out the strategy for what he obviously saw as his operation. He wouldn't just be helping us—he would be in charge and responsible for the arrest.

The second part was fine with Petra. The alternative would be us holding AOD at gunpoint until the FBI could get here from Miami to take over. It was the first part that stuck in her craw. Local law enforcement was not supposed to be running the show.

We had all finished our meals by then, and when Petra started to raise her objections, Linda suggested we adjourn to the living room to discuss Phil's plan.

We took seats as before, except Phil sat alone on a love seat that sat perpendicular to the sofa, giving him easy eye contact with the rest of us. Metaphorically, that put him at the head of the conference table.

"You had an issue, Dee," Phil said. "Let's hear it."

"Sheriff, I have no problem with you locking up the assassin in your jail. But on what charge will you be making an arrest?"

"Murder, of course. And conspiracy to commit murder. What else do I need?"

"But how do you know these things?"

He stared at her for a moment, then he nodded and smiled. "I see what you're trying to do. But we use informants all the time to make arrests."

"I'm more than an informant. I'm an agent of the Central Intelligence Agency, which is working with the Federal Bureau of Investigation to capture an international assassin. You have no direct knowledge of her crimes and will be acting solely on my say-so. In fact, you depend on me to identify her for you. Informants lead to arrests, certainly. But the perps have to be caught engaging in criminal activity to be arrested, correct?"

Phil smiled again. "Not necessarily. Fugitives from the law can be located through informants, as you have done. At the very least, based on what you, Alex, and Vic tell me, she would be a person of interest, subject to interrogation." His smile disappeared. "You have no authority to arrest this woman in my town."

"That's correct. But the FBI does. And they're standing by. One call from me, and agents can be here in a few hours. We came to you because this is your territory and you know the area. And Vic and Linda trust you. We'd appreciate your help, but this is a federal operation." She glanced at me again. Petra was throwing her weight around, but I knew it was a bluff. We had to have everything in place by the morning, and getting the FBI up to speed by then was problematic. We could lose a day. And that was what had convinced Petra to ask for the sheriff's help.

Phil stood. "Well, go ahead and make that call. Good luck with the takedown. Vic, you can drive me home now."

The sheriff was no dummy. He could bluff too.

"Phil," I said, spreading my hands, "we want you to make the arrest. You and the department will get the credit, and it'll make national—and international—news. Dee has to remain covert, so she can't have any publicity, but it's her authority that makes the arrest possible."

"That's right," Petra said. "We're working together on this, okay? I'd like to have your help. You need me is all I'm saying."

Phil stared at us for a few seconds, then with a sigh, he sat down. "All right. We'll have to bring four deputies here tonight in Vic's truck. One will be Vic in the morning, two will play FBI agents, and one will stay in the house. It'll be your job, Dee, to identify her, and my deputy will call me. We'll block the street and surround the house." He smiled at Petra. "That okay with you?"

"It is." She smiled back.

"And I'll open the door," Linda said.

"No!" Vic protested. "That's Dee's job."

Linda spoke up. "Her job is to make the ID. With our security camera she can still do that. But as you said, Victor, this woman might know what I look like. If she sees Dee at the door instead of me, she could bolt before we get our ducks in a row."

"Too dangerous, hon. She could shoot you in the doorway! She needs the house, not you."

Vic had a good point. AOD could have planned to kill Linda right away then wait for Vic to come home from work.

"How do we get around this, Phil?" I asked.

He looked at Linda. "I can't let you do that. Vic's right. The woman is a killer, and she doesn't need you to stay alive—only to let her into the house."

"So get me one of those vests you guys wear. I'm doing this. We can't let her get away. I'm not going to spend my life worrying she'll come back. Besides, Dee can ID her before she even rings the doorbell."

"She'll probably be in a disguise of some sort." Petra eyed Phil. "I might not be able to ID her soon enough."

"What strangers come to your house?" Phil asked Linda.

"Kids, mainly, selling stuff for school drives, and Girl Scouts selling cookies. Delivery people sometimes. Jehovah's Witnesses showed up last year, but there were two of them. We're not expecting any deliveries. And this woman isn't a kid."

"That's the solution, then," Phil said. "Any adult showing up at the door, we go into action and take her into custody. Linda doesn't even have to open the damn door."

Maybe I'd seen too many movies, but I spotted a flaw in that. "Phil, what if AOD tests the security by paying somebody to ring the doorbell while she watches to see what happens? You guys come rushing in, and she knows we're waiting for her. We have to wait for her to make a move. We can't afford a false alarm."

"That settles it," Linda said. "It has to be me at the door."

"Phil, can a Kevlar vest stop a bullet from point-blank range?" Vic asked.

"Yes, but Linda wouldn't like it. Hurts like hell."

"I don't like living in fear either." Linda folded her arms over her chest in her now-familiar determined pose.

Phil shook his head. "My neck's on the line here, Linda. Something happens to you..."

"I'll sign a release. Will that work?"

"No changing your mind?"

"You know me, Phil. C'mon, man up."

He raised his hands in the air. "Okay, you win. Maybe I can find another job somewhere."

"Good. Now make the arrangements with your people."

Katarina was thinking about how she would go about gaining entry to the McNally house when Sergei called her.

"What's happening down there?"

"I'm working on it."

"You checked out the house this morning?"

"Yes. It looked like you said. McNally left for work, and an SUV followed him."

"An SUV?"

"A white one."

"That wasn't the car I saw, Kat."

"So?"

"Probably nothing. We caused them to change their focus. Could be a new team of watchers now."

"I went by tonight. The same SUV was outside, but there wasn't anybody in it."

"Maybe they were introducing themselves to the target."

"That's what I thought. What have you been up to?"

"I pretended to check out Stearns's house and followed him to the gym and the grocery store. The FBI is watching everything I do. Not being very subtle about it."

As she expected. "You should leave now, Sergei."

He was silent for a moment. "Why?"

"The FBI wants you to know they're following you. You're an experienced agent, but they're experienced too. If they wanted to make tracking you a secret, they'd do a better job of it."

"That doesn't mean the distraction isn't working."

"I agree. But it's time we gave them another. Go to Topeka. And this time use more stealth. Just enough to show you're trying to evade them. But if you lose them, so much the better."

"What then?"

"Take two days to surveil Clancy's routine, then I'll meet you in the embassy in Washington."

"I should come back to Key West, Kat. You have no backup."

"Sergei, I'll be fine. My plan will work. And if they detect you coming here, they'll know I'm still here."

"All right. I understand. It's been a pleasure working with you, Katarina Petrovic."

She forced a chuckle. "I'm not dead yet!"

"Keep it that way."

Vic took Phil to the sheriff's office and waited while he lined up four deputies—three men and a woman.

"The county won't like the overtime bill," Phil griped. "This better work."

One by one, the deputies arrived in civilian clothes, carrying gym bags. The ones impersonating Vic and the FBI agents would double back after taking off from the house in the morning to be part of the takedown team.

They climbed into Vic's truck, and Phil stepped to the driver's-side window and asked Vic, "We all set?"

"What about the vest?"

"Oh, yeah." Phil went back inside the building and returned a few minutes later with the Kevlar. "Good luck."

"Thanks." Vic started the engine and headed to his house. He glanced at the dashboard clock. Ten p.m.—eight hours before the operation would begin.

Petra walked through the house with Linda and Alex while Vic was away with Phil.

There were three entrances: the front door, the back door at the end of the hallway that extended from the front door to the rear of the building, and the access to the kitchen from the garage. Across from the living room was a formal dining room. A hallway split off the main one at the kitchen to service a wing to the right that contained the master bedroom, two other bedrooms, and a guest bath.

The backyard was fenced, abutting the yard of a house on the next block. A single gate leading to the backyard at the left side of the house didn't have a lock, but the six-foot fence would provide an escape barrier to the rear. The next-door neighbor on the left had no fence, only a row of wax myrtles at the back, but the neighbor on the right did. Escape routes were all what-if scenarios, though. Hopefully, they would be irrelevant.

The number of bedrooms presented Linda with a logistical problem. Six additional people would be spending the night. She went in search of bedding and a blow-up bed.

"Let's go over the plan again," Petra said to Alex.

"Let's."

"When Linda opens the door, a deputy will be standing to the side out of sight. You and I will be in the living room."

"Phil insisted. We're backup only."

"Right. Had to give him that, Alex. He's in operational control. So AOD comes to the front door disguised as... something. Phil is notified and moves the troops into position. Linda opens the door. Now what?"

"She points a pistol at Linda and forces her back into the hall, where the deputy gets the drop on her."

"Or she shoots Linda immediately and steps around her." That was a real—and logical—possibility. AOD wouldn't want to guard Linda all day until Vic got home.

"But then she'd still get shot by the deputy," Alex said.

"She could shoot the deputy, too, if he hesitates at all."

The brainstorming session was making her less confident, not more, as she'd hoped. "Okay, by then, Phil's been notified, and he comes roaring up the street with the troops. She focuses her attention to the front of the house and backs up in the hallway, toward where we have the second line of defense."

"If she gets past the deputy, we can't hesitate, Petra. No 'Freeze!' or 'Hands up!' She might have been a childhood friend with shared experiences, but you have to ignore that."

He was right. In her mind, usually at night before going to sleep, she'd seen herself taking Katarina down without hesitation. She'd killed before, but never someone with a personal connection. "Of course. I'm concerned about Vic, though. He'll be in the kitchen with his shotgun. He hears gunfire and thinks Linda could be injured or dead, so he storms out, and AOD guns him down before we get her."

"We have to convince him to stay put."

Petra shook her head. "I don't like the setup. Behind the door is not a good place for the deputy. As you said, he's vulnerable there. He should be in the dining room. Or maybe in the kitchen to keep Vic from doing something rash—and to hit AOD if she gets past us. Think about it. Once she sees the cops outside, she'll run to the back of the house and be a fast-moving target for us. How's your marksmanship? We need an additional deputy."

"I agree. I'll try to get ahold of Vic before he leaves Phil."

Thanks to Sergei's original idea, Katarina had the makeup and clothing she needed for the transformation. She needed two props, though, to complete the disguise. No stores were open at that hour, so she would have to get them in the morning—after she'd seen McNally and the FBI agents drive away from the house as had been the routine.

She checked the Glock 19 Sergei had left for her, along with a silencer and an extra magazine, just in case. She couldn't think of anything else she had to prepare for. After finishing the last of her wine, she got ready for bed.

Chapter 26

I couldn't reach Vic before he was halfway home. I asked him for Phil's number and called the sheriff. I told him our concerns, and surprisingly, he agreed right away.

"That occurred to me too. I was just about to call Dee about it. A deputy in the kitchen and one in the dining room makes sense. No way AOD escapes all that. And it happens I have an additional man for it. He was going off shift, heard what was going on, and wanted in."

"What about Vic, though? It's his wife who'll be at immediate risk. If he hears shots fired, I'm afraid of what he might do."

"Well, we can't take his shotgun away from him. I know Vic. The deputy in the kitchen with him will have to make sure Vic stays put. Hold on a sec."

I waited for a couple of minutes, during which Vic arrived with the deputies. Phil came back on the line. "I talked with Deputy Hager. He knows the situation and will take care of it. Is Vic there yet?"

"Just got in."

"Let me talk to him."

I called out to Vic, and he came into the living room. I handed him the phone. "Phil wants to talk to you."

"Hey, Phil... Okay, another deputy is good... The dining room instead? That'll leave Linda alone at the door. I can take that position, like we talked about... Then get me a vest too... Thanks, Phil. I feel better... Don't worry, I won't... I'm on my way." He gave me back my cell and left for the kitchen.

"What was that about?" I asked Phil.

"We have the problem solved, kinda." He told me the change in plan. "I don't like having two citizens at the point of attack, but Vic always wanted to be there with Linda. I couldn't say no now. He has a right to protect his wife. And it'll keep him from being a wild card."

I liked it, though Vic would have more risk. "I hadn't considered that option."

"That was Vic's idea to begin with, but I talked him out of it. Couldn't do that again."

"I understand. See you in the morning, Phil."

"Try to get some sleep."

He hung up, and I turned to Petra, who'd been listening quietly to the conversations. I told her the new arrangement.

"Much better," she said.

"Let's meet the deputies and see what sleeping arrangements Linda's made."

"Alex, it would make things easier—for her and us—if we stayed at the hotel. We can be back here at five. AOD won't be watching now. She has to get some sleep too."

"Good idea. I'll get a spare key from Linda."

Katarina's alarm went off at five in the morning. After a quick shower, she dressed in shorts and a sweater, gobbled down a piece of toast, and went to the car in the garage.

At a quarter till six in the morning, she parked on Washington Street, where she had been the day before in front of a house-construction site. Workers usually wouldn't start arriving so early, but cars and trucks coming and going at the site all day was the norm, and a car there wouldn't attract undue attention from neighbors.

Down the street, the white SUV was in front of the McNally house as before. She saw two heads in the front seat through the rear window. So far, the setup was the same.

At six o'clock, right on time, the pickup backed out of the driveway and drove off, then the SUV followed. Over the next ten minutes, she watched for any more activity. Seeing none, she headed back to the house. The store would be opening soon.

The McNallys and the deputies were having coffee when Petra and I returned from the hotel in the morning.

Petra had been right. We needed a shower and a fresh change of clothes before beginning the crucial day. And our absence had eased the sleeping-arrangements issue facing Linda the night before.

The female deputy and a male colleague shared the room with two twin beds the McNally daughter had used for sleepovers when growing up. They left shortly after our arrival to take their positions in our SUV.

Deputy Barlow went to the garage and McNally's pickup. The other two deputies, Hank Hager and Ken Morrissey, sat with us and the McNallys in the kitchen. The security camera covering the front entrance fed into a monitor there.

I heard the garage door open then close a few moments later. Thirty minutes after that, Hager received a call on his radio.

"Morning, Sheriff."

"All set there?"

"Yup."

"Everyone's in place here. Like I said last night, call me when she makes a move, but not before."

"Roger that."

"Good luck. Out."

"Where are they?" I asked Hager.

"Behind a restaurant that's not open yet. About half a mile from here. You think she'll try something today?"

"Yes. If not today, then tomorrow for sure."

"What if she doesn't?"

"Then we were wrong about her being in Key West," Petra said.

"It has to be today," Vic said. "I was able to reschedule my charter for tomorrow, but we can't do this again."

"You could see if Troy can take over for you," Linda said. "He doesn't usually take his boat out on Sundays."

"Yeah, maybe. But if he can't, and I have to go out, you're not doing this without me, Lin. Are we clear on that?"

"Whatever you say."

Vic checked his watch. "We have about eleven hours to wait until I supposedly return after a long day on the ocean, right, Hank? That's the window?"

"Yup."

"I'm gonna see what's on TV."

"I'll join you," Linda said, and the two went into the living room.

Hager and Morrissey started chitchatting about schedules and preparations for the Saint Patrick's Day Parade in town, and I led Petra into the dining room for some privacy.

"Any idea what you'll be doing after your AOD assignment is over?" I asked her.

She shook her head. "I've been on this for so long, it'll be strange to be assigned to something else. Nothing's been mentioned about what that will be yet."

"Do you have any other interests besides being a spy?"

She tilted her head and frowned. "What are you getting at?"

"Just curious. I was thinking you can't do this type of work indefinitely."

She chuckled. "You mean what am I going to do when I get too old for the job?"

"Well..."

"There's more to the CIA than field agents. We're the ground troops, but the Agency is a bureaucracy structured like other government organizations with different levels of responsibility." She grinned. "When I can no longer run in high heels, there are other positions I can take."

"So you get vacations?"

She laughed again. "Of course. Last year was my fifteenth with the Agency, so I'm entitled to twenty-six days of paid leave annually. In case you're wondering, I plan to take a big chunk of that when this is over." Her eyebrows shot up.

My move. "Unfortunately, New York isn't very appealing this time of year."

Her smirk told me she was enjoying this. "Is that where you take *your* vacations?"

"Not really."

"I hear Aruba is nice."

I smiled. "I'll have to look into that."

The amusement left her face. "Alex, are you wondering if this will work out?"

"If she does what we're planning on, I think we'll get her. Still concerned about possible casualties, though."

"No, that's not what I meant. *Us*, Alex. You in New York and me... who knows where?"

"That did cross my mind."

She grabbed my hand. "Being a covert operative is terrible for a relationship. All the pretending, the fake identities, the constant travel. Our affair is the first *real* relationship I've had since leaving that boarding school so long ago."

"Maybe you're giving it more importance than you should as a result?" I hated saying that, but I had to get it out in the open.

She released my hand. "Because of the novelty?"

"Something like that."

"How about you? Did my being a spy make it more exciting?"

I grinned. "And how! But if you remember, we had a thing before I knew you were a female Jason Bourne."

"True. You thought then I might be an assassin who wanted to kill you." She grinned back at me. "That excitement factor again?"

I nodded. "Can't deny it got my juices flowing. Danger stimulating the libido and all that. In fact, while we're waiting for AOD to show up, I have the urge to take you into a bedroom and ravish your body."

She placed a hand over her sternum and looked at me in mock astonishment. "Oh my!"

"Seriously, I've gone beyond accepting your line of work to looking at us in practical terms. I'm a businessman anchored to New York, and you work for the government all over the world. I want to be with you, Petra. Not Dee the spy, but the woman I care about for who she is, not what she does for a living. I want us to be together. Can we?"

She sighed. "I want that too. Believe me, I'm not attracted to you just because you're the first nice, honest man I've met in a long time. And we *can* be together... Just not all the time."

"Truax had his doubts about us. I'd like to prove him wrong."

She smiled sweetly at me. "I'll do all I can to help you with that."

We leaned toward each other for a kiss.

"But we have to put an end to AOD first," she said.

Phil had been up all night, making the arrangements. He was sitting in an armored truck with four SWAT team members, all dressed in full combat gear. Four other deputies, including the three who had left the McNally house earlier that morning, manned two patrol cars and waited by the truck behind the closed restaurant.

"What armament are we looking at?" Don Aiken, the SWAT team leader, asked.

"We think handgun only. But she might have confederates. The one we knew about tried to lead us off track by leaving town."

"What's behind the house?"

"Fenced backyard, totally enclosed. There's an unlocked gate to it at the side of the garage. Back door off a patio. It'll be unlocked."

Aiken addressed his team. "Ed, Mario—you're the rear entry. Stan, you and I will go into the front with the sheriff."

Phil grabbed the radio mic. "Car One, when I give the go signal, you will proceed Code Three to Washington Street and block its intersection with Leon Street. Confirm."

"Copy."

"Car Two, you will follow the SWAT truck Code Three and block the intersection of Washington Street and Tropical. Confirm."

A deputy acknowledged the order.

"Out." Phil turned to Aiken. "Anything we've missed?"

"I think we're good, Phil."

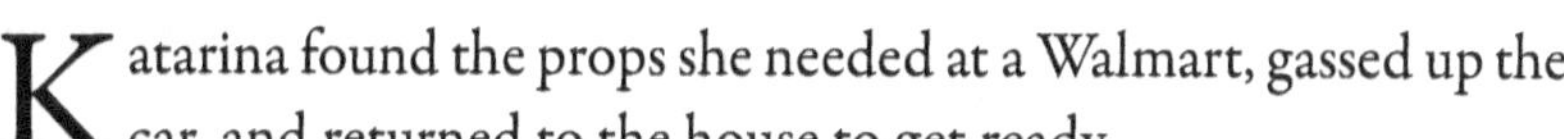

Katarina found the props she needed at a Walmart, gassed up the car, and returned to the house to get ready.

An hour later, she drove to South Street and parked in front of a wooded side yard of a large, two-story home. She climbed out and walked east to Leon Street, then south to Washington Street, where she headed west and began her act.

"We have somebody!" Deputy Hager yelled from the kitchen.

We rushed in to view the monitor.

An elderly woman stood on the sidewalk, looking around, a black beret perched on her mop of gray hair. She wore a dark-blue, car-coat-length fleece jacket over black sweatpants. She held a cane in one hand and what looked like a dog leash in the other. She was saying something as she surveyed the neighborhood, but the camera feed didn't capture sound. I did hear shouts coming through the walls, but I couldn't interpret them.

"That's her!" Petra said. "Remember? She was going to be Garin's mother on the boat."

"Do you recognize her?" Hager asked.

"Not with that getup. But if she comes to the door, it has to be her."

"She's nobody I know in the neighborhood," Linda said.

"Looks like it's starting." Hager went to unlock the back door. When he returned, the woman was walking slowly up the walk to the front porch. We hadn't moved yet, mesmerized as we were with the unfolding drama. "Ken," he said. "Call me now on your cell and keep the line open."

"We should call Phil," Morrissey said as he tapped out the number.

"Not yet. He said she could be a decoy, so she has to make a move first." He accepted the call.

"What would that be, exactly?"

Hager glanced at Linda. "You'll hear what's going on at the door. If she forces her way into the house, give me a tap, and I'll call Phil."

An idea that would solve the uncertainty suddenly hit me. "There's another way to know." I quickly told them.

"I think that'll work," Petra said. "But you'll have to say it right away, Linda. As soon as you open the door. And then you'll have to do some ad-libbing."

"No problem. Beats the hell out of getting shot!"

The doorbell chimed.

Chapter 27

We got into our positions: Hager in the kitchen, Morrissey out of sight in the dining room, and Petra and me in the living room. We'd moved the love seat so that the back faced the hallway, and we crouched behind it, weapons drawn.

Linda and Vic walked to the front door. Vic would be standing to the left and hidden when the door opened. I heard the click of the lock disengaging.

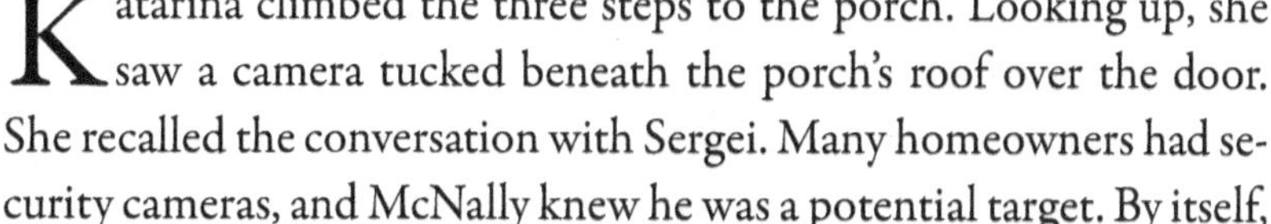

Katarina climbed the three steps to the porch. Looking up, she saw a camera tucked beneath the porch's roof over the door. She recalled the conversation with Sergei. Many homeowners had security cameras, and McNally knew he was a potential target. By itself, the camera meant nothing. But it did increase the importance of an effective disguise.

The weight of the 9mm in the pocket of her coat comforted her. She'd practiced dropping the leash and drawing the weapon in one fluid move. The silencer made the gun too cumbersome, so she'd left it in the car. But with a resident down the street using his loud leaf blower, the pistol's report would likely not be noticed.

She took a deep breath and pressed the doorbell.

After waiting for what seemed more than a minute, she was about to ring the bell again when she heard the door being unlocked.

The door opened. Linda McNally, dressed in a housecoat, stood in the doorway.

"You must be looking for your dog," she said right away, catching Katarina by surprise.

The camera?

"Yes." Katarina brought the leash up to the level of her gun pocket as if to confirm her answer. She loosened the leash in her grip, ready to let it fall.

"I think I have her! A Maltipoo?"

The woman's playing along with Katarina's pretense meant only one thing. *They know!* "Yes," she said as she scrambled to come up with a plausible exit. But too late, she realized she hadn't taken advantage of the opportunity McNally's question had given her.

"She was in our backyard. I keep telling my husband to fix the latch on that gate. I hope you don't mind, but I gave her something to eat. She's in the kitchen, chowing down. Must have missed her breakfast, poor thing. Come on in."

Where I'll be ambushed. The solution popped into her head. "What color is the dog?"

"White."

"Oh, darn it! Mine's brown. That must be Alice's dog. She's always getting loose. Sorry to bother you." Katarina turned to go.

"Do you know Alice's number?"

"I can't remember it. I'll call her when I get home." She started down the steps.

"I'll keep an eye out for yours. What's her name?"

"Muffin," Katarina said over her shoulder as she headed to the sidewalk, maintaining the act of a slightly disabled gait. It could still be an amazing coincidence, she thought. Maybe there *was* a Maltipoo loose in the neighborhood. But the woman didn't ask for *her* phone number, which was strange if she'd been sincere.

Then she heard the sirens.

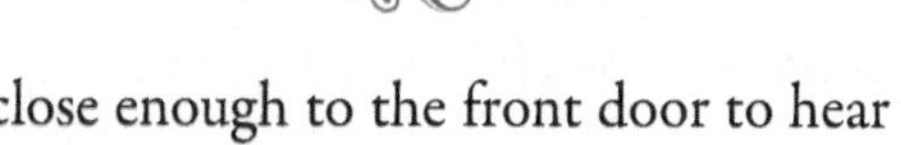

We were close enough to the front door to hear the conversation. My idea developed the way I'd hoped—that as soon as Linda said she had the dog, she would be protected because AOD would know a trap had been laid for her. Then she wouldn't accept Linda's invitation to come into the house, thus giving herself away as AOD, and Morrissey would signal Hager.

The dog story would also eliminate the possibility of a decoy. A woman paid just to ring a doorbell wouldn't have a script ready to go.

Though it was infinitesimally small, there was a chance it could all be a coincidence. The woman *had* lost her dog, and it happened to be a Maltipoo—Linda almost blew it there—and of a color not often found in that breed.

"I'll keep an eye out for her. What's her name?"

"Muffin."

The woman's voice was more distant now. She was leaving—without telling Linda how to contact her. It had to be AOD! I peeked around the corner of the living room. The woman had reached the sidewalk and was headed west. I joined Vic and Linda at the door as the wailing sirens of Phil's team reached us. AOD had passed the garage when she dropped the cane and leash and took off running through the neighbor's side yard.

I was about to go after her when a patrol car raced down the street. An armored truck followed it closely, but it stopped abruptly in front of the house. Five heavily armed men in combat gear poured out of the back. Two ran into the backyard through the gate, and the other three rushed to the porch. One of them was Phil.

"She got away?" he asked.

"She caught on to our trap. Took off through the neighbor's yard." I pointed. "You just missed her. Black beret, dark-blue coat, black pants."

Phil spoke into his mic. "Cars One and Two, suspect on foot headed to South Street. Block it off." He turned to the men next to him. "Let's go get her."

Katarina tossed the beret and wig to the ground as soon as she reached South Street, thankful she'd taken the precaution of parking on the next block. She jumped into her car and sped to Leon Street. After making the turn to the north, her rearview mirror showed a police car behind her. But it stopped on South Street.

She slowed to the speed limit, took a left on Catherine Street, then north on White Street to Olivia. Arriving at her house, she parked in the garage and went into the house from the patio. After throwing clothes from the closet and dresser into her suitcase, she grabbed her makeup bag and rushed out to the garage.

She calculated it would take her an hour to get past Seven Mile Bridge, the natural place for a roadblock. Hopefully, a hunt for her in Key West would give her that time.

She froze. *It won't work!* She couldn't make it in time. They might still look for her on the island, but the call would go out for the roadblock right away.

The airport was out. That was one of the first things they would think of, and it could have been covered days ago.

She could hide out and wait for things to cool down—they wouldn't have a permanent roadblock, after all. But where? The rental period on the house was ending soon, and the stolen credit card number might have already been discovered. Plus, the cops might have taken note of the make and model of her car when she drove away from South Street.

She cursed herself for persisting in the McNally attempt, but she had to put that behind her. She decided waiting it out was not an option. *I have to get off this fucking island! There has to be a way!*

And there was.

She'd forgotten about it after their hijacking scheme failed. *The marina!* They were going to drop off McNally's fishermen on an uninhabited island after killing him then use the ship's registration to rent a berth at a marina Sergei had picked out. It was close to US 1, and they would drive off in the second car waiting in the parking lot—the one she now had.

The marina must have boats to rent. Sergei had said the controls were straightforward, and she wouldn't need a huge fishing boat. She would call Sergei to arrange for someone to pick her up when she got close to the mainland after hugging the Keys along the way.

I can do this. I have to do this!

Morrissey stayed behind with the two SWAT deputies who had come into the house from the back door, while Phil and the other two SWAT guys took off after AOD. Hager drove Petra and me to the embarkation point at the restaurant so we could retrieve our car and Vic's truck. We returned to the house.

Upon reaching South Street, Phil spotted the discarded beret and wig. He and the deputies spread out to explore escape routes through residential lots. Patrol cars were at the intersections at both ends of the block, light bars flashing. Homeowners stood on their porches and front lawns, watching the spectacle. Some had cell phones out to capture the activity.

After searching for ten minutes, Aiken said through Phil's radio, "I found a way through to Seminary Street. She could have had a car stashed there."

"Or she had one on South and got away before we closed it down. Or she was parked on Washington the whole time and doubled back. Whatever, I think she's gone, Don."

"Could be hiding, waiting for us to leave."

"Stan, come in."

"Here, Phil."

"I want you and Don to check out all parked cars in the Seminary Street block and get their license numbers."

"Roger that."

"Car One, come in."

"Go ahead, Phil."

"You heard that, Jerry?"

"Yup."

"You and Chris do the same for South Street. Return to the house on Washington when completed."

"Will do."

"Car Two," Phil said, "return to Washington now."

"Roger that."

Phil slung his M4 rifle and pulled out his cell phone as he began to retrace the route back to Vic's house. A man in his sixties stood in the side yard AOD had used to escape.

"Sorry for the intrusion, sir. I'm Sheriff Landry."

"What's going on, Sheriff?"

"We're looking for a fugitive who was spotted in the neighborhood. A woman. Did you see her?"

"A woman ran through my yard about twenty minutes ago. She was wearing one of those beret hats and dark clothes. That her?"

"Yes."

The man eyed Phil's gear. "She must be dangerous."

"She is. But she's gone from the neighborhood now and won't be coming back here."

Aiken and Stan Pitts caught up to Phil. "No cars parked on Seminary," Aiken said.

"Okay."

They started to walk away.

"If I see her, I'll be sure to call 911, Sheriff," the man said.

Phil acknowledged him with a wave as he walked off. He tapped a number on his phone.

"Highway Patrol, Marathon," a female voice answered.

"This is Monroe County Sheriff Phil Landry. I need to speak with Lieutenant Kennedy ASAP."

"One moment."

As Phil waited, he walked through the front door of the McNally residence, the other two men close behind.

"Hey, Phil," Kennedy answered. "What's up?"

He stopped in the foyer. "Are you at the station?"

"At home. They patched me through."

"I need a roadblock on Seven Mile as soon as you can arrange it. A woman wanted by the CIA, the FBI—and me—should be headed your way from Key West."

"Wow. You have a car description?"

"Negative."

"What about the perp?"

"Don't know what identity she's using now. Late twenties to early thirties. Should be traveling alone, but that's not definite. And she's good with disguises. I'll be coming from my end to meet you with someone who can make the ID."

"Okay, will do. Anyone close to the description will be detained until you get here."

Phil stepped into the living room, his eyes on us. "Be careful, Susan. She's armed and dangerous."

"Roger that."

"See you in about an hour."

— ❧ —

The two SWAT deputies who had stormed through the back door had taken off their heavy equipment and sat in the living room with the rest of us, waiting for orders from Phil. Linda had made a fresh pot of coffee.

Phil walked in, talking into a cell phone held to his ear. He finished his conversation with someone named Susan and addressed us. "Highway Patrol in Marathon will put up a roadblock on Seven Mile Bridge. Dee, we need you to make the ID. Wanna take a ride with me?"

"Sure."

"I want to tag along, too, if you don't mind," I said.

"No problem." He turned to the man next to him. "Don, you and your team can stand down. Take the truck back. Tell Henson and McCoy to stay here. Ditto, Masters and his car. But you can take Barlow back to the office."

Don nodded, and the four SWAT guys left.

"Vic," Phil said, "can you print up copies of AOD's picture?"

"Yeah."

"Okay. Ken and Hank, take those copies to the airport with Henson and McCoy in their car. Cover all the airlines. No woman trying to buy a ticket today will be allowed to fly out. I'll talk to the airport manager."

I thought of how Garin introduced himself to me on the boat. If he and AOD had been posing as a married couple...

"She could be using ID with the name Neumeister," I said.

Phil said to his men, "Neumeister. Write it down."

Hager and Morrissey went with Vic to get the copies, and Phil turned to Linda. "That was a brave thing you did. Thank you."

"I was scared to death!" She looked at me. "I shouldn't have said the type of dog."

"Doesn't matter. By then, she knew what we were doing and would have asked you what kind of dog it was. So it worked out."

"But we didn't catch her."

"We will," Phil said. "We have her on the run."

"How far away is Seven Mile Bridge?" Petra asked.

"About forty miles," he said.

"There are other keys between here and there, right?" Petra asked.

"Yes, but they're all in Monroe County—my jurisdiction. And they're sparsely populated. She can't hide in one of them for long."

"Maybe long enough for the roadblock to be discontinued."

Phil nodded. "She might do that, sure. But she won't know when that would be. Hell, she won't know about the roadblock to begin with."

"Phil, she knows there are only two ways off the island, and she'll assume a roadblock and coverage of the airport. She's no amateur."

"Hiding out in another key would be harder than staying here. Her only real chance to escape would be to get out before the roadblock goes up. But if she hasn't shown by the time we get there, we can backtrack and check out the keys between Seven Mile and here."

"There's another way off the island," I said. "By boat. For all we know, that's how AOD got here to begin with."

Phil stared at me for a few seconds then made a call on his cell.

"Kathy, call every marina in Key West... No, I *don't* know, but it can't be that many. I want to know about any woman who takes her boat out or tries to rent one... Tell them to stall her and call you."

He disconnected and looked at us. "Land, air, and sea are covered. She's not getting away."

Katarina pulled into the parking lot of Sunset Marina and went into the office. She stepped up to the counter. Behind it stood a forty-something, medium-height man with a muscular build talking on the phone.

"See you then." He hung up and smiled at her. "Help you?"

"Do you have any boats to rent?"

"Motor or sail?"

"Motor. Something not too big. I just want to go to Little Duck Key for the day. I hear it has a nice beach. My husband is out fishing and will meet me there."

"Do you have a boating safety ID?"

What? "I didn't know I needed one."

"Depends. Let me see your driver's license."

She fished it out of her handbag and handed it to him.

As he perused it, the phone on the counter rang.

"Sunset Marina," he answered and listened for a couple of minutes. "I think I have what you're looking for... I'll try to save it for you, but it's first come, first served... Okay."

He hung up. "Sorry for the interruption." He gave her back the license. "It says you were born in 1994."

"So?"

"The law in Florida is that anyone born after 1988 has to take a boating safety course in order to operate a boat with a motor over ten horsepower."

"Do you have any boats with ten-horsepower motors?"

He laughed. "To take out in the Gulf? Besides, with that amount of power, you wouldn't be able to get to Little Duck Key and back before it got dark."

Katarina pouted. "Oh shoot! What am I going to do? Charley should have told me!"

"How old's your husband?"

"Thirty-six."

"He probably doesn't know the law. He got grandfathered in when it passed in 2010."

She turned to go but had a sudden thought. "Is there a test you can give me?"

He shook his head. "You have to take the course. It's online."

"How long does it take?"

"About three hours."

Three hours!

"Look, I sympathize with your problem, Mrs. Neumeister. Tell you what I can do. I've got a computer and a printer in the back room. You take the course, print out a copy of the completion confirmation, and you'll be good to go."

"Very kind of you. I'll have to call Charley, see what he says. Maybe he can pick me up here."

She went out to her car, wondering what she could do. Three hours was too long. Almost an hour had passed since her escape from the ambush. The roadblock had to be in place already. And if Sergei could somehow arrange for a boat from the mainland to pick her up, that would take a lot more than three hours.

She texted Sergei. Five minutes went by, then ten, with no response. As she gazed idly at the parking lot entrance, a patrol car drove slowly in.

We had just crossed over to Stock Island on US 1 when Phil's cell phone rang.

"Go ahead, Kathy... Okay, thanks." He disconnected and turned to the driver. "Bill, take the next exit and head back to Key West, Code Two."

Phil looked at us in the back seat and smiled. "A woman by the name of Neumeister is trying to rent a boat at Sunset Marina. And the process is going to take a while."

Chapter 28

Katarina crouched behind her Nissan and watched the patrol car roll to a stop in front of the marina office. A man in a dark-blue uniform and a man and woman in civilian clothes exited the vehicle and hurried into the building. The driver remained in the car.

Sergei had mentioned a man and a woman on the boat he suspected of being CIA. That couldn't be a coincidence. The CIA and local law enforcement must have teamed up. And somehow, they'd guessed her intention.

She opened the car door, crawled onto the driver's seat, and, keeping her head down, quietly closed the door. She started the engine and drove out of the lot. She headed back to Olivia Street.

"I'm Sheriff Landry," Phil introduced himself to the man behind the counter at the marina. "Did my office call you?"

"Yes. About a woman you were looking for. She looked like she could be the one. The right age, wanted to rent a boat. What did she do?"

Phil ignored the question. "Is she here now?"

"I told her she needed a boating safety ID. She didn't have one, so, like the girl in your office wanted, I tried to keep her here. Offered to let her use my computer to take the online course. She went outside to think about it."

"To the docks?"

"No, the parking lot."

"Did you see her car?" I asked.

"No. Sorry."

"How long ago was this?"

"Ten or fifteen minutes."

"Thanks." Phil rushed to the door, Petra and I following.

We scanned the parking lot. All the cars appeared to be empty. We checked them anyway.

"Damn it!" Phil said. "We just missed her again! Where would she go now?"

"Back to where she was staying would be my guess," I said. "She has to regroup. She doesn't have a boat—we've ruled that out now—and she can't rent one without the special ID."

"So the sea route is out. Which means she'll go to ground, hoping we won't find her while she waits for things to quiet down."

"She used the Neumeister name," I said. "Hardly a common one. That's how we'll find her."

"Yes," Petra said. "Garin used the same alias. Chances are they were posing as a couple, and one of them rented a place to stay on the island. Too much exposure for a hotel. Has to be a private home or apartment."

"I'll call Kathy." Phil took out his cell and called the office again. He put it on speaker this time. "Kathy, we just missed her at Sunset Marina. We think she's back to where she was staying on the island. I've got another list for you."

"Thanks, Phil."

"Hey, you found her once, you can do it again."

She sighed. "Go ahead."

"Call all the rental agencies—"

"Oh, jeez."

"And ask for any houses or apartments rented to a Neumeister, last name, going back a week ago."

"How do you spell it?"

"I don't know, just how it's pronounced. 'New-Myster.'"

"Not a common name."

"Exactly."

"Okay, Phil. But do you know how many agencies we're talking about? It'll take a while."

"Get all the help you can from the staff. I'm headed back to you now."

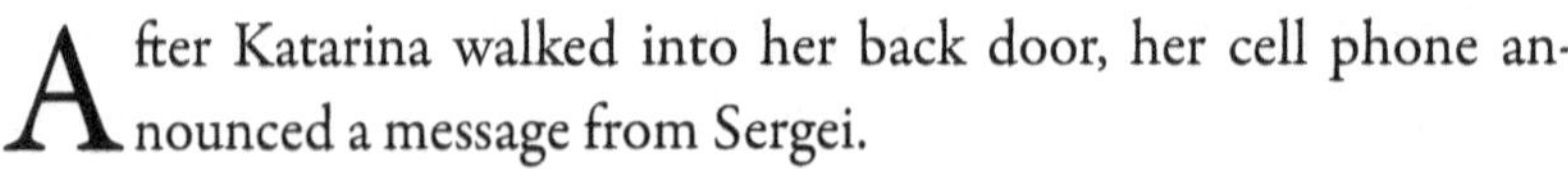

After Katarina walked into her back door, her cell phone announced a message from Sergei.

Finally! She sat at the dinette and read it.

Sorry for delay. Left phone in hotel room. Where are you?

She tapped her response: *At the rental house. Where are you?*

Minneapolis. Going to Topeka tomorrow.

I need help to get out!

Roadblock?

Think so.

After a few seconds, he responded with, *Rent a boat.*

Tried that. Need a license. She waited again, longer this time.

I'll see what I can do. Stay in house.

Thanks.

She took the phone and makeup bag into the bedroom and dumped the bag's contents onto the bed. The Cher wig wouldn't do. She couldn't be a young woman. Or an old one now either. That left only one possibility.

Phil dropped us off at the McNally house.

Vic and Linda looked at us expectantly. "Well?" Vic asked.

"We just missed her," I said. "She tried to rent a boat at a marina but couldn't."

Vic nodded. "Didn't have a boat safety ID."

"Right."

"I could have told you that. But I thought you were going to the roadblock."

"She must have assumed it was there and didn't chance it."

"So where did she go?" Linda asked.

"Back to where she was staying, we think."

"Where she can hide out until the coast is clear." Vic shook his head. "We let her get away, thanks to that plan of yours."

Petra glared at him. "Would you prefer Linda got shot? Sure, we could have stopped her in the house, but at what cost?"

He raised his hands in the air. "Hey, I'm sorry. You're right. It was a good idea you had. If only Phil could have gotten here sooner. Now she's still on the loose and could come after us again."

"She won't," Petra said. "She has to save herself now. You're the last thing on her mind."

"But if she gets away somehow, I'm still on her hit list. It'll never be over until she's caught."

"We have a lead that could tell us where she's hiding." I told them about the Neumeister idea. "She's not going to get off the island."

"Well, let's hope for that," Linda said with a grimace. "Meanwhile, it's lunchtime. How does grilled cheese sandwiches and tomato soup sound?"

The staff, including his administrative assistant, was busy making phone calls when Phil got back to headquarters. He gave Kathy a thumbs-up when he passed her desk on the way to his office. He closed the door and, exhausted from a day and a half with no sleep, plopped down on his couch, hoping to catch a nap.

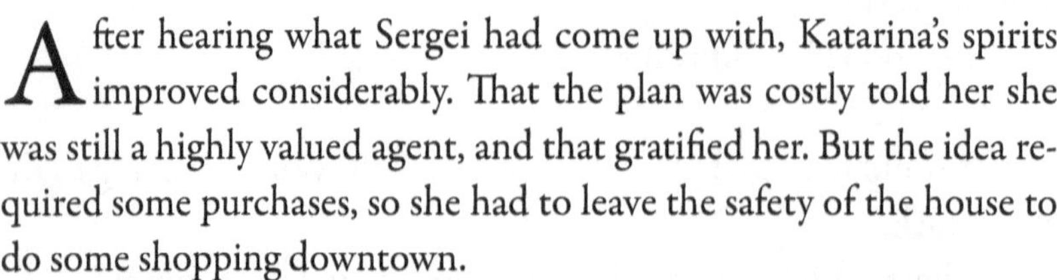

After hearing what Sergei had come up with, Katarina's spirits improved considerably. That the plan was costly told her she was still a highly valued agent, and that gratified her. But the idea required some purchases, so she had to leave the safety of the house to do some shopping downtown.

She returned with what she needed and went into the bathroom, opened up her phone to the photo Sergei had sent her, and began applying makeup. Thirty minutes later, she got dressed in the outfit she'd bought and checked her appearance in the mirror. Satisfied, she got ready to leave the house for what she hoped would be the last time.

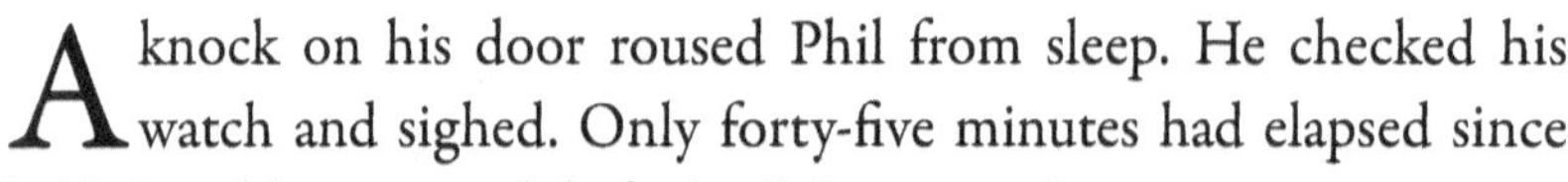

A knock on his door roused Phil from sleep. He checked his watch and sighed. Only forty-five minutes had elapsed since he'd closed his eyes and drifted off. "Come in."

Kathy entered, carrying a slip of paper. "We found the house."

Petra and I went back to the hotel after the lunch Linda made for us. We had nothing to do but wait for any developments from Phil's search, so we decided to lounge by the pool. It was a clear day, with the temperature in the seventies.

After applying sunscreen Petra had purchased in the hotel's sundries store, I lay back on a chaise and dozed off. A ringing cell phone woke me up. It was Petra's, I could tell, because the ringing stopped, and she was holding her phone to her ear as she spoke into it. *What a detective I am.*

"Great news, Phil. We're at our hotel." She paused to listen. "Okay, call me if you get her. Fingers crossed." She put the phone on the table between us and smiled. "Phil found a house rented by Erwin Neumeister last week. He's headed there now."

Phil drove an unmarked sedan by the aqua-colored house on Olivia Street. He noted a detached garage in the back, its door closed. He circled the block and parked at the curb, two houses down.

"All cars, stand by. I'm going in for a look."

He had deputies covering both Olivia Street and Pine Street to the rear.

Dressed in civilian clothes, he left the car with a handheld radio and strolled to the driveway of the bungalow. He walked up to the garage. There were no windows to peek through.

Entering the backyard, he drew his Glock and approached the back door. He found it partially ajar and crept into the kitchen, where he had a view of the front door.

"This is the sheriff! Come out with your hands up!"

Hearing no sounds, let alone a voice, he stepped into the living room and saw the hall that led to the sleeping quarters. He unlocked the front door and spoke into his mic. "Cars Three and Four, converge on the house and stand by. No sign of suspect yet." His gut told him she wasn't there.

He entered the short hallway. A bathroom door was open to his right. He did a quick peek to confirm it unoccupied and noticed the tub's closed shower curtain. He would check later, but hiding behind a shower curtain was too obvious.

He shut the door and stepped to the bedroom entrance across the hall. After another quick peek, he went in, searched the closet and under the bed, then returned to the bathroom. Standing to the side of the bathtub, he yanked open the curtain. As expected, no one was hiding there.

"House is clear," he said into his radio and went out to the garage. He lifted the door and found the garage empty.

His cell phone rang. It was Hank. "Stand by," he said into his mic and answered the call.

"Whatcha got, Hank?"

"Just checking in. We showed the photos to the airlines. Nobody can remember seeing her, and they'll call if any woman shows up to buy a ticket. Want us to go check out Signature?"

"Signature?"

"Yeah, Signature Flight Support. It's the fixed-base operator here. Where private planes come and go."

The FBO had completely escaped Phil's mind. *Of course!* "Get over there, Hank. I'm on my way."

We had just returned to our room to get ready if Phil had been successful when he called Petra. I could tell from her face as she listened that it wasn't good news. The house tip must have been a bust. But then she brightened. "It makes sense, Phil. She's that important. We'll meet you there."

She disconnected and looked at me. "How can you fly out of an airport without needing a ticket?"

It suddenly dawned on me. "Private plane!"

We got dressed in a flash and were out of there five minutes later.

Chapter 29

When we arrived at the Signature terminal, two of Phil's patrol cars were parked in front of the entrance. I'd never flown out of an FBO before, and the absence of magnetometers and ID checks surprised me when Petra and I walked in.

Phil was talking with a man wearing a gray blazer sporting the company logo we'd seen outside the entrance—a white "S" that looked like a coiled snake on a blue background—below his breast pocket. Hank and Ken, deputies I knew from the operation at Vic's house, stood by along with two other deputies.

The large room featured cushioned armchairs in conversation groupings and a small dining area with plastic-and-metal tables and chairs and vending machines. A hallway on the right led to restrooms and a pilots' lounge, according to a sign on the wall. A reception desk occupied a rear corner of the room. The picture window that comprised most of the back wall provided a view of planes of various sizes—propeller and jet—sitting on the tarmac; beyond that was the airport runway.

A private jet had just landed and was taxiing toward the terminal. A Gulfstream, I saw from the G450 painted on its tail.

Phil ended his conversation with the Signature employee and noted our arrival. He came over to us. "No planes have picked anyone up here since yesterday."

"What about that Gulfstream?" I pointed at the window. The jet had stopped, and its built-in staircase was being lowered to the ground.

"The manager said it's a flight from Dulles in Washington en route to Mexico City. Refueling only. No passenger pickup."

The G450 was a fairly sizeable plane, and it made me wonder. "Do you know the distance between DC and Mexico City?"

"Not offhand. Why?"

I pulled out my cell phone as two large men in suits, a man in casual clothes, and two pilots descended the steps from the plane's cabin. I had the answer in seconds. "Twenty-three hundred miles."

"So?" Petra asked, frowning.

I did another search. "The range of the G450—the jet that just landed—is almost five thousand miles. Why would they need to refuel?"

I could tell Phil understood where I was going.

"They wouldn't," he said. "But no passengers are supposedly being picked up."

"So let's make sure nobody else gets on that plane."

The jet's passengers and pilots entered through a rear door. The pilots headed for the hallway, and the suits went to the vending machines. All had facial features consistent with eastern European ancestry, but perhaps my working hunch slanted that assessment.

The third passenger had a medium height and build. He sported a straw fedora, sunglasses, and a brown mustache. He wore an oversized, long-sleeve denim shirt untucked over baggy jeans. He took out a pack of cigarettes from a shirt pocket and headed for the entrance.

"Phil, the guy in the hat," I said.

He followed my gaze. "Looks like he's going out for a smoke."

"Yes, it does." I felt a tickling of excitement. After the fedora-wearing man went through the door, I went up to it and peered through its glass.

Katarina watched from her car in the Signature parking lot as a patrol car drove up to the building entrance and parked behind one that had been there when she'd arrived ten minutes earlier. The same uniformed man she had seen at the marina climbed out and went inside. *They've figured it out?*

Her first impulse was to flee, but she had no options left. She tried to relax by telling herself it would be logical to check out the FBO in their coverage of the airports.

As she looked anxiously at the sky over the runway, the arrival of another car in the lot caught her attention—a white SUV like the one at the McNally house. And the same man and woman she'd seen at the marina got out.

This was no routine check. They had gone after her most likely escape possibilities one by one. *And ended up here.* What Sergei could think of, they could too. So far, she'd kept one step ahead of them, and she would have to do it once more. Getting away via private plane was a good guess, but they couldn't possibly know *how* she would do it.

The plan has to work!

She saw what she assumed would be her means of rescue land on the runway. Ten minutes later, a man in a beige fedora emerged from the terminal and lit a cigarette. He started strolling through the lot, scanning the parked cars.

She put her own fedora on the dashboard as the man neared the Nissan. He spotted it and stepped to the passenger door, looked around once, then quickly climbed in.

"Neumeister?" he asked.

"Yes. Did you see the officers in the terminal?"

"Five of them."

"What were they doing?"

"Just standing around. Didn't show any interest in me."

That's good. "Who else came with you?"

"Two pilots the embassy uses who know what we're doing and two armed bodyguards. They're all in the terminal now, waiting for the plane to be refueled. Shouldn't take long. The bodyguards are the only ones inside wearing suits. When you go to the plane, they'll be behind you. Do you need a weapon?"

"No." She took the Glock 19 from the center console and tucked it in the waistband of her jeans at the small of her back.

"Do you have another ID? The cops know the Neumeister name."

He lifted his shirt and reached into a fanny pack at his waist. He retrieved a small leather case and handed it to her. "You're Lawrence Carter, the owner of a patent for a new kind of solar energy cell. But you don't have to show ID to anyone besides the main pilot." He smiled. "And, of course, you're already a passenger."

"What do you think? Will I pass for you?"

He chuckled. "My mustache is fake too!" He looked her over. "Not like looking into a mirror, but close enough to pass casual inspection. I don't see your boobs. Can you walk like a man?"

"I think I can manage. Do you know Sergei?"

"Yes. In fact, when he called the embassy about you, he asked if I was available since I was the right size. And I've passed for a woman before."

"What's your name?"

"You don't need to know... Lawrence."

She nodded. "Thank you."

"Good luck."

She donned the fedora and was about to get out of the car, when he stopped her.

"You'll need these." He handed her his sunglasses.

"Right." She put them on.

"Look." He pointed at the runway. "Another plane landed and is coming to the terminal. It should provide a distraction for your policemen. Especially since it looks like those people—" He pointed again. "Are going to be its passengers."

A man and a woman climbed out of a taxi at the entrance, took luggage from the trunk, and went into the building.

As I watched Fedora stroll into the parking lot, Phil came up to me.

"Another private jet has landed." He grinned. "It's from Minneapolis and here to pick up passengers."

Minneapolis! "Who's the pickup?"

"The manager didn't know."

I followed Phil to get a better look through the window. The plane taxied to the terminal's pad and stopped behind the Gulfstream being refueled. Its steps descended. A pilot went down them and headed toward the terminal.

"Must be the passengers," Phil said, looking at the front door.

A man I immediately recognized as Chris Pratt, the actor, had entered carrying a large duffel bag and rolling a suitcase. An attractive brunette accompanied him, wheeling her own suitcase.

Though I doubted AOD could have somehow hooked up with the well-known actor—or found a lookalike to play the role—I closely examined the face of the woman as the couple approached the pilot now talking to the manager at the desk.

She was not wearing any significant makeup I could detect, and her hair appeared real. Plus, the facial structure was all wrong. It wasn't AOD.

The transaction at the desk completed, the pilot, Pratt, and the woman went out to the plane.

"Tired of me already?" Petra had a slight smirk on her face. "I saw you checking that woman out."

"I wanted to make sure she wasn't AOD."

"She isn't."

"I know." Petra followed me when I went back to the entrance to look through the door. Fedora was on his way back. "That guy in the hat got off the Gulfstream and went out for a smoke."

She looked over my shoulder. "And?"

"Something about him. The baggy clothes, the sunglasses, the mustache. It's like he's wearing a disguise."

"But he got *off* the plane."

"And the first thing he does is go out to the parking lot."

We stepped aside as he came in, walked quickly past us, and joined the two suits at the manager's desk with the pilots.

"Are you thinking what I am?" Petra asked.

"A switch."

One of the pilots had settled up with the manager, then headed for the rear door. Fedora followed, the suits behind him.

I went up to Phil. "That man wearing the hat. He might not be the man who got off the plane."

His eyes got big. "Traded places in the parking lot?"

"Maybe."

"Hank, Ken, come with me."

Petra and I followed Phil and the deputies out the door. The group ahead was halfway to the Gulfstream. The other plane was taxiing to the runway.

Phil drew his sidearm, and the two deputies did likewise. "This is the sheriff!" Phil yelled. "You people going to the plane, stop right there and put your hands up!"

The pilots in the lead obeyed and turned around to face us. Fedora did the same.

The suits separated and kept walking, their right hands now hidden by their bodies. One of them shouted something, and they whirled around, guns in their hands. They fired, and Ken fell to the tarmac.

Phil and Hank returned fire. One of the gunmen went down; the other, his gun arm hanging limply at his side, tried to switch his weapon to his left hand and was immediately hit with more rounds. He, too, fell to the ground and lay motionless like his partner.

Fedora stood facing us between the fallen suits. His right hand came down and disappeared behind his back.

"Katarina, don't!" Petra shouted, advancing toward Fedora, her 9mm held in a two-hand grip and aimed at the remaining threat.

Fedora hesitated for a second before bringing a pistol around and shooting two quick rounds. Hank, in front of me, groaned and stumbled before falling backward to the tarmac. I had a clear shot and was pulling the trigger when Petra fired her weapon. The gun dropped from Fedora's hand, and he stood staring at us as if in surprise. Then his legs crumpled, and he fell onto his back.

The other two deputies ran out of the terminal.

"Mack!" Phil yelled, crouched over Hank. "Check on Ken. Gil, secure the pilots and those bodies."

Petra and I went to Fedora, who was still alive, but in extremis, blue eyes wide and darting back and forth in panic, breathing rapid and raspy. The hat had come off, and a brown wig was askew, exposing a head of blond hair. The mustache hung down to one side. Blood soaked the front of the denim shirt. I kicked AOD's gun away. Petra stared at the dying woman, her pistol held loosely at her side.

Phil joined us as Gil called out, "The two suits are dead."

"Call for an ambulance," Phil told his deputy as he stood with us looking down at the assassin. "She doesn't look like much of a killer."

"If you only knew," Petra said, not taking her eyes off the woman. "We meet again, Katarina."

"Who... are... you?" AOD asked, gasping for breath.

"Petra Nikolic. Remember me?"

"Petra?" The woman's eyes showed recognition for a moment before they became still and lifeless.

I knelt to feel for a pulse, knowing there wouldn't be one. There wasn't.

"The war," Petra said softly.

"What?" I stood.

She stared at the body of someone she had known when they were both young girls, shaking her head. "War and its collateral damage, Alex. Lives forever changed if not destroyed. In Katarina's case, it turned her into a killer, motivated by blind hatred. So sad—and scary—that the sweet little girl I once knew ended up like this."

"You experienced the same war and had your own grief, Petra."

She looked at me with moist eyes. "I know. And I almost took the same path as Katarina. That could be me lying there."

I put an arm around her shoulders. "But it isn't. You *chose* to hunt down terrorists instead of being one. It's not karma. You're proof of that."

I looked back at Phil and a deputy I didn't know helping the fallen deputies to their feet. They looked like they would make it. I turned Petra away from the woman she'd been forced to kill. "C'mon, let's go inside."

Ken Morrisey's vest had saved him, but he was taken to the hospital to be evaluated for blunt chest trauma. Deputy Hager suffered a fractured scapula from the round to the shoulder. No surgery was required.

Phil met with airport security and KWPD officers who had rushed to the scene, and later, he talked with two police detectives summoned by the patrolmen. After hearing about FBI and CIA involvement in the case, KWPD gladly ceded authority to the Sheriff's Office.

A local funeral home picked up the dead.

Petra and I had a reunion with Tom Blankenship and Gwen Michaels when they arrived three hours later to collect the IDs of the dead Russians and take the pilots into custody.

"We won the bet after all," Tom said and gave Gwen a high-five.

"What'll happen to the pilots?" I asked.

"You got me. I'd guess they'll just be deported, though the Russian embassy says they're criminals."

"Really?"

He chuckled. "Oh, yeah. They claim this whole operation was conducted by rogue agents and they never heard of Katarina Petrovic. And they want their jet back!"

Petra and I drove to Vic's house after the FBI and Phil and his people left. Troy Ingram was there. They'd seen the news of the shootout on TV, but as usual, the talking heads only guessed at the particulars of the event. Phil had told a reporter that a press conference would be held in the morning.

We gave them the good news.

"So it's over?" Vic asked.

"Yes," Petra said.

Linda heaved a long sigh. "Thank God. We've got our lives back." She looked at Petra and me. "What are you two going to do now?"

I smiled. "I'm going to collect the signed contracts from my new employees and see about getting the Key West tours ready for the summer."

"I brought mine with me," Troy said.

"And you, Dee?" Linda asked.

"I'm sure the CIA will find something for me to do. But first, I'm taking some vacation days."

"Any idea where?"

Petra looked at me and grinned. "I was thinking Aruba."

About the Author

After graduating from the University of Vermont College of Medicine, John L. DeBoer, M.D., F.A.C.S. completed his surgical training in the U.S. Army and then spent three years in the Medical Corps as a general surgeon. Thirty years of private practice later, he retired to begin a new career as a writer. When not creating new plot lines for his novels, Dr. DeBoer pursues his interests in cooking, the cinema, and the amazing cosmos. He's an avid tennis player, and his yet-to-be-fulfilled goal is to achieve a level of mediocrity in the frustrating game of golf. The father of two grown sons, he lives with his wife in North Carolina.

Read more at www.novelsbyjohnldeboer.com.

About the Publisher

Dear Reader,

We hope you enjoyed this book. Please consider leaving a review on your favorite book site.

Visit https://RedAdeptPublishing.com to see our entire catalogue.

Check out our app for short stories, articles, and interviews. You'll also be notified of future releases and special sales.